HAUNTED BY SHADOWS

MAGIC WARS: DEMONS OF NEW CHICAGO
BOOK TWO

KEL CARPENTER

Haunted by Shadows

Kel Carpenter

Published by Kel Carpenter

Copyright © 2021, Kel Carpenter LLC

Edited by Analisa Denny

Proofread by Dominique Laura

Cover Art by Covers by Juan

 Created with Vellum

To the future us.

You, me, and everyone that is struggling right now. Hang in there.

It's going to get better.

There are two kinds of guilt: the kind that
drowns you until you're useless, and
the kind that fires your soul to purpose.

— SABAA TAHIR, *AN EMBER IN THE
ASHES*

THE STATIC CRACKLE in my ear was driving me fucking crazy. I shoved my gloved hands into the pockets of my new leather jacket to keep from swatting at the thing like an unwanted fly.

"Whatever you're doing over there, you need to stop. I can't scout out for Ronan with this thing crinkling like a plastic bag in my ear," I said under my breath.

"Sorry, I'm trying to figure out the frequency. If I could just ask Barry—"

"No," I said, cutting her off. We'd had this conversation a dozen times in the last three days. "It's already bad enough you got the tech from him. I don't want him butting into my business."

Nathalie sighed into the mic that fed to the tiny

speaker in my ear. "Have I mentioned how much your trust issues are a pain in my ass?"

"Only a time or twenty," I replied. "Now hush. I haven't seen Ronan yet, and if he sees me talking to myself, he might not show."

"Somehow I doubt it'll matter if you're crazy when he's more concerned with getting in your pants," Nat commented dryly before cutting the mic, and by extension the static that was driving me nuts.

My boots were silent as I walked the length of the Navy Pier. It was beautiful this time of day. The sky was painted the same shade of creamsicle as the ice pops Bree and I would eat while our parents strolled side by side next to us. Those rose-colored memories were still marred with the signs of bite marks on my mother's neck and the glint of steel on my dad's hip, but it was a better time all the same.

And it was long gone. While there was still the odd light from the city, most of the streetlights were either broken or didn't work. The cobbled walkway was covered in graffiti and bird shit. There were no strolling couples or children milling about. Anyone I ran into at this hour wasn't someone I wanted to make nice with.

I pivoted on my heel, turning to walk the length of it again, when a figure standing at the end caught my attention.

My pulse quickened. I started walking toward

him, my hands itching to reach for the two pistols strapped to either side of my hips. A long hunting knife was wedged in my boot. My leather jacket didn't have all the nifty compartments my old trench coat did, so I had to forego the rope and hook that often helped me out of a pinch. Not that I saw that being a thing with Ronan. The nearest roof was through a museum that had long since closed. The odds of me getting that far weren't high given I was headed straight to him.

Just like he wanted.

"You came," he said, his voice a rumble of thunder and night. The very sound caressed my skin and sent a trail of goosebumps up both arms.

"You didn't exactly give me a choice."

His hands dropped away from the railing over-looking Lake Michigan as he turned to face me. Silver eyes edged with black fire swept over my form hungrily. While it was freezing in New Chicago, heat touched me in that moment. I hated it.

"But I did. You told me pursuing as I was didn't work. You didn't have a choice, so I gave you one. You're choosing to be here of your own volition, despite your desire to run." His eyes focused on the edge of my long-sleeved shirt. It wasn't a turtleneck for once. The very edge of one of my brands peeked out from the faded black fabric.

"Fine. You forced my hand. Either way, I'm only

3

here for Bree. Where is she?" I made a show of looking around even though I was damn sure she wasn't nearby.

"Safe," Ronan said, his eyes flaring with a touch of anger. He extended a hand to me. I didn't take it. "Come. We'll talk over dinner."

I reeled back, my hand instinctively reaching for the pistol at my side. I'd shot him once, and he got back up. Maybe if I just kept shooting, he'd stay down long enough to find a way to incapacitate him. A crackling in my ear made me pause. "If you're reaching for your gun, that's stupid." The fact that she knew exactly what I was doing—but couldn't see me —was annoying. "You need to get more info out of him if we're going to find Bree. Go to dinner. Talk to him."

Ronan waited expectantly as I waffled in indecision. "Dinner," I insisted. "That's it. We eat, and you tell me where Bree is."

His lips curled in a cruel smile as he regarded me. "We'll see. We have much to talk about." I didn't like that answer, but what real other choice did I have? Either I walked, and our odds of finding Bree were zero-to-none, or I went with him.

I straightened my back and took his hand. Instead of threading his fingers through mine as I expected, he pulled me slightly in front of him and then released my hand, possessively placing his on my lower back. I lifted an eyebrow at him, and he mimicked the motion mockingly as he led me around the pier.

"For someone that says we have so much to talk about, you don't say much."

The corner of his mouth curled upward. "I'm just admiring that my atma finally came to me willingly. What can I say? After chasing you for weeks, I'm savoring victory."

And will be for the last time if I have my way.

"Don't get used to it," I said instead.

He chuckled. "You're wary of me. Understandable to an extent, given what you've been through—"

"You have no idea what I've been through," I said sharply. Ronan paused, and his hand fell away. I turned back after walking a few feet.

"Oh, but I do," he said softly. There was a dark edge to his voice. A dangerous note. "What do you think I've been doing when I'm not chasing you? Claude Lewis' memories gave me a starting point. I followed those pieces of information I gained like a trail of breadcrumbs, finding people you've worked with or for. I've tracked places you've been. People who've hurt you. These last few weeks I've immersed myself in your world for *you.*" He stepped forward, and I stood my ground. "I know the Magic Wars hurt you and your family. That made you power hungry. Desperate. You would do anything to save them and save yourself. You've always been proactive that way, and it led you down the path you're on now."

"Don't talk like you know me," I spat. "You hunted down people who haven't known me. What they saw was a phase of my life. A mask. A child. You invaded my privacy—"

"I wouldn't have to if you weren't so stubborn," he said quietly, but not harshly. Ronan lifted a hand to run one finger down my cheek.

"Exactly. I'm stubborn. Willful. I don't like change, and I like magic even less. It ruined my life, and you can't change that. You can't make me love it or you. So I don't understand why you keep trying."

"It's not about love. It never has been. Love is for humans."

"Then what's it about?"

"You're mine," he said, as if it were that simple. "I've existed for a long time, Piper. The world I come from is different, but also the same in that I stopped caring. It didn't matter where I was or who I was with. Numbness was settling over when you created the door and called out. I felt your magic, and for the first time in a very long time, I was *alive*. I smelled you and knew it was a scent that could intoxicate me. You're an enigma, and I find that fascinating. I want to know you. I want to *own* you. Not because of some misguided love, but because the first moment I laid eyes on you, I knew there was no going back. I couldn't, even if I wanted to—and I don't."

My lips parted, somewhat in shock, because he wasn't lying. He truly believed that, and I knew in that moment there was no going back for me either. Ronan would never leave me alone.

"Surprised you, have I?" he mused, a cruel smirk playing on his lips. Then he reached around and rested his hand on my back and guided me toward the water. "Come. Let's eat." I moved mechanically at his side as he led me onto a riverboat. It was the only one in the harbor. A wooden board bridged the gap between the walkway and the ship. In my ear, the piece crackled once more, reminding me Nathalie was there and had heard every word.

"Hot damn, are you sure you don't want to reconsider this bond business?" Nathalie said. "He might be a demon and a stage five clinger, but—"

I reached up and flicked the earpiece, knowing it would get my point across.

Nathalie groaned in my ear right as Ronan gave me a look. I didn't bother giving either of them a response.

The riverboat was upscale. Only half a dozen two-top tables were seated on the deck. Twinkling lights ran along the edge of the overhang. A waiter was already standing at one of the tables, a neutral expression set in place. She was a few inches shorter than me, but she had pointed ears. Half-fae, if I had to guess. Explains how she managed to land a job at a place like this.

Ronan and I sat across from each other with only a two-foot table between us.

I squared my shoulders as she placed the menus on the table and then poured each of us a glass of water. The wind whipped over the lake, batting against the thick siding around the deck that was designed to keep the worst of the cold away.

"Welcome, Mr. Fallon," she began. The rest of her speech was lost on me.

My eyes narrowed on Ronan, who was now smirking widely. As if sensing my rising ire, he lifted a hand and said, "Thank you, but we'll need a moment to look over the menu."

She bowed her head graciously and moved to give us space.

"You took my last name," I said. Both my hands were clenched into fists on top of the table in an effort to not reach for my guns.

"I didn't have one," he said with a shrug. "Where I come from, we're known as the son or daughter of our parents. That's not the way of your world, though, so I adjusted."

"How gracious of you."

"I thought so."

My fingers twitched, and it was like he knew what

I wanted to do, even if I was stopping myself. "If I thought I could shoot you enough times to keep you down, I would."

He inclined his head, not at all bothered by my death threat. "But then you'd never find Bree, assuming it worked—which it wouldn't."

"Unfortunately."

The server chose that moment to reappear. "Have you had a chance to look over the—"

"I'll have whatever is most expensive on the menu," I said. "Since *Mr. Fallon* here is paying."

The waitress opened, then closed her mouth. Ronan simply continued to smile. I wondered if he knew it was pissing me off.

"Make that two," he said, "And a bottle of your best red."

She nodded once and went to place our order, leaving us.

I squared my shoulders like we were at a showdown and not dinner.

Considering he was holding my sister hostage to get me there, it wasn't far off.

It was why I didn't expect his next statement.

"Tell me about your life." He demanded it. Expected it. It wasn't a question at all.

"If you already know everything, I don't see the point."

"I know pieces of it. Things that I've gathered and

then filled in the blanks. I want to hear it from you. I want to know you."

"You want to own me," I corrected. "I don't understand the point in getting to know me." He chuckled.

"They're one and the same in this case. You showed me that. The only way I'll have you is if you choose it. So indulge me. I want to know everything." He settled back with one arm sitting loosely on the table and the other on his lap. Three inches to the right of my left hand was a silver knife. I could put it through his hand if I wanted. Wouldn't kill him, but it would hurt like a bitch. Maybe test that dedication he claimed to have.

The only problem—if it wasn't as strong as he claimed, then I'd be fucked. Again.

"Everything is a tall order," I mused, instead reaching for my glass of water. I took a sip, the crisp cold hitting my throat and grounding me.

"Then start at the beginning. What's your earliest memory?"

I stiffened. Ronan lifted a brow.

While I could push it down and be obstinate in this, there wasn't much point. He already knew, to an extent.

"The day we learned magic existed."

"'We' being the humans?"

"Yes," I said softly. He looked like he wanted to

say something about it but didn't. "I was sitting next to my sister on the floor in our living room, playing with Barbies. We were watching cartoons when the tv started blaring. My parents ran into the living room right as the sound cut out and the screen changed. The forty-three seconds that played after that changed the world."

I didn't tell him what I'd seen. If he looked through my past, he certainly saw it himself. Everyone had seen it that day. Never before had a massacre like that taken place on public television. Hell, I was only a child. I barely knew about such things. My parents weren't the type to even curse in front of us. They didn't raise us sheltered, per se, but we weren't exposed to the darker facets yet. We were only children, after all.

"You're talking about the public execution of your leader and his guards." That was one way to phrase it. Although I suppose they might not have presidents where he came from.

"Yes," I said, though it wasn't really needed. He got the idea.

"I heard he brought it on himself by starting a slave camp for those of magical kind," Ronan continued. Years ago, I might have bristled. To me, the insinuation that we somehow deserved what came after was . . . I didn't have words. Just rage.

But I wasn't a child anymore, and I'd heard those whispers enough times to not lose myself to the anger.

"Rumors," I said stiffly, shrugging one shoulder. "The evidence was scattered, and either way, the crimes to a few hundred never justified the crimes to millions."

He tilted his head. "I never said it did."

I opened my mouth to tell him he insinuated it, but the waitress reappeared, two plates in hand.

"Duck confit on a bed of greens," she said, not clipped, but pleasant enough. She set the dishes in front of us, and Ronan dismissed her with a wave of his hand before she could ask if we needed anything else. I reached for my fork, thankful for the excuse to stop talking.

"You feel wronged on a very personal level by the events that occurred, but it sounds like both sides were ultimately wronged. Magical beings had been hiding for hundreds of years because humans had tried to hunt them to extinction. Only when they forgot did it give them enough time to grow. The attack on their presence had been renewed, and they exacted their vengeance on the man they viewed as responsible."

I stabbed my duck harder than needed, and the plate beneath it clanked when the metal prongs of my fork hit it.

"Maybe he was responsible. Maybe they were

wronged, in some sense. But they killed and enslaved humanity after that."

"Did they?" he questioned, and my temper rose. "It became survival of the fittest, and humans simply weren't. Is that really different to how humans treated other creatures not long before?"

I grit my teeth, appetite diminishing in favor of stabbing him.

"Whose side are you on?"

"Neither." He shrugged. "I was not affected. It makes it easier to look at it without bias, and the way I see it—you both committed crimes against the other. That witch went after someone she deemed had hurt her and her own. It's not all that different from you and your hunt for Claude. Their kind developed a hatred for humans for what was forced on them, and in your kind's ignorance, they were hurt. But in their anger, they lashed out, and you were hurt."

"You feel sorry for them," I accused.

"No, not really. I simply understand them, just as I understand you. Your prejudice was born out of rational and irrational anger from childhood. It says a lot that that's your earliest memory. It shaped you."

I took a bite to give myself a chance to form a response. I wasn't crazy about being psychoanalyzed like this. Nathalie was already bad enough.

As if she heard me, the static crackled in my ear. "He's right, you know."

The most delicious meal I'd probably ever had turned to ash in my mouth.

I set my fork down, noticing he hadn't even touched his meal.

"You're right. It shaped me. I'm an angry person. I'm prejudiced. Speciesist. I'm not nice—"

"You're also loyal to a fault. You put others above yourself when you believe they are worth it. Your trust is hard earned, but once someone has it, you'd do anything for them."

My jaw slipped, and I had to catch myself to keep from gaping. "You don't know—"

"You're sitting here now eating dinner with me. I didn't need to look into your past to know that. You're here for Bree, and that tells me all I need to know."

I looked at my plate and took a deep breath.

"You can't change me," I said eventually. "Fix me. Heal me. It can't happen. It won't."

I waited for him to deny that. To tell me I was wrong. But when he didn't speak, I lifted my eyes. He was smirking.

"You're right to an extent, but fortunately for me, I don't have to," he said. "At least not completely. You've already changed. The fact that you're living with a witch and she's currently listening to every word I've said speaks for itself. You're changing, Piper, but you're changing by your choice. Not mine."

"Oh snap," Nathalie said in my ear. "This guy really knows how to lay it on you, doesn't he?"

I reeled back to jump to my feet, but his hand grabbed my wrist, pulling me down.

"This dinner is over," I hissed.

"But we haven't even had dessert." He grinned. "I was hoping to have you, but I think that might have to wait till next time."

My face flamed from anger and . . . embarrassment? I did not want to assess that. Nope. I wasn't touching it with a ten-foot pole.

"Let. Me. Go."

"But then you'd never hear about your sister."

I froze.

"What about her?"

The grin faded from his face as a more serious look washed over his features.

"I know what's wrong with her. I know why she never woke up."

Those words were ringing in my ears. Salvation within my grasp, and damnation right beside it because I knew that truth wouldn't come free. Not from a demon. Certainly not from Ronan.

Before I could ask him anything, the boards beneath my feet broke apart. A crack like bone shattering registered.

Then the dinner boat exploded.

2

Splintered wood and fire filled my vision.

At first it was just heat. Pain. My head swam, and I didn't know up from down.

Then came the cold. My body crashed into the icy waters of Lake Michigan and I started to sink before I even thought to swim. Magic was singing in my veins as my heartbeat soared, perilously close to stopping. I clawed at the water, kicking my feet. My chest was seizing painfully as the cold pushed the air from my lungs.

I was drowning.

After everything I'd been through, it was fucking drowning that was going to get me.

No. I mentally calmed myself and relaxed my movements to look around. It was jarring. The waters were clear but shadowed from nightfall. I kicked toward the orange glow above me. It had to be fire, which meant there was air.

My body jerked to a stop.

I narrowed my eyes and peered through the darkness.

Something was pulling my jacket, and by extension, me.

I reached for the zipper with numb fingers, still kicking to keep myself from sinking any lower.

The thumping in my ears urged me on.

Come on. Come on. My fingers were slow. Sluggish. They struggled to hold on to the smooth metal. I yanked it, only for the zipper to move a few inches, then stop when I lost my grip.

Goddamnit. I was going to come back and haunt every last motherfucker that played a part in exploding that boat.

I reached for the zipper again, but my feet were failing me. My lungs were failing me. My body was too weak, and whatever was pulling down my jacket was too strong.

Darkness closed in and I made a fist, prepared to let my heart stop if it meant a chance of escape.

Strong arms grabbed me.

I tried to struggle when hands locked on either side of my jacket and shirt, then pulled. The material gave way easily.

Bare hands helped me out of it, rough calluses

brushing against my skin. My head rested against something hard and warm. The sides of my vision were starting to become hazy as a burning built in my chest from the lack of oxygen.

I didn't know we were moving until the cold wind slapped me in the face. Water spewed from my lips, and those warm hands held me tight, keeping my head above water. I took wild, gasping breaths, inhaling as much as I could while urging my heart to slow.

It was so close . . .

Too close. One wrong move and it was all ove—

"Breathe slower. You don't want your heart to stop," a dark voice rumbled. My eyes snapped open.

Ronan hovered, his face only inches away. His expression furious. Something cold and lethal glittered in his eyes. I knew without a doubt I wouldn't be the only one hunting down whoever did this.

"You saved me," I uttered, dumbfounded. It was the same thing I'd said to Nathalie, except where she shrugged it off, Ronan held me tighter. Those eyes like winter winds and steel pulled me in as we drifted in the dark waters. Overhead, a sliver of the moon cast its light upon us. Pieces of flaming debris skittered over the surface of the lake, far enough away to not be a concern, but close enough to bask us in muted light.

"Of course. You're mine. I protect what's mine."

His words snapped me out of my reverie. I blinked and then kicked, trying to swim away. His arms may as well have been iron, for they didn't budge an inch.

"You need to calm down. If your heart stops, you're only strong for a time before the crash will consume you."

His words were . . . right.

I hated that, but I stilled and stopped fighting as much as it killed me.

"Do you know what caused the explosion?" I asked, forcing myself to shut down all emotion and think logically. His bare hands clutching my back made that difficult.

"Magic," he said, confirming my suspicion. "I can smell it in the air. That wasn't a natural fire. Ships don't explode without warning."

Footsteps pounded against concrete about twenty yards from us. I glanced up at the pier right as Nat came to a stop at the edge where the boat had been docked. She bent at the waist, hands braced on her hips, breathing heavily.

"What happened? I saw the explosion and your mic cut out . . ." she said, her eyes moving to the wreckage that surrounded us before zeroing back in.

"I'm not sure, exactly. Did you see anyone up there? Anyone try to run?"

She shook her head, and I cursed. The thumb

rubbing my lower back in slow, rhythmic circles made me hyper aware of how close me and Ronan were.

"Come on," he said, cutting through the water toward the dock with a few strong kicks. "Your lips are turning blue."

"If someone let me swim away when I tried to, maybe they wouldn't be," I said stiffly.

He hoisted me out of the water and halfway up the ladder without comment. My arms shook from exertion as I clutched the slippery metal bars with numb fingers. Water poured from me in a torrent as I hauled one leg up after the other onto the dock. Tiny hairs clung to my arms and my ponytail splayed over my back, sticking to my bare skin.

The cold hit me as I stood there in jeans and a bra. My brands were completely on display for anyone to see, including Ronan.

I started walking, and Nathalie met me halfway, a baggy sweatshirt in hand. She extended it silently, shrugging when I flashed her a look.

"You have a tendency of catching on fire. I figured having extra clothes on hand was smart. That said, I didn't bring a towel because I wasn't expecting you to go for a swim."

I snorted, shoving my arms through the sleeves. It clung to me uncomfortably but took the edge off the cold.

"Were you the target?" I asked Ronan without

turning. I sensed his eyes on my back, making me uncomfortable. He'd just saved me from drowning, though, so I had to face the fact he wouldn't kill me. While I didn't like magic and certainly didn't want to bond with him, it would be stupid to constantly watch my guard, expecting him to kill me when he'd never given me any indication he would.

"Unknown. I haven't been here long enough to make many enemies, but it's possible . . ." He trailed off as if there were more. I turned around, crossing my arms over my chest.

"What's possible?"

"Lucifer wasn't the only demon to cross over through the ages. It's possible others have heard of my arrival and thought to test my power. They might have thought I'd be weakened by the crossing and attempting their coup now before I learned of their presence was worth the risk." He ran a hand through his slick black locks, silver eyes flashing with the promise of vengeance.

"Why would other demons want to kill you?"

"Because of what I am. Who I am."

"Who are you?" I asked pointedly.

"It's not important," he said dismissively. "What's important is finding out if it was another demon, and if so, who. If I was the target, then it's only a matter of time until you're in danger as well." I narrowed my eyes, not missing the way he danced around my question. Whatever he was, he didn't want me to know.

"I'd say she's already in danger given the whole exploding boat," Nathalie said.

"Yes, but it's the difference between actively being the target and simply being here with me this time," Ronan said without looking at her. A slow smirk spread across his wicked lips, like he knew why I was glaring.

"If they do know who she is, is it possible this attack was actually meant for her? Not you?" Nathalie asked, astute as ever. Ronan tilted his head, considering that.

"We shouldn't rule it out. This explosion couldn't have killed me, even if the crossing had weakened me. I wouldn't be surprised if another demon tried it anyway, but if they knew Piper is my atma, then hurting her to get to me isn't unlikely either."

"Who are you?" I repeated.

He grinned openly, almost taunting.

"Does it matter?" he asked me, an echo of the question I often found myself asking him.

"Maybe. Depends." I shrugged.

"Liar. You'd hate me either way just because I'm a demon," he said. I couldn't tell if that bothered him or not.

"Then why won't you tell me?"

Ronan took a step toward me and leaned in. "Because some truths you have to earn."

"Even if I'm your atma?"

"Especially because you're my atma," he uttered.

Seemingly oblivious to the tension between us, though I knew that wasn't the case, Nathalie paced. "Not even Lucifer knew she was your atma until last week. I think it's unlikely this is a demon. He practically owns New Chicago. Very little gets past him. And from what I know of your kind, they can be territorial—"

"We are," Ronan said, looking at me.

"Exactly. For another demon to know where you would be and coordinate an attack, they'd have to have a lot of spies that are close to you. I don't think that's likely."

"It could be Lucifer himself," I pointed out.

"Also not likely," Nathalie said. "He wouldn't endanger you this way."

I wanted to disagree, except I knew she had a point. There was also the obvious fact that I hadn't seen or heard from him since the night in the alley.

"As much as I hate to give him this, I also find it unlikely to be my brother. Besides, I haven't sensed him or his power in long enough I'm beginning to wonder if he died that night or simply entered stasis."

"Stasis?"

"The crash," he said. "All of us experience it in

some form. None like you, however."

He didn't know me, and yet he knew all my secrets. It was an odd feeling, uncomfortable at best.

"Getting back to the point at hand," I said, taking a step back from Ronan. "If it wasn't Lucifer, then who? You can feel magic. Did you feel anything strong enough to be a demon nearby?"

"No," Ronan sighed, the tension easing if not leaving entirely. "It's possible they were working through someone, just as it's possible that it's not a demon at all. Although, I wouldn't have any idea who if not a demon. As I said, I haven't been around long enough to make enemies."

"No," Nathalie agreed. "But this definitely has to do with you. Piper didn't know you were taking her there. Whoever caused it did. Either that or they've been tailing you and got out before any of us knew . . ." Nathalie's lips twisted in a displeased grimace. "Honestly, that doesn't seem all that likely either. Piper is paranoid, and I've been watching the perimeter."

"I know," he said in a way that made me confident he did. "I can sense you both. There were only four other people on the boat at the time, and none of them had the power to actually blow up a ship."

"Well someone had to," Nathalie said. "Someone that clearly knows how to get around all three of us."

I looked out over the pier, knowing that I would

find it empty, but still doing it all the same. "If no one saw, heard, or felt them, we're not going to get anywhere standing here, and I'm freezing."

"I'll look into it. Whoever did this covered their tracks well, but if they're really that intent on hurting you or me, it won't be the last time. You need to stay with Nathalie until then and try not to leave the apartment."

I opened then closed my mouth as what he said registered. "How do you know where I've been staying?"

"I had you tailed coming back from the cabin," Ronan said, completely unashamed.

"But that was three days ago."

"Yes." He lifted a dark eyebrow.

"You've known where I've been this entire time?"

"You made it clear that chasing you wouldn't work. So I didn't." But he still had someone tail me. Even in letting go of control, he was still finding ways to take it without giving me a choice. Not that I'd ever say yes.

I shook my head. I really didn't want to go into this with him. Not now, not ever. "Look, I met you here like you wanted. Time to uphold your end of the deal. I want Bree back, and I want to know what's wrong with her."

"No."

I stilled, anger making my magic prickle in my

palms as my heart started to beat louder, the sound filling my ears. "We had a deal."

"Did we?" he asked, cocking his head. "I don't recall that part."

"But you—you—" I searched for words, thinking back on the note he left.

"I never promised to give Bree back. I simply said I had her and that I wanted to meet you here. As for what's wrong with her—I told you, some truths you have to earn. This is one of them." He stepped back, and I recognized it from my dreams. He was leaving, and with him, all hope of finding and fixing Bree.

I stepped toward him and grabbed his forearm. He stopped, though I certainly didn't have the strength to make him. Something primal ran through his face when he stared at me then. I felt his desire, his need, his hunger . . . and I stood against it even as my knees threatened to buckle. "How do I earn it?"

Ronan regarded me, pausing on my lips for a moment too long.

"The second blood exchange—I want it."

I didn't give myself time to think. To consider. To fear or to hate.

"Done."

He blinked, his full lips parting in surprise. He didn't think it would be that easy. That's how much he didn't know me, because if he did, he would have known I would give anything.

Even me.

I was willing to once, and I was again. Only this time there were no other options.

He made sure of it.

"She's safe with me. I'll be in touch." His lips ghosted mine for the briefest of seconds and then he was gone. Shadows consumed his body and then faded, leaving nothing where he was standing only moments before.

I stared, feeling that prickling of anger. Nathalie fanned her face in exaggeration despite the frigid temperature.

"I can't believe he just did that. What an—"

"Asshole?" she inserted, chuckling under her breath. "Gee, it's almost like you were made for each other."

I glared in her direction and she simply laughed harder. "I said yes. I gave him what he wanted. I kind of thought he'd—I don't know—do it? Ugh." I ran a hand through my tangled hair in frustration.

"Do it?" she repeated. "Out here? Where it's below freezing, and you almost died—oh and let's not forget that someone is out to kill one or both of you?" She snorted again when I looked away. Maybe she had a point.

Not that I was going to tell her that. Nope.

I turned on my heel and walked in the opposite direction.

That just seemed to make her laugh more.

"Are you seriously mad at me right now?" she asked, jogging to keep up beside me.

"No."

"No? You're not mad?"

"I'm not mad."

"You seem mad," she said, as we walked two blocks down the street to where she parked.

"If I was mad, you would know."

"Because you'd shoot me?" she mocked.

"Yup."

By the time we got to her car, I was shaking from the cold. While the sweatshirt helped, it only did so much. My fingers were starting to turn blue by the time the heater actually got going. Nathalie paused at the wheel before pulling out onto the road.

"I know you're busy being not mad right now," she started. "But I just wanted you to know, I'm really glad you didn't drown tonight."

I side-eyed her, waiting for the rest.

"What?" she asked.

"I'm waiting for the part where you crack a dumb joke and then laugh obnoxiously because you find it funny."

She rolled her eyes. "Way to ruin a moment."

"That was not a moment," I deadpanned. "We were not having a moment."

"We so were," she said, looking to the road as she

pulled out. "And for the record, so were you and Ronan. He may be a demon and have this whole alpha male vibe going on, but he sees you."

"What happened to you staying out of it?" I snapped. She lifted her hands off the wheel in mock surrender and the car swerved. I glared at her, and she righted it while chuckling.

"I am. Mostly. It's not like I'm telling you to bond with him—you agreed to that all on your own there."

"He's got my sister," I reminded her. Nathalie shrugged.

"You kidnapped me and I'm still around," she pointed out. I was not nearly as amused as she seemed to be. "I'm just saying, if you've got an itch to scratch, he's the one I'd be wanting to scratch it."

I sighed. "I just want my sister back and to find a way to wake her up. That's it. Whatever else happens . . . it's all a means to an end."

I hoped. The truth was, I would do anything for Bree. But when this was all over . . . I knew there was no way Ronan would walk away, and every time I saw him, I was more convinced.

But these were the cards I had. The choices I could make to save her. As long as that happened, I could figure the rest out later.

Or rather, figure out how to deal with him when the time came.

3

RONAN

MY BLOOD HUMMED. My flesh tingled.

She said yes.

The second blood exchange was in sight, and easier to grasp than I'd thought—but first I had to find out who blew up that dinner boat, and what their intentions were.

If Piper's life was in danger . . . I had to eliminate the threat.

If it were just me they were after, well, my mysterious assailants were in for grave disappointment. Demons and monsters that could tear this world asunder had tried and failed. This would be no different.

I stepped through the void and into the penthouse apartment I'd collected from the Coven Antares. The lights of the city illuminated the living space through the wall of glass that went out to a small balcony. I moved about the space, comfortable but not truly at home as I poured myself a glass of scotch.

"*Someone tried to kill me tonight. Me and Piper,*" I mentally communicated to the boy. He wasn't truly a servant, but close enough. He'd traded his will for power. His freedom for more magic. Ultimately, it was his decency he gave up. In letting me into his mind, I was privy to things about the witch that I never would have allowed if the roles were reversed and it was Piper I was asked to spy on—but that was humans for you. Their greed ran deep, supernatural or not. At their core, they were human, and therefore fallible.

"*Is Nat alright?*" he asked, anxiety edging his mind instantly.

"*She's fine, but I need you to go to the pier and see if you can find any residual magic and trace it. Keep your head down. Don't attract attention. Have you heard anything in the Underworld about this?*"

I knew he hadn't. He would have reported otherwise. Our bargain and the magic that formed it would have compelled him. Still, something wasn't adding up, and I felt the need to ask.

"*No, nothing. People are still focused on Lucifer missing.*"

As was I. My brother didn't just simply disappear without a trace. Just like dinner boats didn't just explode. Something was going on. Pieces were being moved on a board, but the game itself was evading me.

"Let me know if that changes."

"Of course," came his immediate reply.

I sipped at my scotch. Savoring the salty brine undertones for a few suspended moments. While this flesh was not like my previous form, it had some pleasures on its own. I could see why Lucifer was able to make a life here and enjoy it.

The human weakness was its own flesh.

Just as a demon's was its soul.

I set the glass aside and made my way toward the shower, needing one after the dip I took in the lake. I paused at the second bedroom and stuck my head inside.

Bree Fallon lay utterly unconscious, her light brown hair spilling over the pillow. Her limbs were exactly as I'd left them. It was only the bauble around her neck that Piper had paid for with all their family savings that kept her body alive and muscles from wasting into atrophy.

Convinced she was undisturbed, I pulled away and closed the door behind me.

I stripped the disgusting water-soaked clothes from my body as I walked. Peeling the layers of fabric from my skin until I was naked outside the shower. I stepped in and flipped the water on, unflinching against the cold spray.

It cooled my blood. The need to hunt down the fuckers that dared put my atma at risk. The desire to kill anyone involved. But most importantly, my urge to go to Piper.

She didn't need me, I knew that. My woman was strong. She had a soul of blood and fire. An iron will. A mean streak that few could survive.

Piper the woman held strong against the bond, even as her walls were starting to crack. Piper the demon was another case entirely, though she didn't seem to realize it.

I wanted them both, just as I wanted the second exchange.

But first, I needed to find the fuckers involved, because if there was one thing I knew about my atma —it's that she would be out for blood regardless of what I said.

4

I TOSSED and turned in my sleep, stuck in a place that
existed between exhaustion and restlessness. My legs
twisted in the sheets, and my hands skimmed the
surface of the bed aimlessly. I was too hot. Too cold.
Too tired to rise, but too wired to actually rest.

In the back of my mind, I sensed a presence
watching me. It was dark and shadowy. It stayed out
of my dreams, dancing just around the edge of my
mind, ever-present but unseen. In another time,
another place, I might have thought myself paranoid.
That I was imagining things. I'd entered two blood
exchanges with two different demons, though, and I
wasn't imagining shit.

It was only on the cusp of waking that the entity
drifted closer, never taking form, but making itself
known.

He didn't say anything, seeming content to simply occupy the same headspace as me. Even if only for a moment.

I want Bree back, I thought into the void.

My eyes opened as a response came from everywhere and nowhere at once.

Be careful. I'll come to you when I know it's safe.

I groaned.

Safe. It was a stupid word. A meaningless use of four letters. Safety was an illusion, one only the powerful could afford to be ignorant in. Being raised human, even if I wasn't one anymore, meant I didn't believe in such pretty delusions.

I could die walking down the road at the wrong time in the wrong place.

There was no fucking way I was letting a threat that was *maybe* targeting me, stop me from getting out there and finding my sister—especially when Ronan didn't seem in any hurry now that he had me right where he wanted.

I rolled over, groaning lightly when my joints popped. The sky was still a hazy shade of gray blue. Clear, but early. The sun wasn't even completely out, but it would be soon.

I dragged myself out of bed despite the pounding in my right temple begging me to stay. Cool air fanned the skin that my skimpy tank top did little to cover. I ran a hand down my arm, over the goosebumps, as I padded barefoot across the wood floors to the half dresser. It only took me a second to fish out a pair of loose black pants and a long-sleeved shirt. My sports bra was a harder find, and when I did, it was still damp from the unplanned swim I took the night before. I dropped the sopping material to the floor in favor of the only other bra I had that didn't smell like mold and lake water. Changing quickly, I slipped out of my room, AKA Nathalie's official guest room, and down the hall to pee and brush my teeth. Once my mouth tasted like grainy mint toothpaste, I headed back down the hall, my footsteps near silent on the wood floors. It was early enough Nathalie hadn't risen yet, and from the little bit I really knew of her schedule, I had a feeling she wouldn't for a while yet.

I paused by the front door to put on socks and a new pair of sneakers Nat had bought me in her big shopping binge a few days prior. I was severely lacking in clothing due to the move from my old apartment to the cabin, and then here. When on the run, you take the bare essentials. While a few things like my beloved turtlenecks and underwear had made it, things like shoes and such were a goner. Being rich as fuck as she was, Nathalie went on an online shopping binge—a luxury only the wealthy could afford. Even the internet was a luxury. She bought me everything she deemed I needed, from sneakers to leather jackets to lingerie.

I shook my head, thinking of the lace bits she'd presented to me, so proud of herself.

Both cups combined might hold up my left tit, but that's it. While sexy, their functionality left a lot to be desired. She insisted I needed sexy things, though, just in case a demon or two needed seducing.

I rolled my eyes, thinking about how she told me that when all the boxes arrived later that afternoon. Because she hadn't asked my permission, I didn't feel as guilty accepting them from her. Besides, one of us was loaded, and the other wasn't. The fact she even had access to the internet at all spoke to that. There was a time when anyone and everyone could access it, but after the Magic Wars, everything became more expensive. Electricity and electronics were already a luxury item, they just became a sign of wealth as well. Cell phones dropped off when magic was so prevalent, and nothing was secure. The ordinary person had to buy shit at a supermarket or know a guy these days. But not Nat, no, she had certain privileges. Money and magic being the most obvious.

I grabbed a coat and one of the keys that would let me back in, then I slipped out the front door. I moved slowly, closing it behind me. When the mechanism on the handle whirred and the lock clicked shut, I breathed easier.

Now for the last challenge.

Making it out of the shop without any problems. I

was most of the way down the hall when I paused mid-step at the squealing of a hinge. I glanced over my shoulder as a black cat darted out from Señora Rosara's apartment open door. She stood with her arms crossed over her chest, dark hair in a shower cap, and dressed in silk pajamas.

"You were loud last night," she said, offering no further explanation as to why she was confronting me in the hallway at the buttcrack of dawn.

"We tried to keep it down," I replied.

"Hmm." She pressed her lips together, not liking that response. "Nathalie wasn't loud before you moved in."

"So you do know her name," I mused, tilting my head while ignoring her statement. "And here I was wondering if dementia had kicked in, or if you simply didn't care to use it."

Rage flashed in her expression. One moment she was standing at the door, and the next she was right in front of me. Despite my demonic powers and six inches of added height, I had a feeling she could give me a run for my money—if I wasn't broke.

"Now you listen here," she hissed.

I held up a hand to stop her.

"Look, before you go on threatening to turn me into a cat, let's just get this straight. You like your quiet. You like to not be disturbed. Believe it or not, I get that—and I try not to be loud when coming in or out, but we live in a shithole. This entire country is one bad thing away from being classified as hell on earth. Sometimes, shit happens. If you don't want to hear us, spell the building for silence so you don't have to. Or soundproof your walls. Or play music—I don't really care. I'll never try to inconvenience you, but I'm not tiptoeing around you like she does either."

Her dark eyes narrowed, and she hummed under her breath once more. "I don't like you," she said.

"I'm aware."

"I told her you'd be trouble."

"Maybe she needs a little trouble so people will stop walking all over her," I said with a pointed look, crossing my own arms over my chest. The black cat started winding its way around my legs, brushing up against me. I wasn't sure if that was its version of begging for help, or if it was warning me about prodding the witch.

The older woman cracked a smile.

"Perhaps." In the blink of an eye, she disappeared from in front of me and was back at her door. Señora Rosara leaned over and picked up the black cat. It purred loudly, big violet eyes staring at me. "Keep her safe. And don't drink the coffee, you'll need it."

I opened my mouth to ask her what she meant, but the door slammed shut.

I blinked once, the irony of it not lost on me. I shook my head as I stepped into the elevator. The ride was short, and the shop below was empty as I navigated my way through it. A more curious person would look through the various items, anything from voodoo dolls to glowing orbs filled with magic. Shadows moved in this place, though, shadows I was pretty sure were actually her ever-watchful cats. How many she had, I wasn't sure. But I wasn't interested in becoming one of them.

I kept my eyes and my hands to myself as I made my way through the crowded shop, careful not to bump into anything. The shop door pealed like wind chimes when I opened it, despite the fact there weren't any. I stepped outside, taking a second to breathe in the crisp air. The cold heightened my senses. It stripped me of any false senses of security, reminding me to be alert. I stuffed my hands in my pockets and balled them into fists as I walked down the cracked sidewalk. There were a few stragglers out this time of day, but like me, they were minding their own.

Two blocks down, there was a coffee shop that I'd been going to for the last few days. While Nathalie was capable of making the stuff, it was a good spot to watch. To learn. I stepped inside and ordered my usual: black drip, no cream, no sugar.

I waited next to the window at one of the high barstools. The shop was full swing this morning. Not many cafes could boast being packed at dawn these days, but this one could. That's why I came to it.

Walking all over New Chicago wouldn't yield me anything but sore feet and possibly getting mugged. Without a job, my cash flow was limited to Nathalie's generosity and the couple thousand I had in my wallet, which meant paying someone for information wasn't an option either. That left the only other practical solution when trying to keep a low profile. Listening.

But that wasn't the only reason I was here today.

No . . . I needed answers, and I needed them soon if I was going to get Ronan to move ahead with the second blood exchange. So here I was, sitting in the crowded coffee shop . . . as bait.

I leaned back, pretending to watch nothing in particular as I stared at the reflection in the window of what was going on behind me. A few figures were milling about next to the pickup counter. That, in itself, wasn't unusual.

I waited, and when they called my name, I didn't immediately jump to my feet.

Don't drink the coffee. Isn't that what Señora Rosara said? I had to wonder if the old bat had some sort of sight. She didn't strike me as the type to hire goons to follow me and know where I went every morning when not even Nathalie knew.

A few seconds passed, and when no one reached for the coffee, I frowned.

Sliding off the chair, my sneakers let out a squeak as I landed softly against the cement floors. I strolled over to the counter, not in a hurry. The barista's back was already turned as she started on the next drink, leaving it up to me to claim mine or have it stolen.

I grabbed the cup, wrapping my fingers around it. The heat warmed my numbing fingers through the cardboard hand holder. Instead of going back to my seat and listening to the latest gossip about the Underworld and New Chicago, I stepped outside.

Wind rattled the windows as it funneled down the tight streets, bouncing off of building fronts as it looked for a way out. I turned left, going in the opposite direction of the apartment.

My heart rate picked up, but deep, even breathing kept it under control. My feet moved on their own accord, knowing not to go too fast or slow.

I was careful not to fidget much, and even if I couldn't be at ease, I could pretend I was. Stuffing one hand in my jacket pocket, I wandered aimlessly, pretending to have a destination in mind.

Only when I felt eyes on me did I start to actively look at where I was going.

I needed somewhere quiet. Undisturbed. Something like . . .

Bingo.

I paused at the edge of the sidewalk, not looking behind me, though I sensed someone there. I crossed the street quickly and then slipped in the alley.

Luck was with me for once in this shitty life. There was a door at the end with a flickering light over it. I started for it like that was my destination, trying not to slow too much. I made it halfway there, watching the wall beside me out the corner of my eye.

One second my shadow was alone. The next, there was a second one behind it.

I pulled my hand out of my pocket and reached up to pull the lid off my coffee.

The shadow behind me paused.

I leaned forward like I was inhaling the scent of my coffee and hummed happily when I saw them creep forward.

Then I pivoted.

One hand thrust out to throw the hot coffee on whoever was behind me.

The second came up to swing a strong left hook on what I hoped was a head.

The coffee stopped midair. A masculine hiss of pain registered right before my fist contacted with something hard.

A man blinked into existence, wearing said hot

coffee as my punch to his jaw sent him reeling. I registered that he wore dark clothes. Nothing that would
help distinguish him.

Before he could recover from the hit, I slid my foot
back and then aimed a low roundhouse kick for his
thigh.

My mystery man let out a howl, his leg buckling.
He teetered sideways and then dropped onto his
injured side. Now that he was kneeling and no taller
than my chest, this was getting fun.

Part of me was a little disappointed that someone
who had gone through great lengths to track me
wasn't skilled enough to handle me even without my
magic or guns.

I stepped forward and aimed a knee shot directly
into his chest. I could have aimed for the jaw, but I
needed him conscious. The chest, however, worked to
my advantage. Air left his lungs in a strangled exhale
that sent him backwards. His back hit the ground, and
he wheezed hard, giving me the first decent look of
his face.

Dark hair. Blue eyes. Red marks lining the left side
of his chiseled jaw in the shape of my knuckles. He
might have been pretty if not for that.

Such a shame. Or maybe not.

The pretty ones often liked to stay that way.

I dropped down on top of him, planting one knee
on his chest. I used my free leg to pin his left arm to

the ground, my foot crushing his wrist. My right hand came down on the other, holding it down next to his face.

I leaned close, the scent of coffee and cologne washing over me.

"Now that we've got that unpleasantness out of the way—"

He reared back and then his mouth jutted forward. A wet glob of spit smacked me in the face. My eyes hardened.

Using my free arm, I brought my elbow down on his jaw in the same place I'd punched him, eliciting a sound of pain. Then I followed it up by pressing my forearm into his neck, cutting off his air supply.

"Buddy, we can do this the easy way or the hard way. How messed up you are when I walk out of the alley is all on you."

He glared back, cheeks turning a deep shade of crimson.

"I don't have forever, and I'm not dumb enough to wait around for whatever backup you have. I'm going to ask you a question. You get one shot at answering before I stick my thumbs through your eyes and blind you. Hopefully. May kill you if I'm not careful enough—and let's be honest, I haven't done this all that often. It's been a while since the last one, so it's really in your best interest if you want to keep your vision. Got it?"

His glare sharpened, but he nodded once, just the slightest dip of his chin in acknowledgement.

"Good," I said, easing off his throat just enough to let him speak. "Who the fuck are you, and why are you tracking me?"

5

He started to speak.

"I'm just the——"

His words cut off in a pained cry. He seized upwards, as if pulled by an invisible string. His eyes rolled back in his head. Then his skin started to *burn*.

It turned red splotchy, steadily darkening until embers formed and ate away at the flesh. The edges glowed hot and the burning spread, melting his skin from his bones in seconds.

I jumped back before the fire could catch on me or my clothes, and I watched as some magically induced curse killed him. There was nothing I could do. No magic I possessed to save him. No action I could have taken to prevent his death.

When the screaming stopped, there was nothing left but a pile of ashen bones and flakes of skin in the wind. Whoever he was, he wasn't the mastermind. That curse was meant to prevent him from talking.

I pressed my lips together, lost in thought as I turned over what I just witnessed.

I didn't notice the air around me. I didn't sense the thickening of power or brush of dark magic over my skin.

I didn't know he was here until he stepped out of the shadows.

Ronan's eyes flashed, and thunder clapped overhead. The winds stirred, lifting my hair from the nape of my neck.

I glowered.

"What are you doing here?"

"Powerful magic," he said, eyes scanning the alley then landing on the blacked spot of cracked pavement. "Not your magic," he added, "but powerful all the same." He leaned down and swiped two fingers over the dead man's ashes. Black soot stained the tips as he lifted them back to his face and sniffed once.

His nostrils flared.

Magic pulsed once in warning.

He stood, wiping the remains on his tailored black pants.

"What did you learn?" I asked him, slightly begrudging I had to ask to begin with.

"I'm not sure," he mused. "I'll let you know once I follow up."

Ronan-speak for *I'm not telling you.*

My lips thinned.

"Or you could tell me," I said pointedly, not letting it drop. He smirked once, eyes raking over my body. I wasn't wearing anything particularly attractive or revealing, but you wouldn't know it with the way he perused, as if he owned every square inch of it.

Although, I suppose in his mind, he did.

Asshole.

"What happened to staying in the apartment?" he said, voice condemning even if his gaze seemed more interested in undressing me. I crossed my arms over my chest.

"I never agreed to that. You ordered it."

"For your safety," he said, steel-gray eyes coming back to my face. Some of the heat drained in place of frustration. "I assumed you were smart enough to leave this be until I figured it out. You ignored my order to stay in your apartment and then went the opposite way on your morning walk. Almost like you were . . ." His eyes flicked down to the blacked patch and hardened further.

"You're not the only one capable of tailing me, Ronan. I took a gamble that whoever our mysterious attacker was might be as well. Looks like I was right."

The muscles in his jaw clenched. "The curse that killed him wasn't some weak witch. You could have been hurt—"

"Yet, I'm not," I pointed out.

He narrowed his eyes. "You're not even carrying this morning."

"Obviously," I said. "Having a gun strapped to my side wasn't going to lend to my attacker being sloppy."

"You used yourself as bait," he said softly. Anger permeated his expression and flashed in his eyes. "That was—"

"Smart."

"Stupid."

I lifted an eyebrow. "You underestimate me. This conversation is getting old."

He chuckled, deep and dark and sinfully attractive. "I don't underestimate you. Yes, you were fine this time. You didn't end up needing your guns. But what about last night? You were thrown from the boat and almost drowned. What if it had been more than one man? What if the curse was meant to target you as well?"

He took a step closer and my hackles rose. I hated it when he tried to intimidate me.

"I hate to break it to you, but my guns aren't my only weapon."

He lifted a hand to cup my cheek, and then roughly changed his grip to grab my chin and tilt it up. "Yes. Your other *weapon*. The one you detest, yet also rely on to get you out of a pinch. The one that's slowly robbing you of time and eating away at your psyche."

I wrenched my chin away and took another step back, only to hit the wall. Ronan crowded me. He braced both hands against the wall on either side of my head, leaning close to fill me with his intoxicatingly disgusting scent—

"Stop being a prick," I snapped. "Like it or not, you can't control me. I went out for answers since you clearly won't give me any. If you don't like it, you only have yourself to blame."

Black fire flashed in his eyes. "Is that so?"

"Yes."

"Tell me, Piper, how is it my fault that every time you use your magic, your body can't handle the power, so it crashes and goes into stasis? Tell me how it's my fault that you haven't stabilized, and every waking minute you're a ticking time bomb waiting to blow? Tell me how—"

"Bree," I said. "You have Bree. You won't give her back. You won't tell me what's wrong with her. For my sister, I'll do anything. That's why you took her, you arrogant sack of shit." I pushed forward, away from the wall, and the distance between our bodies was only a breath away.

"Did it ever occur to you, I did that for you?" he breathed, anger lacing his voice like the sweetest of poisons.

I blinked. "That's—"

"Think about it, Piper. You were hauling her around the city like a sack of potatoes. I didn't have to break into the cabin. I walked right in. There were no defenses. Nothing to stop me. Anyone could have taken her."

His scent was too much. His words too much.

"But it wasn't anyone," I said, holding onto my reasoning. "It was *you*."

"Yes," he agreed. "Me. The one person in this city that would not hurt you."

"Taking her hurt me," I argued. "And besides that, she wasn't yours to take. She's *mine*."

He grinned, and I wanted to punch him in the face.

"She is yours, but you are mine. I'm simply keeping her safe. Consider that you haven't been able to find her, not even searching with magic. I know you've tried." I pressed my lips together, but my silence confirmed it. He was right. We had tried, multiple times. I had Nathalie scry, and when that didn't yield anything, we went to Barry. No matter how many times, though, we couldn't find her. "If you can't find her, no one else can. Which means no one can use her against you."

"Except you."

He smiled cruelly. "Except me." That he didn't even try to deny that point . . .

I shook my head. Arguing with him was doing my head in.

"You don't even see what's wrong with this, do you?"

Ronan tilted his head. "Wrong? Right? They are all relative. I chased you. I hunted you. That didn't work. Now I don't have to chase. You come willingly."

"Because you stole her."

He shrugged. "I used what was available to me. I told you, Piper, I have every intention of claiming you. For now, that means I need her. One day I won't."

I snorted derisively. "I wouldn't sound so sure if I were you."

He smirked, completely unfazed. "I have no doubts. You'll find that I'm a patient man. I've waited thousands of years for you. I can wait a little longer."

I stood, frozen to the spot.

Thousands?

I couldn't truly comprehend that time, or that he'd actually waited that long for an atma. It was sad, in a way. All that time waiting, and he was rewarded with me.

I guess I wasn't the only one fate liked to fuck over on occasion.

I fell back against the wall, letting my head tilt up as I started to laugh. It wasn't a pretty sound or amusing in the slightest. It was desperate and edged with emotions I didn't want to feel, and it was as cruel as his smile.

Ronan frowned. "Why are you laughing?"

"Because," I said, wiping the dampness from my eyes, "you waited thousands of years for me. A human who *hates* magic. I suppose it makes sense why you're not so picky now. After that long, willing or not, it doesn't particularly matter to you—"

Lips crashed into mine. Hard. Demanding. He moved with a sensual grace and savage need that decimated my carefully crafted walls. His tongue parted the seam of my mouth, kissing me even when I wouldn't kiss back.

My hands shook, and I clenched them into fists to keep from grabbing him.

I wasn't sure if I would pull him closer or push him away.

That scared me.

His tongue didn't brush against mine. It wasn't soft or gentle or hesitant in any way. It took mine. Demanded mine. He claimed my mouth the same way he wanted to claim my body and soul and mind.

I held tight to my sanity. My beliefs. My self-control.

It took everything I had not to kiss him back.

And then the fucker bit me.

"Don't insult yourself or make this out to be

something it isn't. You're my atma, and you're not a fucking disappointment."

Blood coated my lips, and he licked it greedily. My breath hitched. My heartbeat sped up. A groan escaped from somewhere deep inside me, and I crumbled.

He pressed me into the wall, and I arched away. Our mouths met in a clash of passion, desire, and in my case—hate.

I could regret my actions later. Hell, I was certain I regretted it now—but it didn't stop me.

I might lie in bed with self-loathing for company, but in that moment, I was fire—and I was unleashing on him.

He gripped my hips, pulling them into him. I twined my arms around his shoulders and grabbed at his hair. My nails raked his scalp as I pulled it taut, uncaring for the pain I delivered on him.

For what he was taking from me, he could handle a little pain.

Ronan broke away first, but he didn't release me.

He lifted me off the ground, hands wrapped around my thighs as he pressed himself in between them. I hooked my legs around his waist, crossing my ankles behind his back. He pressed his thickness into me, lighting my nerve endings aflame.

I gasped.

His lips trailed down my neck, suckling and biting along the way.

I pulled on his hair, but Ronan didn't move an inch. He groaned into my shoulder, pressing another hot kiss to my neck and then biting *hard*.

I knew without a doubt he'd drawn blood.

His tongue lapped at it, sucking the wound as he rubbed against me. His cock brushing against my sweatpants sent delicious friction over my clit. And without any warning whatsoever, I detonated.

It was quick and hard and blinding. I threw my head back, slamming it into the wall. A crack echoed through the alley, or perhaps that was just in my mind because stars blinded me.

Fire swept through my veins as my entire body seized with desire and then released. The warmth between my legs pulsed, and I pressed into him, driven by that itch I had to scratch.

I shuddered and shook like it was my first time.

It wasn't, but given the way Ronan froze, he might have thought it was.

As the aftershocks stopped and my orgasm faded into languidness, my own unsettling reality closed in on me.

"Put me down."

"No."

I kicked my legs and pulled his hair. "Goddamnit, Ronan. I said—"

One of his hands released my thigh to come under my ass and grab a handful. The other came up to wrap around my neck. He didn't squeeze, but he held tight. Possessive. Owning. I stared at him, letting him see my hate.

"You're upset," he said, his own eyes filled with desire.

"How observant."

The muscle in his jaw tensed, but he didn't release me. "You're upset with yourself. You acted without thinking it through. For a second, you forgot who I was. Now you want to run away and forget it."

All the heat that had filled my body faded into ice because he *saw* me. He saw the truth. I could have denied it, but what was the point? We both knew it would be a lie.

But there was something he did say that was wrong. Something I wasn't going to correct.

He said I forgot who he was.

The problem was I didn't.

I knew exactly who it was that bit my neck and kissed me senseless. I never lost sight of him when I came.

And I hated myself for it more.

It would have been easier to lie to myself had I replaced him with some nameless, faceless entity.

But I hadn't.

I came to his touch.

To him grinding against me.

To his hands grabbing and squeezing and stroking.

To his lips as they unraveled me.

I came for him, and while I might regret it, part of me wanted to again.

"It means nothing," I said scathingly. "I had an itch, and used you to scratch it," I added, thinking back on Nathalie's words from the night before.

He grinned cruelly. "Lie to me all you want, Piper. Your body sings for me. It *begs* for me—"

"You're laying it on a little thick there," I said through clenched teeth. "It's been a while. Stop making this out to be something it isn't."

"How long has it been?" he asked, taunting. His head tilted to the side, and I sensed a slight shift.

Over a year. I didn't say that. Instead, I simply repeated, "A while."

"Good," he said slowly. "I won't share you. Every part of you will be mine." He leaned forward to brush his lips against mine. "Your secrets. Your pleasure. Your fury." He smiled at the last one. I scowled.

"You really don't know how to take a hint, do you?"

"I'm simply not scared away by your pain. That's what this is—this running, this chasing—you've been hurt. Not by a man, but by your world. You wear that pain like armor to keep anyone away that might get close enough to hurt you. You won't allow that, so you push them away. I won't be pushed away. Fight me. Fuck me. Run or hide—it won't matter." He tightened his hold on my neck for a moment, pulling me forward so that I saw my face reflecting in the black fire raging in his eyes. "I always get what I want, and by the time I take you, Piper, you'll want me too. You already do."

It took everything I had not to shudder as he peeled me apart like the layers of an onion. Nat was right. He saw me. He saw too much.

"Pain exists to remind us of the past. It serves as a warning of what's coming when we make stupid choices. And you?" I eased into his grip. "Ronan, you wouldn't just be a stupid choice. You'd be devastating. You'd come into my life, and you'd ruin it. But by then, I'd probably want you to. The guilt, the hatred; it would eat me alive. For as much as you know about me, surely you see that?"

His face was emotionless for a moment, and then the slightest softening occurred. "Your hurt runs deep, and you're confused, but that's okay. We'll get there. I'm not leaving, which means eventually you'll have to accept me. You may break apart from the guilt, but I'll be there to put you back together again."

I blanched, his words hitting something in my chest that squeezed tightly.

"That wasn't what I was—"

My words stilled on my lips as the alley behind him disappeared.

Darkness so black it was void of anything enveloped me. I felt his hands on my skin, but I couldn't see him despite there being only inches between us.

My heartbeat kicked up a notch, teetering dangerously close to the edge.

Then light filled the room. I blinked back against it, feeling blinded even though it wasn't particularly bright.

"Where are we?" I said, trying to twist around and see.

Gray walls. Black wood floors. Minimalist furniture.

"My apartment."

I wrinkled my nose, though it rang true with what I was seeing. "Apartment? Since when did you have time to afford all this . . ." I started, but my words abruptly halted. The fight left me as we walked into a room. My legs were still wrapped around him. His hands were still all over me, but one look at the unconscious girl in her bed, and I settled.

Ronan slid me down his body, letting me regain my footing.

I stumbled forward, sinking to my knees. My hand reached for her and lowered slowly to her skin. It was dry, but it was always dry. Being inside for ten years did that to a person. She looked so fragile against the slate gray sheets. Her brown hair fanned over her pillow in long, wispy strands. The necklace around her neck pulsed with magical energy that kept her body from degenerating. It kept her healthy despite the fact she hadn't eaten in ten years.

"As you can see, she's safe and unharmed. The same way she'll remain."

"Unless I do what you want," I added bitterly.

"No," he disagreed. "No matter what you choose to do, I won't take it out on her. That would only hurt you more, and she's done nothing to deserve it. If I'm angry with you, I'll come to you, but I give you my word she will be safe here."

I lowered my hand to the bed, clenching the sheet in my fist. It smelled like mint and lilies in here. The scent was clean and soothing, but I didn't want to be soothed.

I wanted to be angry. I wanted to rage.

He was so pigheaded, and yet . . . not.

It beguiled me. It fascinated me. It made it harder to push him away, and easier to listen, yet my own guilt and distrust ate at me all the same.

"How do I know you're not lying?" I asked.

"You don't," he said simply. I whipped my head around to glare at him, and he shrugged. "You also have no choice in the matter. I won't let you have her back right now, so your guilt can rest easy knowing you had no other alternative. You'll just have to trust me."

"I don't," I said.

"I know, but you will."

So confident. So sure.

I was beginning to doubt myself in the face of his absolute certainty, and that just wouldn't do.

"Why'd you bring me here?" I said, not getting off my knees. I was content to be next to Bree while facing Ronan.

"A show of good faith. You're worried about her, but you don't need to be. What you need is to stop trying to get yourself killed. I'm handling the incident that happened at the boat. You trying to lure out our mysterious combatant only distracts me."

I grit my teeth. "I'm not going to sit around on my ass. Whoever it was had me tailed, which means this isn't just about you."

"Exactly, which is why you need to stay in the apartment. You're safe there. The young witch's wards are strong, and what she can't handle, I can. If you're going to go wandering about—"

"You'll what? Bring me here? Lock me up?" I snorted. "We'll see how well that goes for you."

"There are other ways to keep you subdued," he said, a rumbling growl in his voice. I sensed that I'd poked at something, and I couldn't resist the urge to dig my nails in deeper.

"Other ways?"

"The blood exchange," he said. My eyebrows drew together in slight confusion. "It'll trigger your magic. You'll enter stasis afterward."

My lips parted.

Well, shit.

I hadn't planned on that when I'd agreed. I suddenly wasn't bothered about the fact he didn't just do it right there on the pier like I'd originally hoped.

"Are you sure?" I asked, looking away.

"Quite," he said. "It's the reason I haven't done it despite the need to claim you . . ." His voice darkened, growing husky. "You test my patience and control, but every time you enter stasis, you put yourself at risk. I know the episodes are getting longer. Eventually you may not wake up. I can't chance that."

I stared at Bree, trying to process the emotions running through me despite feeling overloaded and overwhelmed.

He didn't push me for it because he knew it would prompt the crash.

He knew it was lengthening, and he was trying to prevent it.

And Bree . . . if I never woke up, I'd never see her again. Even if there was a way to save her.

"What's wrong with her?" I asked, knowing he likely wouldn't answer.

Ronan sighed. "I told you my price for that information."

"You also won't do it right now, will you?" I said without looking at him.

"No."

"I could bite you," I pointed out, twisting a lock of her hair with my index finger. "You bit me in the alley. All I would have to do is get a drop and that would trigger it. Then you'd have to tell me."

I heard the smirk in his voice when he spoke. "I wouldn't let you, and you can't stop me."

I growled under my breath. "Why make the deal if you won't go through with it?"

He was silent for a moment. I dropped my hand away from Bree and pushed back onto my heels, then stood. "For the same reason you accepted it without thinking. You'll do anything for her. Once I tell you, all your focus will go into finding a way to bring her back. You don't care about yourself. You won't concern yourself with the danger. You'll just run and dive in headfirst. Maybe you'll find the answer, maybe you won't— but I need to limit the danger you put yourself in first."

My lips thinned, and I crossed my arms over my chest when I faced him. "You want time," I said. "But is it time to find our mysterious attacker . . . or time to try to win me over?"

He smiled coldly, and I knew I hit the nail on the head.

"Both."

"It won't work," I said. "You're just delaying the inevitable."

He lifted a masculine eyebrow. "And what is that?"

I didn't even hesitate as I said, "Me finding a way to end you."

Ronan laughed, not taking my dark threat seriously in the slightest. Anger kindled inside me. A spark of something like fire ignited.

I started toward him. Hands clenched and heart pounding.

My eyes were locked on the crook of his neck.

He must have seen it. My intent.

I got close, but not close enough before black surrounded me. I found myself in the void once more, and while I sensed him there, I had no way of knowing where.

I stumbled forward, swinging my arms around in the hopes of catching him off guard and hitting him. A dark chuckle whispered over my skin.

"Not even you believe that lie anymore," his voice said, coming from everywhere and nowhere at once.

"You don't know what I believe," I snapped.

"Oh, but that's where you're wrong. I know you better than anyone, even yourself. And I want to know you better still." Something like naked fingers grazed my spine, but that wasn't possible. I was wearing a jacket . . . "Take a couple of days. Lie low. Let me follow up on some leads, and if you still want the blood exchange, I'll do it."

Lips grazed my own.

I lunged forward, teeth out, prepared to bite.

Then ran headfirst into Nathalie's door.

The wards activated, and I bounced off it, flying back on my ass.

"Ow," I groaned, sitting up and rubbing the top of my head. A dark chuckle echoed around me as I muttered, "Fucker."

A door opened, but it wasn't Nathalie's.

Señora Rosara peeked through the crack, her brown eyes narrowed on me. I lifted my hands in surrender. "That wasn't me. Blame the demon."

"Mhmm," she hummed, pursing her lips. The door slammed shut, and I sighed.

A couple of days.

Then I'd have the answer I'd been seeking for over a decade.

I'd waited this long; a few more days wouldn't kill me.

Right?

6

RONAN

I'D GROWN QUITE fond of the dark look in her eyes when she threatened murder. The way the lapis blue changed to periwinkle, as the rage magic within her peeked out—using her eyes like windows to the world. Even when she wasn't actively using it, it was there all the same. Watching. Guarding. Always waiting to be unleashed.

But today wasn't the day, and right now wasn't the time.

Not when the magic that killed her stalker in the alley was potent enough for me to recognize it, and yet too faint to trace.

It had the bite of rage.

But the smoothness of spirit.

There was a feverish quality that leaned toward desire.

And a hard, unyielding cold that followed death.

I shook my head and returned to the alley, hoping that I might see something I missed the first time. Some clue as to who the mysterious puppet master could be.

I stepped out of the void, my eyes going to the spot where I'd stood with Piper not fifteen minutes before. There was a crack in the wall from where her head slammed back as she came.

I clenched my fist, trying to push that from my mind for another time. The last thing I needed was to lose this battle I was waging against my own magic. It wanted her with a sort of desperation that leaked into my psyche so easily. But she wasn't ready, not yet. Even if her will was weakening . . .

I tore my eyes away from the brick wall to the spot where the ashes of her attacker were. Where they should have been.

Only someone had cleaned up in the time I was gone.

Not a sign of the ashes or any traces of magic remained anywhere. I walked the full length of the alley and around the block to be sure.

When I picked up nothing, I stepped back through the void and into the penthouse apartment.

"Piper was attacked today. Again," I mentally communicated, jarring the boy from his sleep.

"Wait, wh—"

"Nathalie was not there, but it does not change that my atma was attacked. What have you heard?" Silence greeted me as the boy fumbled with his thoughts.

"It's the same as it has been," the boy insisted. *"Lucifer is missing. There are power struggles going on in the Underworld. It looks like the black-witch families are winning, but the land is being carved up and divided among the supes that can actually hold it."*

"No mention of Piper?" I asked, tilting my head as I felt through his thoughts, sensing nervousness.

"No, nothing. If anything it's only been some mentions of Nat and what happened with her in the pits when Lucifer had her. Piper is the Witch Hunter, so it was not abnormal for her to have gotten in the bad with Lucifer and potentially disappear when he did."

Ah, yes. The witch. She displayed and controlled another's power—a power she did not possess. Only the people of this world were fools and failed to realize she was nearly as rare and powerful as Piper, albeit different. I wouldn't have left my atma with her if she wasn't.

"And me? Have you heard whispers of the harvester or another demon being here?" I inquired, moving about the apartment to check every room out of habit more than anything. I was the strongest demon in this realm, possibly ever—but I also had my atma's unconscious sister and I could not become lax. Even the best can be fooled or overcome when they let

their pride get in the way. I would not make that mistake.

"Everyone that has seen you outside of me, Piper, and Nat —have died. There's no one left to talk about you," the boy answered groggily. I could see him rubbing his eyes and brushing his teeth. Satisfied with the answers he'd given me so far, I asked him one more thing.

"What do you know about chaos magic?"

7

I CLEANED MY GUNS TWICE. The familiar rhythm soothed my nerves.

It had been three days since I'd left the building and gone for coffee.

Three days since I'd watched a man die, magic ending his ability to speak.

Three days since Ronan found me and took me back to his apartment.

Three fucking days, and I was still stewing.

"I'm pretty sure they're clean by now," Nathalie said, from the kitchen. She stood on the other side of the bar, leaning over the edge, a glass of something fruity in hand. Her brown hair was tied up in a messy bun, and she wore a sweatshirt two sizes too large.

"I don't believe I asked for your opinion," I replied, even though my hands stilled. I was on the verge of disassembling them for a third time, just because I had nothing better to do.

Turns out, lying low for days on end could actually kill me.

I felt like there was an irritation under my skin that I just couldn't reach. A nervousness I couldn't rid myself of. My own demons were staring me down from the shadowed corners of my mind. It's not like they weren't there before. They were. But it's easier to ignore them when you're busy fighting for your life.

Sitting around with nothing to do? They haunted me.

Nathalie let out a sigh. "You're being bitchier than normal. Why don't you go pick some vegetables for me? I'll make dinner. You're always nicer when you're fed."

A frown tugged at my lips, but, well—she wasn't wrong.

I was nicer, but who wasn't after eating? But the fresh air would do me good.

"Fine," I grumbled, stuffing one of the guns in the holster at the small of my back. I left the other one on the table, unloaded and with the safety on. I didn't need to warn Nat not to touch my shit. She had no desire to learn to shoot. She figured she could talk herself out of most anything, and what she couldn't, I could do the shooting. Still, the lessons I'd learned growing up were drilled into my mind. While most supes wouldn't die if you shot them—humans didn't have that luxury.

I learned at a young age because I had to. Because the risk of not being able to protect myself outweighed the risk I'd accidentally kill someone.

Nathalie didn't say anything as I donned a pair of sneakers and a jacket. She started a kettle of water for tea, leaving me to bear the cold for dinner.

The roof was frigid. While this wasn't a particularly tall building, the cold was only getting worse and the wind more cutting. I stuffed my hands in my pockets as I shuffled across the flat gray expanse. On the other side, taking up half of the rooftop space, sat a greenhouse—just out of view of the streets. The windows were fogged, and the edges lined with grime. I maneuvered sideways and used my elbow to hit the latch to unlock it. The door swung freely, and I stepped inside, pivoting with my foot to catch it before it let all the warm air out.

I slammed it shut with my hip, and the lock rattled in its latch. Outside the wind howled, but inside the heat lamps kept it warm. I took my hands out of my pockets and slowly uncurled them to pick up a tiny white basket next to the door.

Foliage of all types grew here. From bell peppers and onions, to rosemary, thyme, and tons of other greenage I had no idea about. Even with the heat lamps, I wondered how they got it all to flourish so well. Then again, they didn't have to work the same when they had magic at hand. Señora Rosara probably cast a couple of spells over the place and they had a nearly never-ending food supply. The thought left me a little bitter even if I was currently benefiting from it.

I rounded up anything that looked ripe enough to eat, hoping that Nathalie's cooking was better than my own and she could make something from it. I was just starting my second pass around the room when the air thickened.

I stumbled, the basket slipping from my fingers.

It wasn't darkness and fire that enveloped me.

But the cool touch of ice over bare sensitive skin. Desire so sharp it cut into me. I canted forward, barely catching myself with a firm hold on the oak table as I doubled over gasping.

The greenhouse faded around me, though I could still feel it physically. My feet were firmly on the floor, my abdomen pressed into the wooden table. The rough grain dug into the pads of my fingers—but instead, I found myself in a dimly lit room. Stones lined the floor, steps, and walls. Red dripped from a bloody pentagram in the center of the floor.

"Piper."

It was a wheeze. A cough. Barely a breath whispered in the dark, dank space.

I squinted through the shadows at the figure on the floor.

"Get out of here," he said. Golden eyes flashed, if only for a moment.

I blinked rapidly.

His white hair was flaking and stained dark brown. *Blood*.

I stepped closer in my vision, though my actual body didn't move. "Don't—"

Too late.

The pentagram flared, and with it, so did the candlelight. I winced at the mangled mess of a body that was Lucifer. His branded chest had been carved open. Long slits ran down the inside of his arms, and blood seeped in between crevices in the stone.

"You need to go," he said, then coughed. Blood tinged his lips. "Before they find you."

"Who?" I asked. "Who will find me? What happened here? Why are you—"

A door opened. Footsteps sounded.

Lucifer's eyes widened in a panic.

"Go," he ordered in a whispered roar.

The vision broke apart. Like shattered glass, it fractured and dropped away, leaving me still standing and bent over the table in the greenhouse.

I took several deep breaths, trying to calm myself.

The ice-cold bite of magic drained away, leaving me disoriented and numb. I leaned over and grabbed the wicker basket, putting the vegetables that spilled out back in it. My mind reeled from what I'd seen.

When I lit him on fire, I'd hoped he'd die, but he didn't. I felt it then, just as I knew it now. Ronan assumed he was in stasis and recovering . . . but that wasn't stasis. Or at least not like mine.

Someone had trapped him and chained him up.

Someone he didn't want to know about me.

He was the devil. The morningstar. The blight upon my world. The reason magic existed here.

And he was being held prisoner.

8

I STOOD up and held the basket tightly as I left the greenhouse, taking the stairwell off the roof to the elevator.

Still lost in my thoughts, I didn't register the figure at the end of the hall fast enough.

"Hey, Pipes."

I stopped where I stood and cursed internally.

Does everyone know where I live now?

For fuck's sake, this was getting ridiculous. I knew the wards only worked to keep people who meant harm from entering the building, or uninvited people from entering Nat's apartment—but my ex? Apparently, that was where they drew the line and failed.

"What are you doing here, Flint?" I asked, my voice coming out icy and stiff.

His warm brown eyes looked me over, but I didn't

feel anything. No stir of heat. No flush my skin. Once upon a time, I'd dated him. If you could call it dating. He wanted a life together. Marriage, as outdated as it was. Real marriages rarely happened anymore when there wasn't any sort of true government keeping track of us. Few were religious enough to demand it these days. It was mostly higher ranked supes looking for alliances that bothered with the prospect at all— and even then, it was simply an arrangement for power or influence. The marriage Flint spoke of was a pretty nostalgic idea because humans liked those things. They clung to them because it was all they had. He wanted a white picket fence outside the city where we could raise little blonde-haired, brown-eyed babies.

But that wasn't me.

I was a bounty hunter. A woman haunted by my past and chasing answers for my sister's future.

I was with him out of complacency because I needed something—someone—to feel less alone. That didn't mean I was in the market for marriage.

He looked at me as if no time had passed. As if he hadn't proposed and I hadn't left him that night and never looked back. Most men would be put off by that, but not Flint. He may not grovel, but he had a nasty habit of popping up when I least expected him.

"I wanted to check on you. See how you were doin'. It's been a while."

I lifted my hands and motioned to myself, dark jeans, jacket, and all.

"Well, as you can see, I'm perfectly fine. So if that was all . . ." I let my voice taper off, adding a pointed look over my shoulder, toward the elevator.

Unfazed, he grinned like I hadn't just suggested he should leave.

"I was hopin' we could catch up."

"Not interested," I said, voice harder than before. He didn't respond, but instead kept watching me with brown eyes too intelligent and nosy for his own good.

"I heard you were in trouble. Boys down in the Underworld told me they saw you there. I know you don't like asking for help, but if you're in deep, I *can* help you."

My lips thinned. Now we were getting to the real reason for this visit.

"I can handle myself, Flint. You didn't need to track me down."

I tried to step around him, but he moved with me. "Pipes—"

"I left," I reminded him softly. "You can't just fly in like you're some knight in shining armor. You tried this back then, and it didn't work. What makes you think it will now?"

Flint stared at me and then sighed softly. "I know you can take care of yourself, baby, but Lucifer? Come on, we both know you're no match for a demon. If I could track you here, so could he. It's only a matter of time——"

"I can handle it," I said, trying to keep the bite out of my voice.

"Why do you have to be so damned stubborn?"

I crossed my arms over my chest, not liking the way his tone was shifting with me. "Why do you have to barge in here and try to save the day?"

His lips pressed together. He leaned into me, and I didn't move as he lifted a hand to my cheek. "I miss you, Piper. You're not easy to love, but——"

I lifted my hand, stopping him right there.

"That's where you're wrong. You don't love me. You think you do, but really, you're in love with a different girl that's wearing my face in your mind. A girl that stays home and makes dinner, letting you handle all the scary things that go bump in the night. You need a damsel to save, but I'm not her, Flint. I never was, and I never will be."

Instead of taking it easy, anger settled in. I could see the dark gleam in his eyes as he dropped his hand from my cheek to my neck, holding it just a tad too tight for my liking.

"We were good. We could be good again." The words would be sweet in a way, if they weren't so forceful. "You come back to human patrol and we could be a team again. I won't pressure you to stay home. I heard about your apartment. You could move in with me, and we—"

"I said no," I snapped, stepping back to try to break his grip. He squeezed harder.

"How'd they do it?" he asked.

My brows came together, and I frowned. "How'd who do what?"

"The supes. How'd they get you? Because the Piper I knew was humans first, and she wouldn't be living with a goddamned witch."

My expression smoothed. I went flat. He glared, not seeing the thing he was provoking. As much as I thought of myself as human, Nathalie, Ronan, and even Lucifer were forcing me to come to terms with the fact that I wasn't.

I was anything but.

A demon. A monster. A predator.

And he was provoking me, oblivious to the damage I could cause. Perhaps I was wrong about Flint in a way. It would seem he was taking our breakup harder than I'd thought, and me moving in with Nathalie had somehow added fuel to a fire I thought was nothing more than ashes.

"I'm going to give you one warning, out of respect for the time you gave me and the relationship we once had. Take your hand off me, get in the elevator, and leave."

His thumb brushed over my bare skin and I shivered, but not in desire.

His mere touch made me uncomfortable.

"You wouldn't hurt me," Flint said softly. He leaned forward, lips parted, and I knew what he was going for. I reached back, grabbing the handle of my gun. I'd just pulled it out and was lifting it when his hand on my throat disappeared.

A bang echoed in the hall and I stepped back, lifting my gun.

Standing next to Nathalie in the doorway was none other than Ronan.

He was holding Flint by the throat.

9

"I BELIEVE she told you to leave," Ronan said. His voice was just a sliver of darkness. An echo of death. He didn't raise it. He didn't yell. He simply spoke with absolute authority.

Flint clutched at the hand gripping his throat, his face turning pink, and tinged purple in some places. "Let . . . me . . ." He couldn't get out the last word as Ronan squeezed.

"Put him down," I said. Ronan paused, turning his head and tilting it to the side. His silver eyes narrowed on me.

"He touched you."

The words; so simple. The logic; incredibly fucked up.

"I was handling it," I said.

Ronan seemed to contemplate what I'd said, and Flint reached for his side. My lips parted as a glint of steel registered only a second before it moved through the air—and stopped.

Ronan caught Flint's arm by the wrist. The knife in his hand flashed under the hall lights, only inches from Ronan's throat. The demon's nostrils flared in anger, and Flint gulped visibly.

"Ronan . . ." I said slowly.

A crack echoed, followed by a scream.

Blood splattered the hallway before I knew what had happened. The knife left his hand and hit the floor, the sound drowned out by Flint's cries.

Ronan flung him down as if he weighed nothing. Murderous intent shone in his gaze, but he didn't move an inch.

Flint crawled back, clutching his hand to his chest. I could see now that it was broken, and a shard of bone was sticking out.

He eyed the knife several feet away, but then thought better of it when he saw the look on Ronan's face.

"She has chosen to spare you. Do not return. I will not tolerate your presence near her again."

Confusion filled Flint's features. His eyebrows drew together, and then slowly smoothed. He was starting to get it, even if he didn't have all the pieces.

"What are you?" he asked, but not completely out of fear. He was fishing, trying to find out what I was to the man in front of him.

Ronan smiled cruelly.

"Hope that you never have to find out."

Flint shuddered and got to his feet. He stalled for a moment, torn between whatever he wanted to say to me and being ripped apart by Ronan.

I didn't want to see the betrayal in his eyes. The hurt. I could handle the anger, but the rest of it was deep. Too cutting. Too guilt-inducing.

He stepped closer, and Ronan growled under his breath, only stopping when he stepped back.

"So this is what you wanted? To be some supe's toy? He'll use you up and throw you away like every other human. We mean *nothing* to them. I thought you knew that. I thought you—"

I punched him.

Flint stumbled back, stunned.

"You don't know me," I snapped. "You don't know a damn thing about me, and if you did, you'd know better than to try manipulating me. Stop being a prick who has to have the last word, and just go."

He rubbed at his jaw, and his lips pressed together. His eyes shifted back and forth between me and Ronan. I could tell he wanted to say something, but with a broken wrist, a bruised jaw, and a hurt ego—

he'd taken more pain than he signed up for when he tracked me down. Accepting his cause was lost, at least for now, Flint started down the hallway. I waited until the elevator closed to breathe easy.

Nathalie let out a laugh that made me want to shoot her for being the one to instigate this by letting Ronan in to begin with.

The hall door cracked open.

Señora Rosara peered out, assessing the scene. She looked at the blood on the ground and then lifted her eyes to Ronan. There was respect there. Knowledge. But she was still a crazy old woman with no fucks to give.

"That stain better be gone by tonight," she said. Ronan nodded once. Señora Rosara turned to me. "You need better taste in men," she said with a disgusted glance toward the elevator. "Pendejo."

Her door slammed shut, leaving me baffled and insulted.

I blinked, not knowing what to do with that encounter. I shook my head and started down the hall, stepping around Ronan and a guilty-looking Nathalie. Without speaking to either of them, I put my key, the basket of vegetables, and my gun on the kitchen bar.

The front door closed behind me.

I turned around and crossed my arms over my chest.

"What is he doing here?" I said to Nathalie without looking at Ronan. His stare was drilling into me, burrowing under my skin. I couldn't stand the way he affected me, and while I could lie to them and say he didn't, lying to myself wasn't getting me very far.

Not when he was so damn reasonable sometimes.

Then there were times like the present when he made it clear how much he was not human.

"What is he doing here?" I asked again when neither of them answered.

"He came to see you." She sighed. "You were upstairs, so I invited him in for tea."

She cast a hopeful look toward the two cups sitting on the end table in the living room. I closed my eyes. Had the Magic Wars not happened, I might have prayed to some god for strength. I knew better than to pray to gods, though. Only demons answered.

So I drew on what little patience I had. "We don't invite demons in for tea," I told her.

"But it's just him—"

"A demon."

"But—" My eyes hardened like blades of ice, and Nathalie sighed.

"I told you, no one in the apartment. Especially demons."

"No," she said. "You told me no one in the apart-ment because Bree was going to be here. She is not here. We talked about that. We never had a talk about inviting demons in for tea."

My eyebrows shot up.

Why did she have to be so frickin' pedantic sometimes?

"Fine," I said through clenched teeth. "Consider this that conversation." Nathalie inclined her head, as if agreeing.

"I will not invite demons in for tea, then. Next time, he can stand outside and beat your ex-boyfriend to a pulp." She shrugged, and walked out of the kitchen, leaving me with Ronan. Her annoying sense of reasonableness ate at me.

I didn't love Flint. I didn't want to be with him. But he was human . . . and I took issue with humans dying. Which is what that would have inevitably led to.

But I wouldn't say that in front of said demon. No, Nat and I would have to have another talk. Later, when she was being less . . .right.

"She made me stand outside until the human showed," Ronan said. I glowered.

"You're not helping."

He arched an eyebrow and took a step closer. A shudder ran through me as something warm and languid rushed through my veins. I pushed it away, standing strong.

"And here I thought you'd be happy to see me.

You were so keen for the second blood exchange last time we spoke," he murmured. My pulse fluttered, and my mouth went dry. I swallowed hard, tasting blood. *Had I bitten my lip?*

Yes. Yes, I had. God, why did I react this way to him?

That one was easier to answer, and not so hard to swallow.

Magic. I was his atma. His soulmate. His destined mate.

Magic made me lust after him, and he lusted after me in return.

It wasn't real. Not really.

I focused on that as I nodded slowly. "Right. I do the blood exchange, and you tell me what's wrong with Bree."

"It won't be that easy," he warned, searching my face.

Was that compassion? Was he testing me? Making sure that I—

I stopped myself right there.

Don't question it. Don't look further. Don't dig. This is an exchange for knowledge. Knowledge is power. Power will save Bree.

"Doesn't matter."

"You'll enter stasis," he pointed out.

"I know."

"It will likely be longer than the previous bouts.

You'll need to be monitored to make sure your body doesn't begin to break down."

"Break down?" I asked.

Ronan reached around me and grabbed something off the counter.

A knife.

I didn't realize until he slashed himself over his palm that fear had never touched me. My heart didn't squeeze, and panic didn't rise.

And I didn't like it.

Blood welled in his palm, yet Ronan didn't flinch. Just as fast as the skin split and began to bleed, it also healed.

"Demons are immortal. We do not age or die or break down, but humans do. We do not know how immortal you are, or if the stasis could kill you by starvation, dehydration, and muscle atrophy."

My lips parted. "I . . . I'm not sure," I said, uncomfortable with the prospects.

"Which means you'll need to be monitored."

"Nathalie can do it," I said. He nodded. I wasn't backing down, no matter the cost, but I also wasn't stupid. Nathalie was smart. She'd either find a way to magic me out of dying, or get the physical means needed. I trusted her enough to handle it and not let me die either way, which said a lot, given I didn't trust anyone else.

"There's one more thing . . ." he said, looking

around the shabby chic living room. He picked up a picture frame and examined it for a moment before setting it back down. "Every blood exchange will deepen the bond."

I lifted both my eyebrows, not that he could see them.

"What does 'deepen' mean?"

He lifted his head. Dark fire threatened to consume me.

"It's different for every pair. Some experience what they think is love, some it's simply intense lust, and others feel a merging of some sort. The latter is not common."

Well, shit.

"While unfortunate, I won't let that deter me," I said. "We're doing this exchange."

The follow-up exchange was a problem for my future self. I'd figure it out. Same as everything else I did.

"Very well," Ronan said. His tongue darted out and swept across his bottom lip.

I wasn't sure what to expect. Would he take me back to his place and try to make this out to be something different than it was? Would he just grab me as we stood in Nat's apartment and bite?

Turns out the answer was neither.

Ronan offered me his hand, a devilish, cruel smirk

of amusement tilting his lips. In his eyes was a challenge. To me.

For all my talk, would I go through with it?

Would I willingly enter an eternal partnership and what little was left of my soul?

Yes, I would.

I took Ronan's hand, and the void welcomed me.

WHEN THE LIGHT RETURNED, we weren't in an apartment of any kind, but instead, the cathedral where I'd summoned him.

Candlelight flickered faintly, casting the sanctuary in a soft glow.

"I didn't peg you for the sentimental sort," I said, casting a look throughout. The pews were gone, though the podium remained. No witches or warlocks were here this time. No summoning circle. No people at all, apart from us.

Two demons in a house of god.

"I'm not," he said, and I sensed that amusement in his voice. "If you recall, you shot me after I was first summoned. My blood has been spilled on these stones. My magic will linger here." My eyebrows drew together. I wasn't sure what that meant, but I didn't want to say it. Ronan seemed to read the expression easy enough. "It should be enough to contain your fire, at least to this place."

"You assume the fire will surface."

His expression darkened. "You won't be able to help it."

Something about that felt vulnerable. In the past, when the fire had come out, it was because I was threatened. I needed it as a last-ditch effort to save my own skin. But this, letting it come out for other reasons?

I wrinkled my nose, not liking that one bit.

"Are we going to get this over with or not? I have a crash to go through. Time's a tickin'," I said, falling back on nonchalance as a mask.

"For someone that hates magic, you're very eager to welcome it in."

"For someone that claims to be concerned about me going through the crash, you still demanded I do this to know why my sister is in a coma," I shot back.

He inclined his head, but he seemed in no hurry to get the exchange underway. "It's a complicated problem," Ronan answered vaguely.

"What is?"

"You." With a single look from him, the temperature rose several degrees in the vacated cathedral. "You and your magic are out of balance. All demons feel this to some degree, but I have to assume yours is so extreme because you were not originally a demon. You were born human. The crash, as you call it, will only worsen every time until you are balanced. The only way to do that is to complete all three blood exchanges."

Three. That number bounced around in my mind.

I rolled my shoulders back and twisted my lips. "Three doesn't leave you much time to convince me," I noted.

"Hence the balancing act."

I hummed in response. "If all demons experience this . . . stasis—have you?"

"Once."

I paused. His response was clipped. Cold. I narrowed my eyes, and he simply said, "No, I won't tell you."

"Why not? You seem to think it's fine to dig through my life."

"I'll tell you a great deal about most things, and I won't lie to you, but I'm not ready to share that. Some truths you have to earn."

There was something profound and almost human in that statement. A vulnerability that he was covering. For all his magic, his years, his sheer power—part of him could still be hurt. Part of him was hurt, and he knew better than to share it with me.

I suppose that was where the difference was. He

claimed to not want to hurt me, whereas I threatened to send him back to Hell regularly. In his shoes, I wouldn't share with me either.

"I'm ready to earn the truth about my sister," I said, turning toward him and squaring my shoulders. The shadow of a cruel grin told me he knew I was changing the subject and why, but he didn't push it. Instead, he reached and unbuttoned his suit jacket, letting it drop with a quiet thud to the floor.

My heart sped up.

Tension thickened the air.

He didn't reach for me, though. No. He switched to undoing his cuff links while he held my gaze. Never lowering it. Never looking away.

I swallowed hard when he began loosening his tie.

"I bet you thought I'd have pretty words for you before this. That just because I made you go to dinner with me that I'd try to court you." He chuckled softly.

"Aren't you?"

"No." He didn't visibly move so much as fade into shadow and reappear before me. Close enough I could see my reflection in his eyes. "You don't want to be chased, but you don't want to chase. You have no real desire for romance. Dinners. Flowers. Gifts. They all mean so little to you. It's why the human never had a chance." He reached up to brush a stray strand back, then threaded his fingers through my ponytail bound hair. He pulled, adding just a touch of pain.

"If not that, then what do I want?" I asked, more curious than I should have been.

"To be understood," he said, our faces only inches apart.

"How presumptuous of you," I murmured.

"Get on your knees."

My mouth turned dry. My eyes flicked down to the blood-stained stone and then back up to him. "No."

One side of his mouth curled further up in dark amusement.

"Very well."

His lips came down on mine in a crushing kiss. The hand in my hair squeezed, and he used his grip to pull me to him. His tongue licked part of my lips, searching for entry. I groaned, and he used that slight shift to press forward, taking what he wanted.

Thump.

Thump.

Thump.

Blood rushed to my head. My hands felt hot, yet cold. His tongue twined with mine. Tasting me. Consuming me. A very male rumble came from his chest before his other hand clamped onto my hip.

The crushing grip on my hair slipped away as he dropped to his knees.

I gasped as his face became almost level with my breasts. He cupped one and squeezed, watching my face for a reaction. I closed my eyes, tilting my head back.

"I agreed to the blood exchange," I started, as that hand trailed over my ribs and down my side to latch onto the other hip. A featherlight touch brushed from my navel to the apex of my thighs. "Not this."

"Mhmm," he hummed. I didn't want to look, not when I could feel his nose pressed into me, rubbing softly up and down.

My lips parted in ecstasy. Heat flooded me.

"Ronan," I said in what was meant to be a chastisement and instead came out a guttural moan. Fuck me.

"Gladly," he murmured.

I must have said that last part out loud. "No, that's not what I—"

Words were lost on me as he started to suck through the material of my jeans. That wicked tongue of his snaked out, pressing into the seam of my pants and creating delicious friction.

"Tell me to stop, Piper," he said, goading me then going back to his ministrations. My hips bucked, and my knees weakened.

Thump.

Thump.

Thump.

His fingers dipped into my waistband, then pulled, ripping my jeans from my body like they were made of tissue paper. The very real dry spell I'd been under for far too long was really coming back to bite me in that moment.

"The blood exchange," I said through gritted teeth.

He hummed against me, not lifting his mouth, but he pulled both hands away. I breathed a little easier, at least for a moment.

Then one of those hands skimmed the back of my thigh.

I shuddered, and he squeezed the back of my knee gently, lifting it over his shoulder.

"Now wait a minu—"

With my legs partially spread, he used the better access to his advantage and locked his teeth around my swollen clit. The rough scrape of fabric had me grabbing fistfuls of his hair to hold myself upright.

That was the wrong move.

He moved his hand from my leg to my ass and dropped the other to the one leg still bracing my weight. Lifting me as if I were nothing, he put the other leg over his shoulder and held me there with his face between my thighs and wide palms cupping my ass.

The world tilted. My back touched something cool and rough.

The floor.

That bastard.

"If you're going to tell me no, you should say it now, but you should know it'll be near impossible to stop when the second exchange is complete," he uttered. I looked down the valley of my chest to see him staring up at me from between my legs.

My panties dampened.

His nostrils flared, eyes darkening.

Pulling together the bruised remains of my will, I said, "No sex. I agreed to the exchange. Let's get it over with."

I'd been with my fair share of both men and women. While I wasn't lax with my body, per se, I did take pleasure where I could find it because there was little else that was good in this world these days. Having a casual fuck buddy and having sex with Ronan would be two very different things. I was sure of it.

Much as Nathalie preached about scratching the itch, I wasn't sure if it would instead only burrow deeper beneath my skin.

Unlike past partners I'd rejected and left, Ronan didn't get angry. He didn't lose his shit or try to force me, though I was fairly certain he could if he wanted.

No. Ronan crawled up my body, pressed a searing kiss to my lips, and then flipped us. Now I was straddling his lap while he sat on the stone floor. The new position was better, but not by much.

I placed my hands on his shoulders, and he grabbed my hips once more.

I didn't wait for permission, or for him to try some underhanded manipulation by asking for more. I lunged forward and sank my teeth into the slight dip of his throat where it met his shoulder.

Ronan grunted.

Copper smeared over my tongue.

Thump.

Thump.

Thu—

My heart stopped. My canines lengthened into tiny fangs. Fire and magic funneled through my veins like an angry storm looking for an outlet.

Rage settled over me, and had my eyes been open, I knew red would have tinted them.

I felt the call of violence deep in my bones as I drank from him and lost touch of myself.

The hard bulge pressed against me twitched. I rocked forward into it, my fingers like claws as they pressed into him.

The hands at my hips pulled me closer, thrusting our bodies together.

Pressure built in my core. The blood on my lips and feel of him beneath me ignited something inside. Something primal and powerful.

I clutched at him as he pulled away.

"Piper," he grunted. "I only have so much control—"

I growled as I gulped down another mouthful of his blood.

Fire was sparking in my hands. Those white-hot embers catching on his shirt.

Ronan grabbed the end of my ponytail and pulled sharply. While my strength was far greater than before, it still didn't trump his. I reeled back, taking a chunk out of his neck and making him hiss in pain.

He gave it a full second, and in that time, three things happened.

His neck healed.

My mind cleared.

Then he bit me back.

Those embers turned to a blaze as our clothes went up in flames. Just as I lost myself in him, he seemed to lose himself in me. Pleasure cocooned us both, and without the confines of clothing, I felt his bare cock brush against my entrance. A shudder went through me, and weak to my own desires, I strained to take him.

But that hand on my hip hadn't moved. It held so painfully tight I didn't budge. Even as he brushed over my wet, sensitive flesh, our bodies never joined. I never took him in me and filled that bitterly empty gulf inside.

Black and white fire danced over our skin, twirling and twisting around us.

It burned, and we burned with it.

But without that joining, release evaded me.

I moaned low, a tortured mewling sound I would regret when the fog cleared.

But it was my own fault. I'd said no sex, and Ronan was holding us both to it. Literally.

That didn't mean the prick couldn't find it in him to tease me.

And tease he did. Knowing he was so close, feeling his burning skin hot and hard beneath my hands, was a whole other kind of suffering. My legs stiffened, so close to the cusp, but not close enough. Not without friction.

"I hate you," I murmured, lost in the haze, but trying desperately to hold on to the only thing that may be strong enough to carry me through.

He pulled back, making a popping sound, suckling the skin while not actively biting. The burning ache didn't dissipate, however. The need didn't die down. While my head had cleared from the blood-drunk high, the desire refused to abate.

"No, you don't." His voice was deeper than I'd ever heard it. Thick with hunger. He was struggling, just as I was, yet he had infinitely better self-control. "But you might by the end. If I were a better man, I would complete the bond now and let you go."

He lifted his head from my neck. Our noses were nearly touching. Our breath mingled. "But I'm not a good man, and I don't care because I'll have you all the same."

My lips parted, but I didn't get a chance to respond.

Later I would think about those words he'd said.

Or I would have, had the edges of my vision not begun to darken and the hot flashes come on.

The crash.

Stasis.

I didn't have long.

The void wrapped around us as Ronan teleported me back, still naked and panting, and embarrassingly wet. I felt him moving my body but didn't register that he'd stood up until we reappeared in my room inside Nat's apartment.

Down the hall, an eighties power ballad was blasting, Nathalie's shit-singing along with it.

Cold fell over me, making my skin pebble. My teeth started to chatter as Ronan set me on my pale blue bedspread.

His hands left me, and the cold seeped in deeper, any warmth I'd felt leaving me with him.

I hated it. This feeling of helplessness that was coming.

Ronan stepped back, and my hand whipped out. I

used the last of that strength and rage to grab his wrist and hold him there.

"Tell me," I said, as I slumped to the side, prepared to give in once I had my answer.

"Bree," Ronan started. "Her consciousness was transported to another realm. That's why she never woke up, and why she won't until her spirit is brought back to this one."

Sleep was calling to me. The crash was imminent. A fogginess buzzed in my mind as I tried to fight it.

"Another realm?" I asked, my whispered words hardly a breath.

"My home dimension. Mine and Aeshma's."

I had already lost the battle with my own consciousness, but I was holding on to the very edge of awareness. Black crept in. Heaviness dragged me under. Try as I might, I couldn't fight it any longer.

I heard his final words as a faraway echo when the crash fully claimed me, and they were worse than I ever could have dreamed.

Your sister is trapped in Hell.

RONAN

HER CONSCIOUSNESS SLIPPED DEEPER into stasis with every passing minute. The red of her rage magic draining from her brands. Her eyelids fluttered rapidly for a few suspended moments, similar to when she was dreaming. But she hadn't been under long enough to dream . . .

I peered into her mind and found myself shrouded in a night so black I couldn't see through it. It surrounded me like a cloak, veiling wherever her mind had gone. I pushed harder, but it was to no avail.

Somehow, some way . . . she'd locked me out.

I didn't like it. Not one tiny bit.

But there was nothing to be done. I wouldn't push to the point of breaking her, no matter how curious I was. There were lines even an atman shouldn't cross.

Still coming down off the high of her blood, the taste of her skin, and the feel of her lips—I stepped through the void and into the witch's living room.

The singing cut out in favor of a mumbled curse.

"Really, Ronan? You can mind-meld and cross entire dimensions, but you can't manage to magic on a pair of pants or something?" she groaned loudly. "I swear, just as bad as Piper . . ." She disappeared around the corner and down the hall, leaving me in the living room not having said a word. A few seconds later, she returned and threw a wad of fabric my way. Sweatpants. "Those were thirty dollars. I expect to be repaid with interest."

I lifted a brow at the tiny female, and she crossed her arms, then jutted her chin toward the pants. "You're supposed to wear them, in case that wasn't obvious."

I shook my head but did as she asked and donned the sweatpants, as she called them. My search through the Antares Coven's memories didn't cover the more mundane things in this world.

"Piper is in stasis," I said after a moment. Nathalie walked around the kitchen counter and pulled a teakettle off the stove.

"I figured as much, given you look like you murdered someone. I'm assuming she went through with the second exchange?" she asked without lifting her eyes from the tiny teacup she was pouring steaming water into.

"Yes, but I don't know how it will affect her. You'll need to watch for signs of dehydration and starvation. If she appears to be degenerating—"

"I'll keep her alive, Ronan. If there's magic I need that I don't have, I'll contact you or go to the good Señora. She may give Piper shit, but she wouldn't let her die."

I nodded and ran a blood-stained hand through my hair.

"If the ex shows up again, let me know."

"He won't," she replied in complete confidence. The witch lifted the teacup to her lips and blew softly, hot steam scattering. "I used the blood in the hall for a spell that would make him forget why he was here if he ever entered the building again. He won't be bothering Piper, at least not here."

I cocked my head, taking in the witch with a keen interest. "You don't have the magic for that."

"I never said I did," she replied, then took a sip of her tea. Nathalie hummed in appreciation before setting the cup back down. "Señora Rosara is a very skilled witch. I had her do the spell, and in return she gets two ounces of crushed jasmine leaves."

My brow furrowed. "You trade in tea?"

A gold light entered the witch's light brown eyes.

Mischievous and dangerous in its own way. "I trade in many things. Tea. Food. Blood. Antiquities that are difficult to get ahold of. In that way, I'm much like you. I make bargains to get what I want."

"I trade in power."

"Power is subjective," she replied. "In a war-ravaged world, food has power. So does blood. So do rare and hard-to-find objects. Everyone needs for something, and for some, that's magic. I don't have much of that to trade, but everything else . . ." She shrugged. "Magic is good, but someone can still have all the magic in the world and not be happy. I'm in the business of pleasing people. You'd be surprised what humans and supernaturals alike will bargain with for just a tiny bit of happiness."

Those were profound words for one so young. Wise beyond her years.

"What is it that makes Piper happy?" I asked her, curious what her insight would offer more than anything.

Nathalie set the cup down with a heavy sigh.

"Piper is a difficult one. She's lived alone for so long. Suffered at the hands of my kind . . . I don't think she truly knows happiness. Just existence. Her childhood was about survival, and the people she loved most in the world were taken from her. She doesn't form attachments now as a defense mechanism to keep from getting hurt. The last decade of her life has been chasing answers for how to save a sister she may not be able to save." Nathalie shook her head, clearly troubled. "But if I had to guess what I think makes her feel at least content—I would say saving people."

"Not Bree?" I asked, though I didn't truly disagree.

"No," Nathalie said softly. "Bree is a body. An idea. A memory. She loves and misses the girl she remembers because she associates it with better times. But I don't think she makes her happy. Not when she has so much guilt surrounding her."

She looked away, far off into the distance, and a sad expression crossed her face.

"And when she finds a way to bring Bree back?" I said. "What about then?"

"You assume there's a way to bring her back," Nathalie said. I didn't respond, and her eyes narrowed in my direction. "Assuming there is, though? She'll still struggle. In her mind, Bree is all there is. The sole source of her entire world because of love and guilt. No one can be someone's everything, and once she saves her . . . I think Piper is going to have a tough time shifting the focus of her survival."

I mulled over her answer while the witch sipped her tea in silence.

"You think it will break her," I said eventually.

"That depends." She lowered the cup to the counter and lifted her light brown eyes as they started to glow.

"On?" I prompted.

"If she can find another reason to live."

1 2

THE TRUTH DIDN'T HAVE time to settle in and weigh me down.

As soon as Ronan faded, stone walls and a bloody pentagram took its place. I scented sulfur, the tang of copper, and subtle undertones of sex.

Lucifer still lay on the floor, bound in chains, his body cut open and dripping.

"I told you to go," he said, his voice a quiet rumble.

"I did."

"But you came back."

His eyes were closed. He didn't look at me as he spoke. He didn't move an inch. Lucifer's chest and arms were still carved open, and so much blood had spilled that it stained his pale skin a reddish brown, completely covering the brands. His once white hair now only had flecks of the snowy color peeking through.

I wondered how much pain he was in. He didn't wince or whine or cry. Not that I would expect him to, being the devil and all. But I had to think it hurt to move, hurt to breathe, and that's why he'd remained so still.

"Not by choice. The crash came, and I woke up here . . ." I took another look around the would-be-sanctuary. The low ceiling and lack of windows made me think he was underground.

"You need to leave."

"I don't know how."

He sighed, and for once, he sounded . . . tired. Old. Ronan was thousands of years old, and that meant the devil was too. He'd known Lucifer from Hell, the *real* Hell.

"They're going to be back soon," he said quietly.

"They?"

His eyes cracked open, thin slits of gold staring straight into my soul. "The ones keeping me here."

"You're avoiding telling me who," I noted. "I find this strange since you're chained down and cut up like a sacrifice."

"Exactly. Me, a full demon. A being once considered too great to be challenged." He chuckled under his breath, but it was a bitter sound.

"So that's it? Someone challenged you? That's

how you ended up here?" I motioned to the room around us.

"Yes and no," he said. I waited for him to continue, but he didn't. I crossed my arms over my chest and started walking around the outer rim of the bloody circle that caged him. Last time I'd stepped in it, and the magic flared to life even though I wasn't really there. Somehow it was able to sense me.

"Someone either challenged you, or they didn't," I said. "I don't see how this is a yes and no answer."

"Someone always challenges me," Lucifer said. "That's what it means to be on top. To rule. You're challenged again and again, but to stay on top, you can't lose. Not once."

"So you lost?" I surmised.

"Yes, but not to *them*," he said, a flicker of icy rage entering his gaze. Now that his eyes were open, they never left me.

"Then who?"

"You," he breathed. "Your blood was so sweet, I didn't even notice it poisoning me. It might have killed me, had the fire not burned it away."

I stopped where I stood. "So you're not my atman?"

"No, I *wasn't*."

I frowned. Wasn't didn't mean *isn't*.

"What do you mean wasn't? If you're not my

atman, how am I here? The fire should have killed you, or my blood—"

"Yet, they saved me." Despite the manacles around his wrists and ankles, the bleeding cuts, and the pain he had to be in—his eyes raked over me, and a hint of both mania and lust peeked out. "The fire didn't kill me because of the presence of your blood. Your blood didn't kill me because of the fire. They canceled each other out, and a small amount integrated within me. I survived. Now, I'm immune to both." His tongue darted out, just the slightest flick to lick over his bottom lip.

My stunned stupor faded as my eyes hardened. "You could have killed me," I hissed.

"It should have," he agreed. "By all means, you should have died. Yet here you stand, unhurt." He scanned me from head to toe and then back up. "Curious," he said softly.

"I have a question. If you knew that Aeshma was dead, why pretend otherwise? Why play along?"

Lucifer grinned a little, and blood coated his teeth, though not his lips. I assumed he was bleeding internally. "Aeshma was a cunt," he said. "I hated her. She rejected me because she wanted more power, and I was sent here out of shame. Imagine how surprised I was to find a woman that appeared to be little more than human had killed her and was now my atma? I would not lose twice. I was going to do everything better with you. Do it the right way. In Hell, Aeshma was what you call born great. She was a princess to power, old power, and it gave her a certain status that I did not have. I was simply Lucifer, Second Son. The Morningstar." He chuckled like the name that inspired so much fear was but a mockery of the original meaning. "Here *I* have the power. Here I was king, and you were no one. A human woman with the power of an immortal. I knew of your distaste for my kind. I was going to use it. Start from the bottom and strip it all away. You might hate me now, but when I was done—you'd know every dark deed and awful thought in my mind and love me despite it all. You would have chosen me."

My lips parted. "You're wrong."

He smiled faintly. "Maybe. Looks like we'll never know."

I narrowed my eyes.

"You were sure I was your atma too," I pointed out.

"And despite being wrong, I was still right. I chose you, and fate chose to throw me a bone." He chuckled, then coughed. Red stained his lips.

"You're dying," I said after a few heavy moments when his coughing finally died down and his head slumped back against the floor once more.

"Feels like it," he said. "But I don't think they intend to kill me, assuming they know how. Not a good assumption, mind you. Unless Ronan hired them—"

"Who are they?" I asked him.

"You going to come save me, Piper?" he asked jokingly. When I didn't immediately respond, a sliver of pain crept from beneath his mask. "You'd leave me to rot. I'm the devil, after all. So why do you want to know?"

Because . . .

"I was tailed the other day, and nearly drowned after an explosion shortly before that. Someone is after me. I'm trying to find out who, and why."

Lucifer lay there, seeming to fade in and out for a moment. Just when I thought he wasn't going to answer, he rasped, "The witches."

"Which ones?"

"The old families." A metal hinge creaked somewhere not far away. "They're angry at the restrictions I've kept them under since the Magic Wars. Most of the supernaturals are. If they've learned you're my atma, you need to leave New Chicago. I can't protect—"

What was with him and Ronan thinking I needed to run or hide at the first sign of danger?

"That's not going to happen."

Footsteps echoed from outside the room.

"You don't understand," he said through clenched teeth. "As long as I'm in this circle, my persuasion can't sway them. They will torture you, bring you right to the brink of death, and then heal you up and start all over. I know, because that's what I did to them when Dryanda Abernathy revealed magic to the world."

"You forget, Lucifer, I cut my teeth hunting witches. If they're after me for revenge on you, they'll be in for a rude awakening."

His eyes glowed brighter for a moment and the circle flared to life around him. "*Do not* go looking for them," he said, his magic filling the room. I breathed it in, and the cold it filled me with burned. His jaw was hard, and his fists clenched as he tried to strain past the circle's hold. The footsteps outside became louder, more insistent. The banging echoed through my brain.

"Nice try," I said softly. "But you forget, if you're immune to me, I'm immune to you—even if that circle wasn't blocking your power."

"Piper," he growled. The thick wooden door shot open and slammed into the stone wall behind it. "Piper!"

Witches and warlocks funneled into the tiny room, but none of them seemed to notice me. None but Lucifer.

My name on his lips was still ringing in my ears when the stone room and bloody circle disappeared.

My eyes flew open, and I gasped, shooting up out of bed.

It took a second to recognize my surroundings. That I was in my room at Nathalie's.

What's more, she wasn't sitting next to my bed waiting quietly with a glass of water. She was sitting on my lap, shaking me.

"Wake up, wake up, wake the fuck up!" she chanted under her breath. Her eyes were wide and crazed, a pink tinge ringed them from crying. Tear stains lined her cheeks.

"I'm here," I croaked past parched lips. I swallowed hard, trying to soothe the burn in my throat. My limbs were heavy, sluggish, and sore. I wondered how many days I'd been out.

Nathalie sat back, her hands stilled. She blinked twice but didn't move to wipe the tears away or calm her expression.

She stared at me, unabashed and unashamed.

"Barry's gone."

13

"WHAT?"

Gone? What did she mean by gone?

"He's gone. The Red Crescent pack took him."
She reached down and pulled a crumpled yellow
piece of paper out of her sweatshirt pocket. "They
want to make a trade."

I took the letter and smoothed it out. Dread filled
me, along with that dangerous current of adrenaline.
Nathalie spoke again as I read the short note.

"They want to trade Barry for Lucifer," I said in a
gravelly voice, mostly from dehydration.

Nathalie nodded. "Except I have no idea where
he is. I've scryed two dozen times, and I can't find
either of them. Piper, what am I going to do—"

"We'll get him back," I said, my body already
moving even as my mind was working through the

plan. I nudged her off of me so I could stretch my legs and stand. "That's all we can do."

And deal with some witches who may be trying to kill me while we're at it.

"But I don't know where either of them are."

"The witches have Lucifer," I said, pulling out clothes to dress myself. My skin was dry and uncomfortable. Under different circumstances, I would have showered and brushed my teeth before anything, then ate, then listened to her problems. As it was, her panicked state didn't make me think we had much time for me to dally.

"What—how do you know that?"

"Saw it," I murmured, yanking open and then slamming drawers shut as I tried to find a clean, long-sleeved shirt. *Where were they—*

My eyes slid sideways to the pile of dirty laundry.

"The same way you 'see' Ronan when you're sleeping?" she asked.

"Yep." I almost didn't notice her tone changing because I was debating how gross I could handle being, even if it was just long enough to capture the devil, kill and interrogate some witches, then possibly deal with a werewolf pack that may or may not already hate me . . .

Fuck it. I picked up the gray shirt on top and sniffed it.

Could be worse.

Not a lot, mind you, but I gave it a fifty-fifty shot I'd end up resorting to magic by the end of the day. Which meant no more shirt in the end.

"Is that normal?" Nathalie asked, pulling me from this debacle.

"Nope," I said, pulling on the one decent bra I had left. She was going to owe me another round of clothes by the end of this.

"You seem to be handling it alright . . ." she continued.

"I figure only one of us can be freaking out," I said, only half sarcastically. "Besides, none of this is normal. I'm a demon, living with a witch, on the second blood exchange with Ronan . . ." I wrinkled my nose at that, even if my skin flushed. Nope. Not going there. "What's one more soulmate in the mix? I plan to leave or kill them both, anyway."

I pulled the shirt on and clasped my belt with my holsters around my waist.

"I take that back. The panic just hasn't caught up to you yet."

"Nope," I agreed. "But that's life. I can't change it, and we've got bigger shit to be dealing with."

Arms wrapped around me from behind.

I froze.

"Thank you," Nathalie whispered against my back. The tension in my shoulders eased. "And I appreciate you being willing to wear your dirty, smelly shirt, but you're going to need to take a shower before we go anywhere."

"What?" I pulled away and turned around. "Weren't you just crying and trying to wake me up so we could go find Barry?"

She wiped her nose with the back of her hand and sniffled. "That was before I had a lead, but you said Lucifer is with the witches."

"Yes," I drawled, a statement that I made a silent question. "That's why I'm dressed. So we can go get him. There's probably going to be some guards. Nothing my guns can't handle—"

She chuckled, then sniffled again, sounding stopped-up. "You're making this too hard for yourself."

I narrowed my eyes.

She smiled.

"Take a shower and dress nice. Your guns need to be hidden."

I blinked as she turned to leave.

"Are you going to tell me why?" I called after. She stopped partway out the door and turned back. There was a hard glint in her eyes. A stiff set to her lips. I knew I wasn't going to like what she had to say next.

"I'm taking you to meet my parents."

Well, shit.

APPARENTLY, Nathalie and I had different definitions of 'dress nice'.

Where she wore a stylish and perky blouse that crimped around her waist and flared at the hips, real leather pants, and four-inch high-heeled boots—I wore slacks, a button-down shirt with a high collar, and a black jacket. The latter mostly served as a means to cover the guns I had concealed on me.

She took one look and sighed. "Well, at least it isn't a turtleneck with combat boots."

I frowned, looking down at myself. "You said dress nice, not dress like you're trying to get laid." Nathalie shrugged.

"With witches, it's all the same. Sex and magic go hand-in-hand. Judging from your blood exchanges with Ronan, we get that from demons."

I pressed my lips together and turned away. I hadn't had much time to process everything we'd done, or what he'd said before the crash claimed me. Nathalie woke me up in a bawling mess, and that took priority. Now that there was a brief intermission from the high emotions . . . I found myself very prickly about the whole thing.

"We should get going," I said, changing the subject. My stomach let out a loud rumble in hunger, as if protesting our plans. Nathalie quirked an eyebrow.

"You were out a full week this time. You should

eat something before we leave," she said. Nathalie moved around the counter and grabbed several plastic-wrapped bars out of a cabinet, then set them on the kitchen counter in front of me.

I reached out and grabbed one of the protein bars, recognizing the brand. It was one of the few that boasted enough nutrition that you could survive on two bars a day, and it didn't taste like shit. My stomach let out another hungry rumble, and I tore the packaging off the first.

"I should be a lot worse for wear after being unconscious for a week," I told her. "It's January now, yeah?"

"Mhmm," Nathalie hummed. I frowned at her again as I took a bite of the protein bar. It was a far cry from actual birthday cake, but it could have tasted like tar and I would have scarfed it down all the same.

"If you have something to say, spit it out," I muttered while tearing open the second bar. She brought me four, and I had every intention of eating all of them.

"You're better now than you were after thirty-six hours unconscious. I think Ronan's blood is changing you. Beyond Aeshma's power, I mean." She said it slowly, her light brown eyes watching my every move as I ate the bar with equal rabidness.

When I finished, I took a second to catch my

breath before saying, "There's always been a risk of that."

Her eyebrows drew together, and she tilted her head.

"You're taking this awfully well. I really expected you to crack by now and start blaming Ronan or magic for your problems." She sounded skeptical, yet relieved. Perhaps I would be too, in her shoes. It was my MO. Blame magic. Blame demons. Blame the whole fucking world. The truth was there was only one person to blame.

Me.

I was quickly coming to realize that it didn't really matter who I blamed. That wasn't going to change anything, only action would.

"I knew the risks when I agreed. I made the choice. There's no point being upset about it when I know I would do it again if it meant I learned what was wrong with Bree. My parents died, and she lost ten years of her life for me to become this way. The least I can do is accept the consequences so that she doesn't lose anymore."

We were both quiet for a moment, but I think she understood then—really understood—that I would truly do anything for my sister to bring her back.

I had no idea if it would ease the guilt, the pain, or the loneliness—but I would try all the same. I had to.

"So he told you how to bring her back?" she asked slowly, almost cautiously.

"No," I shook my head, tearing open another protein bar. "But he told me *why* she never woke up, and that's more than I've had to go on for a decade."

"Well, are you going to tell me so we can figure this out, or are you going to keep beating around the bush? You may be immortal now, but I'm certainly not."

I choked on the food I had shoved in my mouth. It quickly turned to a cough that only died down after drinking a full glass of water. I leaned against the counter, panting softly.

"Her consciousness is trapped in Hell. I have to find a way to bring it back here so it can reunite with her body."

Nathalie let out a low whistle. "I didn't know that was possible. I mean, theoretically yes, almost anything is, but I don't recall ever seeing a spell for that."

"Me neither," I breathed. "But if there was a way to send her there, then there's a way to bring her back. I just have to find it." I said it with conviction, with steel, because there was no room for doubt. Not even a seed of it. A seed could grow and flourish and upend a whole foundation, but I couldn't afford that. Bree couldn't afford that.

"And we will—find a way, that is," Nathalie said,

putting a hand on my shoulder and squeezing. "But first, we need to go convince my parents that I want to re-enter the fold and hope they don't kill you on sight."

I narrowed my eyes. "That wouldn't be a concern if you'd let me handle them my way."

"Your way is more likely to get us both killed, and by extension, Barry. In the same way you would do anything to get your sister back, so would I for him. Which means we do this my way," she said simply. "Besides, don't you want to know *how* they took Lucifer, or what they plan to do with him? Knowing my family, it's not something good, but it might be able to help us with getting Bree back."

If I could have glared any harder, I would have. I knew exactly what she was doing by bringing my sister into the conversation, and fortunately for her, it was working. Even if it did piss me off.

"Fine," I agreed. "But if someone tries to kill me, I'm not responsible for what happens after that."

Her lips quirked up in wry amusement. It wasn't what you'd expect, considering this was her family and all. But I was coming to learn that Nathalie was an enigma in her own way. Loyal to those she deemed worth it, and unforgiving to those who weren't.

Blood be damned.

14

"YOU TOLD me you didn't have a mansion," I murmured, as we pulled up outside her parents' house. It was quite a stretch to even call it that. The property was gated over a mile out, and the longest driveway I'd ever seen led up to a four-story building. A white stoned porch rose up from the cobblestoned circular drive that was already packed with cars. Black double doors with sphinxes carved into the wood paneling held brass knockers. Gargoyles hung over the second, third, and fourth-story ledges. Their red eyes glowed unnaturally, giving the whole place an archaic and intimidating front.

Nathalie parked on the grass, and I noted she was the only one to do so.

"I don't have a mansion," she said pointedly. "My parents do, and in the event they die, it goes to my eldest sister and her husband—and if she dies, it goes to the next eldest, and if they all die—my cousins."

"Don't sound resentful about it or anything."

She chuckled. "Not resentful, just making it clear to you. While I am wealthy and a witch, I am not my parents, nor am I like the rest of my blood relatives, for that matter. You need to remember that I'll have to play a part here, just like you."

I tilted my head, assessing her. "You're scared I'm going to lump you in with them."

She shrugged. "You will or you won't. Either way, this isn't going to be easy for you. Try not to speak unless spoken to. Let me handle the talking. If you see the chance to slip out and take a look around, take it. Go down, not up. If my family has him, he'll be in the basement."

"We don't know that they do," I pointed out. "My dream showed me a stone room. Lucifer is the one who told me it was witches. In all reality, there are a lot of witches, not just in New Chicago, but across America."

Nathalie was quiet for a moment. "You said he was in a pentagram, yeah?"

I nodded.

"Then it's likely because they plan to use his magic for something. That's a black-witch siphoning ritual. My family is the blackest line there is." She motioned to the house as if it proved her point. It didn't, but I got the hint. "Regardless, they have him or know who does. No one on earth has captured the devil before, and witches are a boastful lot. They'll talk. We just have to play the part and listen."

I cocked my head, evaluating her beyond the makeup and fancy clothes. Looking past the masks she wore for armor. There was pain there, behind her voice.

If I were a gambling woman, I would bet that being back home was costing her more than she was letting on.

But for Barry, she did it without question.

I almost wondered what that was like; to have someone stick their neck out for you, without magic or money or any cause forcing them to.

"You're a good friend," I said.

She paused in opening the door and looked back at me. "You're only just now figuring this out?"

I rolled my eyes. "Whatever. Let's get this over with. I'm already hungry again."

Nathalie's laugh followed me out of the car, and halfway up her parents' porch. I could have sworn one of the gargoyles canted forward a fraction and tilted its head at me, but when I looked again, they were simply stone.

I narrowed my eyes and pressed onward.

"You know," Nat said, as we got to the door, "for

what it's worth, you can be too. When you're not being an asshole."

I side-eyed her as she lifted her hand to the knocker and clacked it four times. "If that was you trying to 'have a moment', it didn't work."

She busted out laughing at me and a slight grin was beginning to curve its way around my lips when the front door opened.

Her laughter dried up, and any makings of a smile on my face fell as I stared at the girl that was Nathalie . . . and yet not. I'd forgotten about the Le Fay twins until the very moment I found myself staring down at hers.

While she had Nathalie's pretty features, the horrible scar covering the right side of her face and the cruel smile clearly showcased their differences.

"Nathalie," the other girl said in a voice closer to a hiss.

"Piper," the real Nat said, voice resigned. "This is my twin sister, Katherine. Katherine, this is Piper, my familiar."

I made no move to shake her sister's hand, and instead lifted an eyebrow in Nathalie's direction. *Familiar?* We hadn't discussed a cover story, but that was not something I'd even considered . . . and wasn't sure if I approved of. Familiars were people or animals that a witch sacrificed a piece of their soul to save. In return, the witch or warlock could use their life force to siphon energy and create bigger, more powerful spells. Creating a familiar was risky business. More so than most magic. You couldn't be a weak witch, or undisciplined. Otherwise, you ran the risk of losing your soul to the very being you were trying to save.

In most cases, familiars were beloved animals or the occasional romantic partner. Most witches wouldn't run that risk for a friend, but Nathalie wasn't most witches.

Her sister seemed to be calculating that as her eyes flicked between the two of us.

"Katherine?" another female voice called out. "You need to prepare for . . ." The voice trailed off as another woman that looked very similar, but not the same, came to stand in the doorway. She had harsh features that could be beautiful if not for the distasteful expression on her face. "You were excommunicated."

Nathalie shrugged. "I survived the devil's pits and heard he was captured. Figured I'd take my chances that had been lifted."

Both women looked at her, as if weighing what to say. Then the second one looked to the side, as if seeing my face for the first time. Her eyes narrowed.

Oh joy. Another fan.

"What is *she* doing here?" the woman uttered.

"I'm her familiar," I said in a hard voice, stepping

forward. If that's what we were going with, I needed to own the title. Familiars were exceptionally loyal. It came with the territory. If the witch died, so did their familiar.

The witch in the doorway lifted her head, assessing me at the same time Nathalie put a hand on my arm.

It gave them the illusion she was in control when I stepped back. In all reality, it was Nathalie's way of reminding me of the plan.

I had a feeling this one was going to go about as well as the last.

"Very well. I'm sure Mother and Father will be quite curious as to how you ended up with the Witch Hunter as your familiar."

Ah, with that she confirmed her identity as none other than the eldest Le Fay sister.

Carissa.

She gave me one last distrustful look and turned on her heel. My fingers itched to reach for one of my guns, but I held myself back.

Katherine stepped back and opened the door further. Nathalie went first, as was witch tradition, and I followed at her heels like the good lap dog they thought me to be.

Magic pressed against my skin—slight, but there all the same—as I stepped into the mansion. Music was playing softly in a far-off room. I appraised the gothic architecture that looked like something out of a shitty throwback Halloween flick from before the Magic Wars.

"Nice place your parents got here," I murmured. "Your childhood must have been downright peachy with those skulls mounted over the doorframes everywhere."

Nathalie snorted. "That's certainly one way to put it."

We went through a series of rooms where the floors creaked, and the music drifted closer. Both Nat's sisters were dressed in a similar fashion to herself, but a touch more provocative. When other witches and warlocks I recognized started appearing in the hallways and rooms, a slight sense of panic began creeping in.

My guns were loaded, and my shot was good, but there were a lot of people here. More than the cars outside had indicated. I'd kidnapped or killed some of their brothers and sisters and nieces and nephews and sons and daughters. I was responsible for more of their kind's demise than any other single entity in known history, and that little fact was becoming abundantly clear as the talking died down and whispers took its place.

"Nathalie . . ." I started slowly.

"Ignore them," she replied softly enough it shouldn't have reached anyone else's ears. "No one will try anything until we meet with my parents. It's their property, and no witch or warlock will want to be punished for breaking the laws of hospitality."

I knew the laws. I simply didn't trust them.

Maybe that was because I'd spent so long playing outside of them and using them against these very supes. They wanted my blood, and I knew it.

Let them try, the unbidden thought came to mind. Nervousness and I didn't mix. Or rather, we mixed too well. The anxiousness of it made my adrenaline spike and heart start to pound. Rage began to build in my very pores, a magic all to its own.

I tamped it down, breathing harder than I should have been.

Why, oh why, did dangerous situations have to excite me? What was it about bloody violence that called to me when I felt it brewing beneath the surface?

I'd just gone through the crash, and really couldn't afford to slip back into it so soon. Not when I needed to find Lucifer and work out a way to call Bree back.

My silent struggle was brought to a grinding halt when the haunting music cut out.

The whispers stopped. Someone gasped, and footsteps started toward us.

I looked over the top of Nathalie's head.

Her parents stood, as stone-faced as the gargoyles that watched their doors.

A tense, taut moment passed where Nathalie straightened her spine.

"Mother," she said in a stiff, unyielding voice. "Father."

Her words seemed to snap them from their stupor.

"You were excommunicated. You're no daughter of ours—" her father, Jason, began, but her mother held up a hand.

I flinched, though Nathalie didn't. Her face was cold and impenetrable as marble when she stared at them.

"You know the rules, Nathalie. Better than we do, I suspect," Dolores Le Fay started. "You were excommunicated, and disowned. You're no longer a Le Fay, or a member of this household. This is trespassing, and by witch law, we're within our rights to kill you."

"I know."

When that was all she said, my apprehension grew. This was a really bad idea—

"But you won't," she said after another moment. "You've heard the rumors of what happened in the pits. I survived them, and I now have a familiar." She didn't motion to me in any way, but their eyes still flicked up, and slight surprise ran through their features before it vanished like smoke. "I'm the only member of the Antares coven to survive," she continued.

"Because you're a coward and a traitor,"

Katherine sneered. I cocked an eyebrow in her direction that had her shutting up.

"Because I'm not weak like the rest of them," Nathalie shot back, her voice like ice and wind and the crack of lightning. I could have sworn an errant wind swept through the mansion then, despite her fingers not moving. "I've returned to reclaim my rightful place as third daughter of the Le Fay's, and as a member of the Pleiades Coven by birthright and power."

"Power?" Katherine scoffed. "The only thing you have power over is that half-fae bastard—"

A sharp look from Nathalie's mother had the insult drying up like ash on her tongue.

Nathalie stiffened, her brown eyes turning a touch amber.

"What does Barry have to do with anything?" she asked softly. Her wary eyes watched her mother and sister, taking in every odd expression and shifty move. Dolores' face went flat. Unreadable. Her pale skin smoothing, and ice-blue eyes stormy as they flashed toward the elder twin.

Nathalie started laughing under her breath. Katherine frowned in confusion. "What's wrong with you?"

Dolores sighed. "You, Katherine. You and your incessant need to run your mouth."

"It was clever," Nathalie said. "You framed his

kidnapping as the Red Crescent pack knowing that I'd come for him. It gave you a chance to circulate the news as well. Two birds, and one stone."

"Just like I taught you," Dolores said in a bored tone. "You wouldn't come if you knew we had him. At least not so . . . unarmed. I had to improvise."

I reached for my guns at the same moment Dolores snapped her fingers. Invisible binds wrapped around my hands, halting them from lifting the weapons out of my holsters.

"Ah-ah-ah," Dolores said. "Not so fast, Witch Hunter." She made a movement with her hand, and my hands lifted on their own accord as I was thrown back into the wall. I hit it with a thump but didn't fall. She pinned me there in a demonstration of power. One I wasn't predicting. The wind stirred. The ground started to shake. To rumble.

I hung there, pinned against the wall, watching as Nathalie's eyes turned pure, undiluted gold. The windowpanes whined as they tried to contain the sudden torrent of wind. The hangings on the walls rattled, and somewhere in the not-so-far distance, lightning struck.

"Where. Is. He?" Nathalie said, her voice echoing with raw, untrained power that threatened to peel the flesh from my bones. My heart thundered wildly, and it was only my slow, deep breathing that kept it from stopping altogether.

The crowd around us parted. Dolores Le Fay gave her daughter a pitying look, filled with condescension.

And then Barry stepped forward.

Unhurt.

Unbound.

I registered the truth only a second before Nathalie did, and it was an ugly, bitter thing to swallow.

Barry wasn't their captive. He wasn't their prisoner.

He was their bait.

For us.

For Nathalie.

The wind died, and the ground settled, and all that power that she summoned without even realizing it left her at the guilty expression on his face.

"Nat . . ." He sighed, stepping forward. "I didn't mean . . ." She stepped back, and her bitch mother smirked. Goddamn, what I would have given to shoot it off her face.

Parent or no parent, she was a piece of shit, and Nathalie deserved better.

"You didn't mean what, Barry? To betray me? Because that's what it looks like from where I'm standing," she said. She didn't shout. The anger hadn't set in yet—just that deep, cutting pain.

"They knew I betrayed them when I helped you with Greta. They said if I left a note saying the pack took me, and then came here, those sins would be absolved. I could take my place. I could have a place. You've gotta understand—"

"I understand just perfectly, Barry," Nat said. "You sold me out for a spot with the very people that abused you."

"The demon found me, Nat. After that day in the club. But the Pleiades Coven knows a way out. I had to help them. You gotta believe me . . ." His words trailed off as her face closed down. I could sense the anger now rising, but it wasn't hot like mine. Oh no, she wouldn't burn. She went cold.

"The demon?" I asked, drawing their attention back to me. They seemed to have forgotten that Dolores had me strung up like a pig for slaughter.

Barry nodded. "He wanted me to—"

"That's enough," Dolores said, cutting him off. "This has gone on long enough." She snapped her fingers again, and two witches sprang forward. One grabbed Nathalie and the other pulled out a syringe.

She opened her mouth to cast a command, but there wasn't any time.

The needle pierced her skin, and not even a second later, they pushed the plunger.

She wavered, and our eyes met. I saw the helplessness there. The panic. The anger and the desperation.

And then her eyes slanted closed, and she collapsed.

"Don't hurt her," Barry said, reaching with one hand while standing still. Dolores rolled her eyes.

"Get him out of here. Take my daughter down to the cellar to be prepped."

Prepped? What the fuck were they prepping her for? My stomach turned at the possibilities.

"What about the Witch Hunter?" someone asked.

I pressed my lips together, weighing the ballsy move it would be to light up. I could kill them all . . . but I'd probably end up killing Nat too. And on the off chance I didn't, did I have enough juice to get us out before the crash?

Not likely. She'd saved my ass the last couple of times I'd entered it.

"Hmm," she hummed, moving to stand in front of me. "I think I have just the place for you."

Her words might have tipped me over the edge, had she not followed them up with a sharp command in ancient Hebrew.

Black spots appeared in my vision.

The darkness closed in.

But in my moment of weakness, I called out, "Ronan."

15

RONAN

I PAUSED MID-STRIDE.

From the nether, out of the shadows, weak but there, my chosen name reached me.

"Ronan," she called. Her voice was a mere whisper on the wind.

It had been a week since she entered stasis. Mere hours since she came out of it. Nathalie hadn't contacted me in several days, but I felt my atma's presence slip out of the nether. I latched onto the buzz in the back of my mind.

The penthouse faded from me, along with her sister's sleeping form. After the second exchange, I could feel the bond strengthening between us, taking shape. The first exchange let me visit her in her sleep, but the second went deeper. It gave me a general sense of her. A feel.

Twenty minutes ago, panic had started to leak through.

My connection to Nathalie went dead.

Now she was calling to me, not in desire, not in anger, but in desperation.

I retreated to the corners of my mind where our magics mingled. She was there in the darkness, standing strong and proud and gasping for breath.

"Piper."

She wheeled around, her blue eyes tinged violet. She was close to her magic. Close to unleashing it.

My hackles rose. She was supposed to be staying safe. Away from danger, yet here she was so close to breaking. If she did, she'd go back into stasis for even longer.

I couldn't allow that.

"Are you controlling Barry?"

Her question made me stop. The errand boy. She called out to me in a moment of weakness and was asking me about the fucking errand boy?

"Does it matter?" I asked her instead of answering. Her lips thinned, and those violet eyes darkened to the color of mulberries. I shouldn't goad her when she was so close, but the boy's name on her lips incited something deep and primal in me.

"Yes," she snarled, taking a step forward. Her fist clenched at her side.

"Why?" I demanded. She shook her head in anger

and disgust. But instead of taking the swing, she stepped away.

"This is a waste of time. I shouldn't have called."

Her words cut deeper than her hate.

The hate, I understood. It wasn't for me, not truly. But this . . . this *disappointment* . . . no. That wouldn't do.

I grabbed her arm, caging it with my fingers around her wrist. She paused for half a second, then pivoted and swung.

I could have stopped her. If she were anyone else, I would have.

Instead, I took the punch aimed square at my jaw.

A lesser man would have been knocked unconscious.

A lesser demon would have yielded, as Aeshma and Lucifer had.

But I was not lesser to anyone, not even my atma. I was her equal in every fucking way, so I took the hit, and I didn't let go.

The impact was a mere pinprick compared to what she did to me every day. Her eyes lightened as she assessed me with an inch more respect.

I'd take it.

"Feel better?" I asked her, yanking her arm and pulling her in. Her eyes dropped a fraction, toward my lips, and I smirked.

"I'd feel better if you told me why you're controlling Barry. I don't even know the guy. What purpose does that—"

"His job was to keep tabs on you and the witch. To let me know where you went. To run my errands when I asked. That was it." It was an effort to keep the growl out of my tone, but I did. For her sake.

"Errands?" she scoffed. "What errands does a demon have?"

My smirk turned wolfish. She was curious about me. About my world. About who I was. She just didn't want to admit it. Slowly but surely, she was coming to me. Just as I said she would.

"Did you think that I would wait around all day for you to do something stupid and enter stasis?" I asked. She blinked once and scowled, pulling a dark chuckle from me. "You brought me to this world, Piper. I intend to make it mine, but to do that, I have to understand more about it and its occupants. The humans, the supernaturals, my other brethren that have crossed over already . . ." I trailed, my thoughts turning to another problem I'd yet to solve: my brother.

"Make it yours," she repeated. Those damning eyes dropped to my lips again, tugging on my fragile self-control when it came to her.

I lifted my hand to her cheek and ran my thumb over her bottom lip.

Beautiful as they were, I preferred it when my blood was smeared on them.

"You'll come to learn, Piper, that our territorial instincts run very deep. The stronger the demon, the deeper they are. I need to establish myself here and start claiming territory. Your home is New Chicago, so that is where I'll start."

She blinked in surprise, then masked it behind apathy. "Not if I send you back to Hell first."

Her reply was forced. Weak. There was a time not so long ago she threatened me with conviction, but that desire was fading. The blood exchanges, and her own mercurial emotions, were wearing her down.

"Why did you call for me, Piper?" I asked her, grabbing her other shoulder.

She turned her chin, seeming to consider what to say—as though she were deciding whether or not to tell me at all. I wanted to shake her for her stubbornness, but it would do me no good.

"Because I had no one else to call," she said eventually. "Barry betrayed us to the witches. They want Nat for some reason I've yet to figure out. They also have Lucifer, and I suspect they are the ones who've been trying to kill me. But that also doesn't make sense because I'm still here. If they wanted me dead, I would be."

She looked off into the void surrounding us, not seeming to realize that I stiffened or what it meant.

"The witches have you?" I asked softly.

She nodded. "And Nat, and Lucifer. He's in a pentagram. I think they plan to use him to do some kind of black magic siphoning spell."

If they did, that explained some of why I couldn't find him, but not all.

"How did they subdue him?"

"I'm not sure," she said. Her words sounded right, but there was something subtle underneath it. Something almost imperceptible.

"You're lying," I said.

"I have suspicions, that's not the same."

I grabbed her chin and turned her face back to me. "Tell me."

"No," she said. "Some truths you have to earn. So piss off, or better yet, figure out a way to find us and stop the coven. Can't you use Barry for that?"

I sighed. "The boy dropped off my radar shortly after our second exchange. I've been too preoccupied to consider why."

Piper didn't respond at first, seemingly lost in her own thoughts. "He said the witches knew a way out. I'm guessing whatever you did to Greta McArthur you also did to him?"

It was odd to see her question and yet not accuse.

"Yes, but the boy had fewer restrictions. Greta and the Antares Coven were given orders to kill themselves if they talked or tried to escape. The boy wasn't as resistant. He bargained for power."

She nodded once, no doubt reminded of a younger version of herself and the choices she'd made. There was just one difference.

Barry McArthur did it for his ambitions.

Piper did it to protect the very family she lost.

She viewed herself as the villain of her own story, but she was closer to a dark knight. Even after her loss, she tried to protect the humans of this world in her own way. All she knew was violence and death, and she used it to right wrongs—not make them.

"It's not the same," I murmured after a moment of no response. She didn't ask what I meant. We both knew.

"It's close enough," she replied. "I'm waking up. Find Nathalie and figure out what the Pleiades Coven is up to."

"If you think I'm leaving you with them—" I began.

Piper chuckled. "By all means, Ronan, try to find me, but I'm known as the Witch Hunter in certain circles. I suspect whatever they have planned might kill me. Odds are I'll need to save myself first."

Her eyes were still that lilac tint when she faded from the void.

My hands dropped to my sides and curled into fists.

Piper thought she was alone. That I couldn't find her before whatever end the witches had planned.

But I'd found her across worlds. Across dimensions.

I had once said there was nowhere she could hide that I would not follow.

The same was true if she were hidden from me.

The witches didn't know who they were messing with. They didn't understand the power they were testing.

This world feared my brother because he was the devil, but soon they were going to find out that there are worse things to face. Worse fates than being damned.

They took my atma. If they hurt her, they would pay the price.

16

THE COLD TOUCHED me before anything else. I rolled over, and my stiff muscles protested.

"Son of a bitch," I grumbled, still half-asleep.

"Wakey wakey," a voice I vaguely recognized said, just moments before the freezing water hit me.

I sat up straight as a board, spluttering frigid water from my lips. I coughed, and it came out my nose. The cold intensified. My button-down shirt and slacks I'd worn to Nathalie's family mansion now soaked through with water.

"What the fuck?" I groused, peering through narrowed eyes. The lighting was dim. That was good. Made it easier to make out the woman that stood in front of me holding a bucket. My lips pressed together when I noticed her twin at the door, hands on her hips.

Sasha and Sienna.

Great.

It would be just my luck that wherever I was, the first people I woke up to were ones who'd already betrayed me once before.

Fire sparked in my chest as anger took hold. Like a lover cast aside, it was never far from me. Always waiting in the wings for that moment that I would slip and go back to it.

I clenched my fists in the wet sheets as I got a hold on that anger and weighed my options.

"Rise and shine, Piper," Sienna sang in a mocking voice. "You need to get ready."

"Ready?" I repeated, a little of that anger slipping, giving way to surprise. "Get ready for what? Last thing I remember, Dolores Le Fay used a sleeping spell on me. Where's Nat? The coven? And why are you two here? Don't you have a dick to suck?"

Sasha narrowed her eyes. Clearly not amused by my succubus quip.

"The witches sold you. Or more accurately, handed you over," Sienna said slowly. "You're in the pits."

The pits . . .

"But Lucifer—"

"Was taken. You should know that, given you're the one that took his power," Sasha said in a snarky and slightly bitter tone.

"I . . ." Was at a loss for words, apparently.

When the witches knocked me out, I half expected not to wake up. Or if I did, the hundred scenarios that ran through my mind didn't include being back in the pits of the Underworld.

"Get up. We don't have long, and I don't want to be at the end of another punishment because a fighter wasn't ready on time," Sasha said with a roll of her dolled-up eyes.

I narrowed my eyes at her. "In case you forgot, you both lied to me. I really don't give a shit what happens to you, so if you want me to get up, you best start explaining a few things."

Sienna sighed. "Sasha, go get Dannika ready."

"Dannika doesn't need help—" the succubus cat shifter started.

"She does now," Sienna replied in a harder tone. She lifted one eyebrow and jutted her chin toward the door. Sasha looked between us before huffing a muttered insult under her breath and leaving.

The metal door slammed shut, ringing in my ears. I didn't need to look around to figure out I was in some sort of cement cell. There were bars over the tiny window in the door, for fuck's sake.

"Start talking," I said, crossing my arms over my chest.

She silently set the bucket down and grabbed a thin piece of black material.

"Whatever happened between you and Lucifer crippled him. He could barely open his eyes, let alone walk. When the witches came, he was defenseless. They took him, and then they took over the Underworld," she said, speaking low, as if worried someone might hear. "Sasha and I couldn't protect him. We couldn't even protect ourselves. We've had to adapt. Because we were already looked at as objects, it was simply a change of hands."

"So the witches own the pits now?" I asked.

It made sense at least. It was just a form of punishment I hadn't considered.

"More or less," she said. I lifted an eyebrow, silently prompting her. Sienna sighed. "The witches took over the Underworld, but it was gifted to the Morrigan. She owns the pits, and from what I could hear when they brought you in, she asked for you specifically. Do you know why she wants you?"

Shit.

The Morrigan, otherwise known as Morgan Le Fay, was no joke. Witches had mortal life spans, but not her. Rumor had it she sacrificed other witches to stay young and beautiful throughout the centuries. She didn't rule the Le Fay line in the traditional sense, but she was highly regarded among all witches and warlocks.

Mostly because she was batshit crazy and extremely powerful.

The latter mostly came about from being the first witch to possess black magic. Her line spawned from tricking her own brother—dear Arthur—into impregnating her, creating the first bloodline of black magic.

"I would assume it's because of my reputation with witches, but I'm pretty sure she's killed more than I have throughout history."

Sienna nodded slowly. "Well, whatever the reason, you likely won't have to wait long. You're up next, per the Morrigan's *request*."

I pressed my lips together as she extended the black bundle of fabric.

I eyed her wearily.

"I don't trust you." Even as I said it, I took the fabric.

She snorted. "I would be surprised if you did. If it makes you feel better, though, you certainly weren't the first to fall for that act. That was our actual job. Spying, not fucking. Lucifer bought us when we were thirteen, but he didn't touch us until we came of age and we *asked* for it. A succubus' first feed is very intimate. We trusted him more than anything and wanted to go through it together. After some convincing, he agreed." She laughed under her breath, a little bitter as she seemed to recall something. "Everyone assumed the worst of him, but they were supposed to.

Including you. We knew who you were before we entered that room. *What* you were. I didn't want to perpetuate his image that way with you, but it was Lucifer's decision. He said you expected the worst and wouldn't believe it if we told you it was all a front. He said it was best to give you the worst version of him so that when he didn't fuck up, it was a pleasant surprise."

I frowned. Part of me didn't want to know this. Didn't want to humanize him like this. He was the devil, and I was the one that made him vulnerable. Somehow.

The rest of me, the part that didn't shy away from truth, needed to understand why.

"You sound like you care about him."

"I do," she said, without hesitation. "I love him. We both do, Sasha and I . . ." She trailed off, looking at the four concrete walls that surrounded me. "But he's not ours, and he never has been. Not truly. Lucifer cares about us, but he isn't attached. He doesn't love. We were passing fancies to him. But you, you were the real deal. If you could have looked past your own prejudice."

I fisted the fabric in my hand and glared at her.

"Judge all you want, but you don't know me, and I don't know you. We're just two people that have lived two shitty lives in the same city." I turned away to unfold the garment. It was an exact replica of the dress Sienna had me wear that night at the Seventh Circle. I frowned.

"You're wrong," Sienna said.

"What?"

"My life hasn't been shitty. Unconventional? Sure. Lonely at times, and unstable? Absolutely. But I have Sasha, and for a while I had Lucifer. I was protected from the real monsters out there—"

"Look, you said yourself, all I ever saw of him was the devil. If there was a man under the mask, don't blame me for not noticing. He took me against my will. He almost killed my—" I stopped short. My what? What was Nathalie to me, exactly? Best friend had been the words on my lips, but that felt too intimate for how little time had passed. Was friend more accurate? "My friend. He got what was coming. I have a lot to feel bad about, but I won't let you add that to the pile."

"The witch," she nodded. "She broke his rules, you betrayed his trust. Maybe that makes us even . . ."

"No," I said, stopping her short. Her cat tail flicked side to side, and her ears twitched. "Not even close. I was paid help. A bounty hunter. He hired me for a job that I didn't complete, and then he put a price on my head only to kidnap me instead. I simply made a deal with you. You didn't tell him what I was, and in return, I tried to kill him. These aren't remotely similar."

Sienna shrugged. "I never actually told him. He already knew. You still tried, and in a roundabout way, probably killed him. The way I see it, you need me—"

"I don't need anyone," I replied harshly. "Certainly not you. I got myself in this mess, and I'll find a way to get myself out. And since you're clearly so desperate to try to manipulate me into helping you— I'm not interested. You burned that bridge already."

She blinked and then stepped back. Her face turned neutral and detached, like a cat.

"I see," Sienna murmured. "In that case, I'll remind you that most people don't know what you are. Including the Morrigan."

Ah, blackmail. We were becoming old friends.

Misery did love company.

"What do you want, exactly?" I asked through gritted teeth.

"The same thing as you," she said softly. "A way out. We're both prisoners here now, just different kinds. Maybe we can be friends. Help each other out. Friends don't tell other friends secrets," she mused, lifting both her eyebrows.

I blew out a harsh breath. "I fell for that once, and you fucked me over."

She gave me a sad sort of smile. "I'd say I'm sorry, but I'm not. I would do anything for Lucifer, which is why I need your help. Sasha and I can't get out of here alone. But maybe if we find a way to work together, we all can—"

"You're forgetting the part where I can't trust you. How do I know that you won't just run off to the Morrigan, anyway? Or that you haven't already?" I crossed my arms over my chest and tilted my head, waiting for the next bullshit answer to fall out of her mouth.

"You can't," she replied with a shrug. "I lied to you. Like I said, you'd be stupid to trust me now. But the thing is, you don't really have a choice, now, do you? If I'm lying, you're already screwed, but if I'm not, well . . . it could make the difference between all of us getting out of here or finding out whatever the Morrigan will do to you." She gave me a satisfied smile, because she knew she had me. I was stuck between a rock and a hard place. But it was better the devil you know. "So what's it going to be, Piper? Are we friends?"

She extended her hand in a very old, antiquated tradition. It was a human gesture, not a supernatural one. I wondered if she used it to appeal to me then. As if I could forget the black cat ears, and fluffy tail swishing side to side with a mind of its own.

"Fine," I snapped, taking her hand in mine. I squeezed a little harder than necessary as we shook once, and the bite of her cat claws in the back of my hand conveyed her own warning. "But fuck me over again, and I'll end Sasha—and then you."

Her slitted eyes dilated for a moment as the threat hit its mark.

"You're a cold woman," she murmured, releasing my hand first.

"And you've been talking to Anders," I replied. "He end up mixed up in this too?"

She opened her mouth to reply when a fist pounded twice on the door.

"Where's the Witch Hunter?" a raspy male voice called.

"Almost ready," she called back without lifting her eyes from me. "Get dressed. Your first match is any minute now. If you survive, we'll continue this conversation then."

The starkness of her statement didn't do much to warm me. I pressed my lips together and stripped out of my sopping wet clothes that had begun to stiffen from the cold. They hit the concrete floor in wet smacks. When the last of it dropped away, I slipped on the skimpy dress.

"Do I get any shoes?" I asked her, trying to stop the tremble in my chin where my teeth were beginning to chatter.

Sienna silently pointed to a pair of strappy heels at the end of my cot. I scowled at them.

"Not happening."

She sighed. "The Morrigan—"

"Can kiss my ass. I'd rather her curse me than wear those damn things," I said stubbornly. "If I'm fighting, I'm fighting on my own two feet."

"Be careful what you wish for," Sienna said sarcastically, as she stepped aside and motioned for me to go to the door.

I reached for the handle, and a zap of electricity shot up my arm.

I jumped back, holding my hand to my chest.

"What the hell was that?"

"A spell. If you try to leave, the door will stop you. The Morrigan had it done specifically for you. The voltage increases with every attempt. As your friend, I'd strongly advise you don't attempt an escape plan alone." Her voice wasn't gloating, but there was an edge to it. Like she was making her point about working together being the only option.

Little did she know, it wasn't.

It was just the only one that wouldn't land me in stasis.

For now.

"Duly noted," I muttered, as she reached past me and opened it with ease. The metal hinges squealed, and the big, burly man at the door stepped back to allow me a foot of space to squeeze through. His face was squashed like he'd taken one too many hits and they didn't heal right. The nose was bent at an angle, and his left eye drooped. His cheekbones were different heights, and his hair was buzzed short. He wore plain clothes, the tight t-shirt showing off his broad muscled chest. Even if the face wasn't much to look at, he was clearly built for this sort of thing.

"Move," he growled. The rumble of his voice resonated deeply, and I suspected he had some werewolf in him. As much as it killed me to turn my back on a supe, I stepped through the door and started down the hallway.

The hairs on the back of my neck lifted as footsteps followed close behind.

I could have run and possibly gotten away—if I knew where I was going. But the concrete walls, floors, and ceiling boxed it all in. Faint light bulbs flickered every fifty feet, illuminating just enough to point the way. Hallways branched off, and other metal doors lined the walls. My roommates. I peered through one of the cells a moment too long, and a hiss came from the inside before a hand shoved me hard in the back.

"Keep walking."

Not needing to be told twice, I did.

After five minutes of being directed around in what I was fairly certain was a circle meant to keep me from knowing the way, we came across a set of stairs. They went up.

My bare feet slapped the concrete as I started climbing. At the top, a set of double doors stood directly in front of me. To either side it was open hall-ways with a few other supes milling about. They cast me curious and cautious glances while I stood there.

Behind me, my jailor muttered, "All ready here."

He must have had an earpiece of some sort because the next second the double doors opened.

Rough hands shoved me from behind and I stumbled forward, temporarily blinded by the light from the arena. My eyes watered as particles of sand hit them, but I stayed on my own two feet.

Weaponless.

Near powerless.

Without decent clothing or shoes or much of anything at all, I faced the pits.

Trenton McArthur, the fuck boy, was the last person I expected to see.

17

HE WASN'T the same rich, pretty boy he had been a
month and a half ago when I'd nabbed him and
turned him in for a bounty. His hair was streaked with
gray, and scars lined the parts of his body I could see
beneath the leather and dirty linen clothes he wore.
While his eyes were the same, they held a dark
contempt within them that should have scared me.
Especially when I was without my guns and not
supposed to use my magic.

"Well, well, well, look what we have here. The
Witch Hunter. Lucifer's toy. A mere human girl whose
reputation is whispered in fear as though she were a
legend . . . I have to say, I'm disappointed," a lilting
voice said. Deep and raspy. Full of seduction and
madness in equal parts.

The Morrigan.

I angled my body sideways so I could look at her without taking my eyes off Trenton. He might be a fuck boy, but he was still a warlock—and a moderately powerful one with a grudge against me.

My eyes swept up, but despite the packed stands, I saw her right where I'd expected. Sitting in Lucifer's chair like a queen. She didn't wear a crown, but the dark purple wisps of magic wafting off her bony fingers were meant to intimidate all the same. She was interesting to look at, in an odd kind of way. Striking, but not quite beautiful. Her red hair was deep and shiny, like a ruby. Her skin was porcelain pale and appeared near white against the dark chair and stands. The black dress with intricate beads and jewelry sewn in lightened her complexion further. Her nose was too thin, and her bottom lip too full. But the most startling thing—the one that made me stare— was her eyes.

Even fifty yards away I could tell that they were the same exact shape and shade of light brown as Nathalie's.

I shivered.

"What?" she asked, narrowing her eyes shrewdly. "No words? No sharp barbs? For one that's slain so many of my kind, you're awfully quiet without your weapons or Lucifer protecting you."

I tilted my head. There was something about the second half of her statement that stuck. Lucifer . . .

protecting me. It's not that I didn't believe it now, but more the acidic tone she used while saying it. She almost sounded . . . jealous.

Ah, shit.

"Maybe I don't have anything to say because I know it won't make a difference," I pointed out, straightening my spine, only to shrug in feigned nonchalance.

Meanwhile, my pulse was the sound of a ticking time bomb echoing in my ears.

I held my shit together through an exploding dinner boat, being attacked in an alley, and even being subdued by the darkest black magic witches on the planet.

I could handle Morgan Le Fay.

I'd have to, or this whole place would go up in flames. Any chance of rescuing Nathalie and stopping her family from whatever they had planned for Lucifer would burn alongside it.

"It won't," she agreed after a moment. "My children only consented to hand you over if I made sure you suffered. But . . . suffer too much, and it's no fun. You're only human, and I want to play with you as long as I can." Her voice started to trail, like she was talking more to herself than me. She muttered low in a language I didn't understand, but I was fairly certain it was Gaelic, or one of its sister languages.

She went on for a few minutes. The crowd started

to stir, both growing bored and uneasy. One of the warlocks a few feet behind her throne stepped up.

"My lady," he began.

She stopped. The mist seemed to clear, and in its place was a vindictive glint in her eyes. She waved her hand. "Not now, Jebediah."

The warlock stepped back, a deep frown marring his features.

That didn't bode well for me.

Morgan Le Fay uncrossed her legs and stood. She walked to the edge of the platform that overlooked the pit. Her bare feet padding quietly, the beaded hem of her dress scraping the concrete were the only sounds . . . apart from everyone's tense breathing, whispering echoes in the whole damned underground arena.

"Show me what Lucifer saw in you, Piper Fallon," she commanded in a single breath, then smiled with a hint of insanity. "Show me . . . or die."

A ball of fire missed my face by inches.

I stepped back, and my neck cracked when I whipped around to find Trenton. He was muttering quietly, and while I could read lips, I wasn't that good. The second ball of fire in his hand was fairly telling, however.

I jumped to the side as it came flying at me. My breath hitched at the acrid air. My muscles weren't as limber. The cold, and lack of food and water, were taking its toll.

"Is that the best you've got?" I called, as his fireball hit the cold sand where I'd been standing only a moment before. It disintegrated, the spot turning shiny as the top layer melted and solidified into glass.

Trenton narrowed his eyes but didn't pause in his casting.

So much for that plan working. I'd just have to try harder.

I started running to the side, and the stiffness in my body eased even as my feet started to slip on the loose sand. Two more fireballs missed me.

The third grazed my bare calf.

"Motherfucker," I grunted. My next step faltered as pain lanced through the muscle where the fire touched.

I wanted to pause and take a look, but this wasn't the time or place. Not with Trenton aiming to kill. I needed to end this, but I had no magic and no weapon. I was barely clothed and trying to avoid the dress going up in flames. My feet were bare, and glass littered the pit with each new attack—

That thought stopped me mid-stride. I pivoted, and instead of running around the edge of the circular cement wall, I slowly worked my way closer.

Not exactly easy. The closer proximity meant less chance of him missing.

Still, I rounded him once more and managed to evade another three fireballs before miscalculating where I stepped, taking a shard of glass straight to the heel of my foot. My knee buckled, and I dropped.

A hiss escaped my lips as Trenton started walking toward me.

The fireball forming between his palms was growing bigger and bigger with every second. Twenty feet. Ten. Six.

I bent forward and lowered my head. Cold sweat dripped from my brow. The sticky strands of my hair tangled around my neck and face. Sharp, cutting pain took precedence over the burn in my calf. My blood pulsed. My heart pounded.

I had moments at most, and only three choices.

Surrender, then die.

Give in to the magic—kill Trenton, the Morrigan, and probably some other fuckers that deserved it— and still possibly die.

Or the third.

Scuffed black boots came into my view. Shadows darkened, and the heat of the fire between his palms actually calmed me in a way. The cold was what hurt. Warmth . . . that was what I knew. Heat was rage. Fire was fury.

"You threw me in this hellhole," Trenton said, finally pausing in his casting. "I was excommunicated because of you. Shunned from my coven. Now I'm going to earn my freedom with—"

He didn't see the grin that curved its way around my lips as my fist clenched.

But he choked on his words when I threw that handful of sand at him—straight through that dying fire.

The particles turned to glass. Some hit him, some fell, and some crossed that barrier of his parted lips. His hands convulsed, and he grabbed for his throat.

While the glass was fragile and weak, it was still glass—and swallowing it would have hurt like a bitch.

He tried to let out a garbled curse. To use some magic—whether to save himself or kill me, I wasn't sure. All I knew was his little show was about to come to an end.

I launched myself up, using my good foot. My right elbow twisted with me, coming up to slam into the side of his face.

Blood splattered the sand.

Trenton wavered on his feet.

I brought up my other leg to nail him in the crotch with my knee.

He bent at the waist and rasped in pain.

I brought my left elbow down on the back of his neck where it met his skull.

His body shuddered as he slumped to the ground.

Two weak coughs racked his whole body; salty tears mixed with blood and snot as he cried.

"Rule number one of surviving: don't talk shit before the deal is done," I said under my breath. I lifted my head and twisted around to look at Morgan Le Fay.

She stood at the railing, a slight smile on her lips, and bloodlust in her eyes.

I didn't say anything, but the silent question was there.

For all the time the pits had run, there were only two rules. No outside interference, and the fight was only over when one contestant was dead.

Not long ago, I wouldn't have questioned it. I wouldn't have paused and lifted my head, waiting for an answer.

I would have killed him and been done with it.

But I didn't.

"The rules haven't changed," Morgan said.

I licked my upper lip, tasting blood on it. "Very well," I replied in a deep, scratchy voice.

I turned around and hissed from the sting that ran through my left foot. Trenton wasn't unconscious, but the vacant look in his eyes said he wasn't far from it.

If I didn't kill him, he'd die anyway.

And while I fucking hated messy kills, I'd have to make do.

I grabbed his shoulder and pant leg, then rolled

him over. He twitched, but he didn't fight as I pressed his face into the sand.

Trenton's fingers curled into claws and his back arched. His heart began to race as I moved my hand from his leg to his back, pressing down on him. He shook his head, and I fisted his hair, holding it there while he fought and failed.

Minutes passed by in absolute silence.

I'd never reveled in killing. Not truly. If anything, it was just a means to survive. Me, or them.

But this death was slow and painful for more than just the victim.

Never in my ten years had killing a supe bothered me.

Not a single time.

But as his struggle faded, and the jerking slowed, and his entire form went limp—I knew this one would.

It might have been me or him, and I wouldn't regret saving myself, but that was a hard way to go. Too hard for some punk with a gambling problem, even if he was a warlock.

18

I RELEASED a tight breath and lifted my head.

Morgan Le Fay watched me, her features impossible to read. After a suspended second where I wasn't sure what to expect, she gave me a dismissive shrug and turned her back.

"You may prove interesting yet," she said, not looking in my direction. If not for my advanced hearing, I wouldn't have picked up on it. She took her seat and clapped twice. The doors on either side of the pit opened.

On the side where I came from, Sienna and Meatface stood waiting. Sasha was off to the side of them, her head turned stubbornly and black tail swishing with annoyance.

I hauled myself to my feet. Pain lanced through

me with every shift of my weight as I walked toward them, trying to stand tall. My lips pressed into a firm line, dispassionate apathy my chosen shield, refusing to show them and everyone else how much a single glass shard could hurt me.

Only a foot past the door did I stop and turn. In the center of the pit, a young witch murmured the rights of passing, an incantation that when she tossed the salt in her hand on Trenton's body, it burst into flame.

The last thing I saw was the skin melting from his face before the door slammed shut in a spray of sand. I closed my eyes to avoid the grit as it clouded the air.

The scent of burnt flesh made me want to gag.

Yet another reason I needed to keep myself under control.

My fire might wipe them all out, but I would be smelling it for a long time after.

"Get moving," Meatface said. A thick hand barely had time to grasp my arm before a grunt came from behind me, and the appendage dropped away. I opened my eyes and turned back to them.

"Back off, Rafi." Sienna stood too close for my liking, with her hands on her hips. Meanwhile, my so-called bodyguard took a step back, clasping his eye. "We had a deal. She won the fight."

"You better watch yourself, kitten. I'll hold up my

end, but—" Rafi started. Sasha chose that moment to interfere, stepping between them, and grabbing him by the balls.

"No, *you* better watch yourself, Fido. The girl won, so she's off limits. We need her alive for this work, or have you forgotten the pup you have on the line?" Her saccharine voice made him melt against his own will, but the mention of a pup had him bristling. He took another step back, a hard line puckering between his brows.

"You too?" he asked softly, then laughed once, but it rang with a cynical tenor. "Sienna I get. She's always had a soft spot for the humans. But you? Sasha, have you forgotten what she's done—"

The movement was so fast, had I been human like he claimed, I would have missed it.

One moment, Sasha stood there fuming. The next, her outstretched claws raked across his chest. Blood splattered us and the sand. He took a tight, pained breath.

"I know who she is and what she's done. I do not forget, and I don't need reminders from you, *pup*." She spat the last word with venom, and then turned her chin to lock eyes with Sienna. "Get her back to her cell. We're too close now to fail because this dog wanted to pick a fight."

Sienna didn't say anything, and she didn't argue.

She just grabbed my arm and swung it over her shoulder before walking me to the stairs.

"I can walk," I objected.

Her ears twitched. "You limped out of the pit. Forgive me for wanting to make sure you get back to your cell in one piece before someone else intervenes."

I sighed. While I wanted to argue, my foot really did hurt like a bitch, and every step just agitated it more.

"What was his problem with me?" I asked under my breath, hoping that talking would make it easier, and my winces less noticeable.

"Girlfriend's a witch. You either killed her brother or collected a bounty on him and he was killed." She shrugged.

"I've got a lot of enemies here," I noted.

"You're the Witch Hunter, and beyond that, you're the last person Lucifer was seen with before he disappeared and the witches took over. A lot of people are speculating about your part to play in that."

I frowned. "I hunted witches. I'd never work with them."

"Nathalie is a witch."

"She's different," I said gruffly. Sienna chuckled.

"She is, but that doesn't mean everyone else sees it that way. Even those that think you'd have nothing to do with the witches assume you're part of the reason for everything going downhill now."

"Now?" I asked. "This city has been a shithole for twenty years. Your kind and every other magic user took advantage of humans—"

"I'm not debating you," Sienna said with a deep sigh. We came to a stop before a door that I could only assume was mine. "We could spend eternity going back and forth with who wronged who. Neither side is innocent, and playing the pain game for who suffered the worst just means everyone loses."

She shoved the door open, and it let out a shrill screech. She held the door open, letting me hobble over to the bed. I half squatted before collapsing back and let out a relieved *umph*.

"So Lucifer was actually a saint, and now everyone blames me for that as well?" I said, staring at the ceiling. Something twisted in my chest. I didn't like it. "Oh, the fucking irony."

"He wasn't a saint," Sienna said, picking up the rubber bucket beside my cot and taking it to the water pipe coming through the wall. "He was a king, and the only thing that kept New Chicago from truly falling apart. His hold on the supernaturals kept them in line, and before you go on saying how much they still did—I know. We all know. But it was better than nothing. Better than now." She turned the nozzle and mostly clear liquid sprayed. She emptied it when the water ran clear and then refilled it with the cleaner stuff.

"Either way, I don't really see how it's fair to blame what happened to him on me. He held me prisoner. Of course, I took the first chance I had to get away. People being angry at me for having a survival instinct is not just stupid, it's hypocritical. None of them would have stayed."

"It's not about you leaving. It's about what happened after you left."

I started to ask what exactly she meant when cool fingers touching my bare foot made me tense. I lifted my head. "What are you doing?"

"Trying to figure out why you're limping. You probably need human medical help, but unfortunately I'm the best you've got." I frowned as she prodded at my foot.

"I stepped on glass and took a fireball to my calf."

She looked over the bottom of both feet, then my calves. "You did?"

I sat up completely, ignoring my protesting muscles.

"Yeah, right here—" The words died on my tongue.

While smudged and dirty, neither of my calves were damaged in any way. That couldn't be right. I brought my legs up, sitting crisscross so I could examine both of them better. No burn marks, and despite the sharp pains that still ran through my heel, there was nothing there. Only a smudge of dried blood and caked sand.

My frown deepened.

"Do you have a rag?"

She tore part of her own shirt off and extended the strip. I dipped my foot in the cold water and used the torn cloth to dry the bottom pad. It hurt to touch, but there was no mark. No cut. No blood.

"How sharp are your claws?" I asked quietly. She lifted a finger, the nail wicked enough to probably cut someone's throat out with a single slash. "Cut right here." I pointed at the spot on my heel.

She lifted her golden eyes to my face, studying me. Instead of questioning it, she nodded once and lowered her claw. The cut was quick, I'd give her that. I had to swallow the hiss that threatened to break free.

Blood welled instantly. I reached down and grabbed both sides of my foot, parting the broken skin, squinting to see what I could find.

"There," I said, thrusting my chin toward the shiny sheen of glass now stuck in my heel. "Dig it out."

"It looks deep. Are you sure—"

"Dig. It. Out. Quickly. I can't walk right with it in there, and it's not like you guys are going to get me to a doctor. Just do it."

The words were barely out of my mouth when

she stuck two claws several inches deep in my heel. I couldn't stop the grunt I gave as my chest constricted, but of all things, this I could handle.

She locked onto the piece of glass and squeezed, then yanked.

The long shard that came free had me biting into my own shoulder to keep from screaming.

In that brief flash of pain, I felt something familiar, or rather, someone.

Warmth touched me in a ghostly embrace, despite the chill of the pits. Breathing hard, I looked around. But he wasn't there. He wasn't—

"No wonder you were having trouble walking," Sienna said, examining the jagged glass between her claws. I was more concerned about the blood gushing from my foot. I released the two sides I'd parted to try to stem the flow.

Meanwhile, the pain died down, and my suspicion rose.

"You were telling me how I'm somehow at fault for what happened to Lucifer," I said after a suspended moment. She lifted both her eyebrows, surprised I wanted to continue that talk.

"He went after you, and then several hours later he showed up on my doorstep half dead. His skin was simultaneously peeling off and healing. Before, whenever he'd been injured, he healed like, well, you." She purposely dropped her eyes to my heel, which was now perfect and smooth, just bloody from being opened only a minute before. "That didn't happen this time. He said your name, and then he passed out. Sascha and I took care of him for days with no improvement, and then the witches came. He was too weak to do anything about it."

I released a heavy breath. "I set his ass on fire because he bit me. I don't know how much you know about demon blood exchanges—"

"I know enough," she said. I nodded.

"It wasn't welcome, so I lit up and then walked away. He disappeared before I was even out of the alley. I didn't know what happened to him, Sienna, and that's the truth—not that you deserve it."

We were both quiet for a moment, and I dipped my foot in the water to let the blood run off.

"I don't," she said after a while. "But thank you for sharing it with me. I realize this might be pushing my luck, but can I ask another?"

"Another truth?" I leaned back, my foot still in the rubber bucket, my upper half resting against the cold concrete wall. As far as witch-punishments went, this wasn't so bad.

"Yes," Sienna said, rocking back to sit on the ground. She crossed her feet at the ankles and rested her elbows on her knees.

"That depends," I said, after some thought, staring at the cracks in the ceiling. "What are you asking?"

"You have the markings of a demon. Lucifer said you're his atma," she started. I wasn't technically, but there wasn't much point in correcting her.

"I'm not hearing the question."

"Yet, you talk like you're human. You *act* like you're human." I heard the frown in her voice. "I don't understand why one with so much power would pretend to be human, but you also don't seem like you're pretending."

"That's because I'm not," I said. "I am human . . . or, at least I was."

"I . . ." she started then stopped. "I don't understand."

"No, I suppose you don't."

"Will you explain it to me?"

I lowered my chin and looked down at her. Not so long ago, this was my deepest, darkest secret. And yet she already knew a portion of the worst parts. She knew what I was. She didn't know how or why, but maybe if she knew, she would see . . .

Maybe she would understand.

But then, did it really matter if she understood?

Her pity couldn't give me absolution. Her sorrow wouldn't change things. I could tell her the story—my story—but at the end of the day, the only one it really mattered to was me.

"No."

She tilted her head, unoffended but curious. Her cat eyes glowed and her tail flicked. "Because you don't trust me?"

"Because it doesn't matter. I was human once, now I'm not. What does matter is us finding a way out of here. You want to save Lucifer. I want to help Nat. Who or what I am doesn't impact that, and for all your talk of friendship—we aren't friends. By your own admission, you don't feel bad about lying to me. I don't blame you for that, but I would blame myself if I trusted you just to be lied to again." I lifted my foot out of the water, ignoring the numbing sensation as I wiped it on the edge of the bare sheet that covered my cot.

"I understand," Sienna said. She got to her feet and dumped the bucket in the corner, then set it down. "I suppose I should probably give you a truth too." I lifted a single eyebrow, waiting. "Whether you help or not, I won't betray you again. I will be getting you out because I love Lucifer—and he needs you. So try to stay alive because the first chance we see, we're taking it—and you're coming with us."

They were nice words. A rousing speech, really. If I had it in me to give second chances, she might have gotten one. After all, she did claim to have done it for love.

But fool me once, shame on you.

Fool me twice, eat lead.

I already had enough shit going on. People that needed me. My metaphorical dance card was full.

That was until my cell door blew open. The metal panel slammed into the side wall, the sound piercing the air like a car backfiring.

I sat up straight, and Sienna hissed—until we both saw who it was.

Sasha stood panting with both her hands braced on the outer doorframe. Her caramel skin was tinged red from exertion. She took a couple of hard breaths after what I could only assume was running.

"We need to leave now." She put a hand to her lower abdomen as if helping a cramp. While lithe in form, I got the feeling she wasn't used to running.

"Already?" Sienna said, frowning in uncertainty. "Are you sure—"

"*He's* here," Sasha replied in a low tone.

I kicked my legs off my cot and used all my strength to haul myself back on my bare feet.

"He?"

Sasha didn't answer.

A brush of warmth sent a shiver up my spine. I inhaled the scent of dark magic and fire. It burned in my lungs and sent the embers in my chest in a frenzy.

I knew without a shadow of doubt who was here.

The tremor in the very foundation of the pits said it all.

"Ronan," I whispered.

Sasha nodded. Her eyes solemn. "He's going to bring the whole place down if he keeps this up. I don't plan to be here when that happens. So, are you in or are you out?"

I pressed my lips together. Ronan's magic called to me. It wasn't kind or good, but it enticed me all the same as it tried to draw us together.

He was a demon. One who wouldn't enter stasis after using his power. Odds were the whole place would be rubble within the hour, and Morgan Le Fay just another legend.

I could go to him . . . but would he do what I asked? Would he help me rescue Nat from her shitty family? Would he save Lucifer so they couldn't kill him for some twisted ritual?

I wasn't sure.

So I had my answer.

"Let's go." I nodded. Sasha eyed me a moment longer as Sienna stepped around her and out of the room. She nodded too and jutted her chin toward the direction her twin went.

I followed after, letting Sasha bring up the end of the line at my back. It wasn't the most comfortable of positions for me. I half expected her to slit my neck. But Sienna's words came back to me.

They loved Lucifer.

And to them, I was his.

I shook my head. Both love and magic were fucked up, but I wasn't sure which was worse at the end of the day.

The walls shook. Loose grit rained down on us as we moved at a brisk pace through the underground tunnels. The lights flickered in and out, and when we rounded a corner to come across three other people, I raised my hands for a fight, right as Sienna raised her flat palms in a sign of peace.

"Just us," she said. Meatface, a heavily pregnant woman I could only assume to be his witch girl-friend, and a young witch with strange, color-changing eyes regarded me with barely checked hostility.

"What's happening?" the werewolf, Rafi, asked.

"Demon," Sienna answered. "Looks like he came for her, after all. We need to get out now——"

"If he's here for her, won't having her put us all at risk?" the pregnant witch asked. She wore patched clothes, and dirt smudged her cheek and hands. Her auburn hair was tied back in a loose bun, and she cupped her stomach protectively.

"She's coming with," Sienna said in a dark voice. "We had a deal."

Her eyes flashed. "Last I checked, you need Ruth more than we need you—"

"We can stand here and debate this until the ceiling falls down on us, or we can run and argue once we're out of here. It's your choice, Belmarina," Sasha interrupted. I opted to stay quiet, figuring that would be our best bet to get the witch to comply. Her brown eyes settled on me with thinly veiled hatred.

"For my pup," she said eventually. "Once we're out of here, all bets are off."

She looked at the younger witch who couldn't have been much older than sixteen. The girl's eyes changed from burnt orange to steel gray as Belmarina nodded once.

"Ruth and Sienna in the front. Belmarina in front of Piper—"

"I will not—"

"You will, because I say you will," Sasha snapped. "We don't have time for this. Rafi can walk behind Piper, and I'll go behind him. We're all stuck here, and she's just a human without her guns. Are you really that scared of a human?"

Sasha knew for a fact I was *not* human. But she and Sienna also accepted the one universal truth.

Knowledge is power.

There was no reason for this witch to know. It's not like I'd use my power. Not unless I was left without a choice. Better to let her think I was harmless because time was ticking. I knew from experience Ronan might be patient, but not by much where I was concerned.

"Fine," the witch said in an exasperated voice. "But if she—"

A crack appeared in the ceiling that cut her off. Seeming to finally understand the importance of what Sasha had been trying to say the whole time, we got in a line and started down another dark and dusty corridor. Sand leaked through larger cracks the further we went, creating a cloud that was hard to breathe in or see through. Every door we came across, though, either Sienna or Ruth seemed to be able to handle.

I could tell we were getting further away from the pit when the dust died down and the cracks became fewer. The trembling was less violent, making me wonder what the hell was going on above us, but I wouldn't let my curiosity stop me from saving Nat. She was the one that needed me now. Not Ronan.

We stopped at the end of a hall. I peered over Belmarina's shoulder to see Ruth muttering under her breath. Whatever spell she was trying wasn't working.

"What's the hold up?" Sasha demanded from the back.

"Door won't open," Sienna replied.

I listened to Ruth command it to unlock, to open, to break.

Seconds ticked by. Sound pricked my ears as footsteps thundered through the hallways, still far off, but moving closer. Behind me, Rafi stiffened. He heard it too.

"They know we're missing and that we took her," he said.

"I can't get it," Ruth exhaled in a growl. Frustration and desperation leaked into her voice. "The spell isn't responding. I can't tell if it's not reaching the locking mechanism, or if I'm just not strong enough."

I gnawed on the inside of my cheek.

Those footsteps drew closer.

"Keep trying. It's gotta work," Belmarina started in a low tone meant to be encouraging, if not for the pressure behind it.

"It's not going to work," I said quietly. "You're attacking the lock, not the spell. They're banking on that. You need to unravel the secondary spell acting as a barrier, *then* go after the lock."

They all went quiet. Ruth turned back to look at me over her shoulder, her eyebrows drawing together in confusion.

"You're not a witch," Belmarina said, rounding on me. "How dare you—"

"How do you think I took so many witches out in so little time? I studied your kind. Your magic. I learned about you. And then I used that knowledge against you. The pits are meant to keep supes in. If the locking mech won't open, odds are they used a secondary spell just to bide time for their guards to get here if someone tried. If witches are the only ones that can open this, then whoever set this up relied on your general weaknesses to counteract witches wanting to get out. You're slower than the other species. Your bodies are as human and breakable as mine. There's probably a backup mechanism set to explode, or somehow slow us after the door opens to account for that as well. I know because it's what I would do if I were designing a prison for your kind."

Her jaw fell ajar, but before she could recover, Ruth's voice piped up. "She's right. I got it."

The lock clicked, but instead of flinging the door open, Sienna put a hand on Ruth's shoulder. "We should send Rafi through first, just in case."

I shuffled to the side, pressing against the wall to let the hulking man slip past me in the tight corridors. Ruth and Sienna backed up a few feet as he opened the door.

And then, in the most predictable way that would have been satisfying were I not trying to escape with them—all hell broke loose.

A siren alarm sent Rafi to his knees. I would have been right behind him if not for the gas that seemed to come out of the very walls. My muscles slowed, and bright flashing lights blinded me. I lost my bearings and direction as my senses were overwhelmed.

My skin prickled as a cold breeze brushed against it painfully.

The combined reactions made black spots appear in my vision. It was only just starting to clear, and my senses coming back to me, when I registered it was not the cold, hard concrete beneath my feet anymore.

It was sand.

I was in the pit. Again.

19

RONAN

I STEPPED into the Underworld and it trembled.

My rage was barely contained. Only thousands of years of hard-won control kept me from unleashing it all on the very city I intended to conquer.

There was a time in my first millennia or two that I would have let my power rule me, but that time was gone, and the Harvester before me ensured it would never happen again—except under one condition.

The death of my atma.

I wouldn't let that happen.

Power coiled between my fingertips. I closed my hands into fists, and the buildings bowed. Boards threatened to snap, concrete shook, small fissures forming as it threatened to crack and crumble.

Everything in me pulled taut, but I held it there at the edge of darkness. Of death.

I wasn't here to punish the city. I was here for Piper—but the witches needed to know they'd made a grave mistake in going after her. One that would cost them—once I could find them.

The second blood exchange deepened my connection to Piper, but it didn't finish it. While I could sense her nearby and drawing closer, I couldn't pinpoint where. Not without her using her own power as a beacon. Something she wouldn't do when the price she paid afterward was time.

And time was the one thing neither of us had.

"Well, well, what brings you here, Harvester?"

I stopped when a being close to chaos—but not quite there—walked out of the shadows before me. Her light brown eyes were as wicked as the serpentine tongue she used.

"Where is my atma?" I spoke quietly, barely containing a power that would crush most beings.

She smiled, unsurprised. "Atma . . . tell me, how does one of your kind bond to a mere human?"

The female wanted to play games with me. I stepped through the void, appearing in front of her, then grasped her neck in my fist.

Red bloomed in her cheeks, but she didn't stop smiling. The smooth skin against my fingers melted into shadow and mist.

She disappeared.

No . . . my eyes tracked the black cloud that sunk

through the ground beneath me. She didn't disappear, she simply changed form. That was not a witch ability, but she was not a shapeshifter. The taste of her magic was . . . tainted. Raw yet rotten. Strong but brittle. It was a cumulation of flavors that blended into something monstrous.

The sort of beast I hunted through the eons.

But she was not of my world.

Entering the void, I traced that unusual magic. When a flicker of pure rage hit me, followed by the scent of smoke and roses, I entered the physical realm.

Then stopped in my tracks.

I'd seen the pits in memories I'd stolen from several witches and warlocks when I'd come to Earth, but I'd never seen the way they were now. Filled to the brim with supernaturals, and utterly silent.

Instead of the cheers I'd expected, it was the ghostly quiet that made me realize there was something more going on.

The fact that Piper stood in the very center, lips parted and fists clenched, said even more.

"I do enjoy a good choking every now and then, but I wouldn't try that again," the woman—the creature—said, standing behind Piper, cupping her neck. My hunter's eyes flashed a shade violet as she shrugged her off and gave the woman in the dress a look of pure loathing. I lifted one hand and extended it to her, the other I lifted to put an end to the nonsense. "I've spelled her blood to turn to acid if any harm comes to me."

My atma had just started to lift her hand, hesitance and the smallest amount of trust warring within her, when she also stopped short.

Her breath caught.

"It was you." Piper rounded on the other woman. "You had the man in the alley tail me. You spelled his blood to turn to acid."

"Pity I did. Damien was pretty, and the best at his job. Both of them." She grinned salaciously, and Piper's face morphed in disgust.

"Why? What is the purpose in killing me?"

"You assume we meant to kill you," the other woman replied. "Though your name sets a precedence, it may come as a shock to you that as a human, your greatest use is *bait.*"

Both their eyes shifted to me at the same moment.

SHIT.

I brought my hands together in a slow clap. A callous laugh slid from my lips. "The riverboat was never about me either."

The Morrigan narrowed her eyes quizzically, but answered, "No. I was testing the demon."

"And the guy in the alley, Damien, you said—that was for Nat, wasn't it? But when that failed, you went to your backup plan. Barry."

She tilted her head, watching me closely. "You're bright. It's a pity you were born a human. You would have made a good witch."

Then she snapped her fingers. A gate rose behind Ronan. His dark gaze drilled into me. Four warlocks came forward. Two were holding a set of heavy chains. Dread thickened in my gut. My fingers itched to reach for my guns, but they weren't there, and a handful of glass and sand wouldn't work a second time.

"Answer me this, creature. Why go through the trouble of protecting yourself from my wrath when I could simply take my atma and leave?" Ronan asked. His eyes didn't leave me, though his question was clearly directed at Morgan Le Fay. Judging by the clench of her jaw, she didn't care for that much.

Her hand twisted, and a knife appeared in it.

"Because you're not going anywhere," she said. The knife pressed into the heel of her palm, and I lurched. My blood quickened. My heart pounded. "Not if you want her to survive, that is."

"Son of a bitch," I growled under my breath.

I clenched my hands into fists and stayed on my feet through sheer force of will.

"Stop," he commanded, and Morgan Le Fay hesitated. Her light brown eyes darkened.

"Chain him," she told the warlocks. They wearily moved closer to Ronan. "He won't stop you, will you, Harvester? If you hurt them, I'll cut deeper, and then we'll really see what the human is made of." Her grin was malicious, but sure.

She had him, and we all knew it.

Ronan took a deep breath, and then extended his

hands. They clapped large manacles over his wrists, muttering a binding spell to seal. Then they knelt around him and secured the other end of the chains around his ankles. His dark jeans bunched around the metal. The brands on his bare chest pulsed.

Dark magic and devastation poured from him, gravitating toward me. I felt heat and flame against my skin. My arms pebbled from a mere look. This bond, this intimacy, it was too intense. Too coarse. Like sandpaper brushing over skin.

It had been that way with us since the very beginning.

But when Morgan Le Fay spoke again, that connection flatlined.

That darkness I felt in him dissipated.

That invisible tether that pulled me toward him snapped.

Ronan frowned, then blinked. His lips parted right before he fell to his knees.

"No." It might have been a command as well, were it not for the deep anguish put into those two letters. "*No.*"

"Oh yes," Morgan said. She twisted her hand again, and the blade disappeared. "You see, Harvester, after we took your brother, we knew it would only be a matter of time before you took his place, and from the things he told me . . . well, I couldn't run that risk. We've been held back for hundreds of years under the control of others. But now . . ." She looked at me and smiled. Then, in the most unexpected turn of events, she cupped my cheek. "Now with the help of a human, *the* Piper Fallon, no less, we're taking this world back—starting with New Chicago."

I yanked my face away, and she switched her grip, twisting it to grasp my jaw and hold it into place. "I still don't know what's so special about you, but I very much look forward to finding out."

Her smile was cold and calculated. I didn't know what she had planned, but I knew it wasn't good.

"Now, send her back to her cell—"

"You think my brother was bad?" Ronan interrupted her. "When I get out of these chains, you will wish for death." His voice was gravel and thunder. The black brands pulsed, seemingly alive with power. But the pit did not tremble. The Underworld did not bow. And Morgan Le Fay did not cower.

She laughed softly, her hair falling forward to block out her features.

The sound was melodious, almost childlike in a way. She lifted a hand outward, and a short sword appeared in it. My heart skipped a beat, making my chest constrict painfully.

The Morrigan was hundreds of years old, but you'd never know it with the way she strode forward and swung without hesitance.

Ronan grunted.

A trail of scarlet appeared on his chest.

Not deep, but still painful all the same.

When Morgan Le Fay dropped the sword, I frowned and stepped forward.

"Restrain her," she commanded. Two of the warlocks moved onto either side of me as she knelt in front of Ronan. Her dress sprawled in the sand, and she tucked her bare feet under her body as she leaned forward and pressed her lips to that angry red line.

I gasped as spots appeared in my vision, and it was only the two men who'd suddenly grabbed my arms that kept me restrained.

My blood hummed.

My pulse raced.

Faster.

Faster.

Fas—

"Get your hands off my atma," Ronan said quietly. Most alphas would have roared that command. Any male fated mate or bonded partner would be falling into their own frenzy. I knew because I'd used it against the supernatural kind more times than I could count. But Ronan didn't. And somehow, his calm, even voice that promised death was enough to anchor me.

I blinked and took a shaky breath.

"I wouldn't give commands if I were you,"

Morgan said, lifting her head from his chest. "These chains were my own design. I created them to hold demons. While I can't drain your power without a siphoning spell—or rid you of it entirely—I can confine it. Anger me. Threaten me. Disobey me—and next time, your atma will pay the price. She's only human. How many cuts will it take before her blood runs out? How many spells can her mind handle before it breaks?" She asked these questions, and Ronan's fangs lengthened, cutting into his own bottom lip. His silver eyes glowed with power. "Very good. I like you quiet. We're going to have so much fun." She lowered her head once more, licking his chest like a dog lapping at water.

Fury rose in me. Anger I couldn't control. It was different than the guilt or resentment that had plagued me for over a decade. Not more, but not less either.

Something inside me gnashed its teeth and extended its fangs at the sight of her hands on him. Fire rose when her tongue darted out, trailing his skin.

I clenched my hands into fists, only vaguely registering the warm wetness that smeared across my palms as my fingernails pricked them.

He wasn't mine. The magic was the cause. These feelings were a lie.

And yet. And yet. And yet—

"You do realize that too much of my blood will

kill you," Ronan said, risking her ire. I wondered if he knew his voice was the only thing grounding me. I wondered if he felt my magic rising, despite his being confined. "Only soul-bonded demons can withstand more than a couple of drops."

"Your concern is appreciated, Harvester," Morgan said, leaning away. "But I am no ordinary witch. Your atma is safe. For now. But question me again, and she won't be." She licked her lips, then used her fingers to gather the excess from around her mouth and licked that too.

It disgusted me.

It angered me.

It . . . confused me.

Because the bond had flatlined. I could no longer sense him the same. And yet . . . I was jealous.

That realization stopped me cold. I quit fighting and focused on my breathing.

Later, I could think about what it meant. Alone, I could ponder my own feelings. But right now, I had bigger problems. Namely keeping the most dangerous witch to have ever existed from learning that I wasn't actually human, but a demon made.

Easier said than done when I had to save Nat from her own family.

I wasn't sure when my priorities had changed. When I'd changed.

But what I did know was that Ronan was right that night on the pier.

I was changing because of Nat—and despite knowing it, I wasn't going to stop.

For once in my life I had someone that had my back, and now it was time for me to repay the favor.

Not that I would tell her that when I got her out.

I liked keeping her on her toes.

"If you're done with me, I'd like to be sent back to my cell now."

Her saccharine smile froze. As if remembering I was still standing there, Morgan Le Fay turned her head and stared. Behind her, Ronan frowned. He didn't know what I was playing at. That made two of us. For as much as Nathalie made fun of my style of planning, though, I would figure this out. I always did.

"Oh? Are you bored with us now, Witch Hunter?" I could practically hear the creeping madness in her tone. She had wanted to send me away anyway, but now that I had her attention, I also had her ire.

Lucky me.

But I was running out of options.

"You said yourself, my best use is bait. You have Nathalie. You have Lucifer. Now you have—" I paused. The name Ronan had been on the tip of my tongue. It was his chosen name. But she didn't seem to know that, and I wouldn't be the one to share it. "The Harvester," I supplied. "You have everything you want, and no use for me. After being drugged, forced to fight in mortal combat, and failing to escape —I'm fucking exhausted. Besides, as you like to remind everyone, I am only human."

My pulse didn't change. My gaze didn't waver. I had no verifiable tells that I was lying through my teeth—at least partly—but her inscrutable gaze made me wonder if she questioned it, or simply questioned why I was speaking at all.

If there was one thing I'd learned about her, it was that she liked to talk. At this point, it was all show for the people in the stands. She captured a demon. I was no longer the same sort of entertainment, which meant my presence could only be used as a bargaining chip to make Ronan dance.

My nerves were too frayed for that. Not unless I wanted to commit suicide via burning her alive. Although, my accelerated healing made me wonder if I'd really die . . . I wasn't sure, but I didn't exactly want to test it either.

"You want to go back to your cell? Very well. But first, you must do something for me."

My stomach dropped. Motherfucker. I just had to say something, didn't I?

"What?" I said, snappier than I should have been considering the way her lips twisted like she'd bitten something sour.

"Such arrogance," she said almost wistfully. "That

won't do." She tapped her chin with her index finger, hips swaying as she strode toward me. "Beg."

My eyebrows lifted. "For what exactly?"

"For me to let you go back to your accommodations," she said. I should have dropped to my knees, but instead I froze.

"Or?" I asked quietly.

A wicked glint entered her eyes. "I'll have you whipped." She twisted her hand and a cat-o'-nine-tails appeared.

Under ordinary circumstances, I'd rather be whipped.

Pain was temporary, and I now knew my body would heal, but that was just the problem. If my body healed, then she would know I wasn't human. She would put me in chains like Ronan's, and then I would be truly powerless and at her mercy. At least this—this was by choice. Until I figured another way out of here, I still had that backup plan. Even if time was running out.

Which meant, despite the way my gut roiled, I dropped to my knees.

Silence filled the arena stands. I could sense Ronan's eyes on me, but I refused to look.

Flames flickered in my chest, but I doused them with cold water and lowered my forehead to the sand.

My voice was almost animatronic, as I said, "Please let me return to my quarters."

She tsked. "Is that the best you've got? Beg me not to lash you for your cowardice."

I closed my eyes and tried to calm my beating heart. Fire rose with every breath even though I stuffed it down. I was not a selfless person. Nor was I a coward.

But I also refused to be a hothead that blew my only option in a fit of rage, especially when it might very well end in my death.

I had to do this. I had to—

"Beg me, Witch Hunter. Show the supernaturals gathered here just how lowly you are. Show the Harvester what a mistake of a mate fate gave him. Show them your true colors, you pathetic human."

My breath quickened.

Fire rose and rose and rose, not wanting to be tamped down.

My hands clenched into fists in the dirt.

Darkness rose alongside fury, the shadows flickering next to my flame.

I had to say it, but I couldn't form the words. Not even to save my own life.

I might not be human anymore, but I would not disgrace that identity.

I couldn't.

Not for—

"Think of Nathalie," Ronan's quiet voice said. A voice of reason. "Think of Bree."

My breath came hard in heavy pants. "You can save them," I said. "You can—"

"I *can't*."

My neck snapped up, and my eyes met his. In those silver depths, I saw he meant it. I might be able to deal with the chains. I could free us both, but he couldn't save them.

He wouldn't.

For as much as the words might pain me, knowing that Bree would never wake up, and Nathalie would be used in some sort of sacrifice, would be more painful than I could live with.

I had no choice.

I had to beg.

My head fell to the sand, and I felt a tidal wave had risen inside me to douse the fire and its embers. Until there was nothing left. Nothing but cold, desolate desperation.

"Please, I'm begging you. I'm just . . . just a pathetic human. Please let me return to my accommodations so I can rest. Please don't whip me."

The words may have fallen from my mouth, and they may have sounded real.

They were anything but.

In my heart, something else was taking up residence beside the guilt and resentment. A new emotion. One that didn't simply come from a child's ignorance and prejudice.

Hatred.

A true hatred.

And I vowed in that moment—for myself, for Bree, and even for Nat—Morgan Le Fay would feel every ounce of it if it was the last thing I did.

21

LUCIFER

I COUNTED the passing seconds by the little puffs of breath she released. Her chest rose and fell over a thousand times before a shudder ran through her.

She blinked twice, then opened her eyes.

They were pretty. A shade of brown closer to cider rather than walnuts. They were the eyes of an ex-lover of mine, but the way that she slowly took in her surroundings was anything but. It wasn't wide-eyed innocence or scalding anger that came to the forefront.

No. It was . . . disappointment.

And despite the pain of a hundred cuts bleeding my body slowly, for the first time since I'd set eyes on Piper Fallon, I found myself intrigued by someone else.

She lifted her arm to wipe the corner of her

mouth with the back of her hand, and she winced at the movement. Her lips pushed together as she swallowed hard. Her pink tongue ran over the cracks forming in the dry skin of her lips as she tried to wet them.

"How long have I been out?" she croaked without looking at me. I regarded her still. My curiosity piqued further.

"Four hours," I rasped, my own voice equally hoarse, but for a very different reason. "Maybe five. It's hard to know exactly without a window or clock."

She nodded once, then put a hand to her temple and let out a grunt. "Did they drop me on my head?"

My muscles were weak. My bones ached. My skin cracked and filled with my blood, but despite the sheer amount of pain I was in, my lips curved upward on their own accord. As if they too took notice of the little witch in our presence.

"One of the women kicked you in the head when the boy left. I believe she was a relative of yours." My vocal cords twinged with every syllable, but still I forced the words out, keeping any and all emotion from my face. I'd lived thousands of years, and while I'd escaped several close calls, none had ever been this close. The end was near. If the witch was here, it meant they succeeded, and Piper failed.

There would be no rescue. Certainly not from Ronan. No, he would be blood bound to go after his atma. His very instincts wouldn't allow otherwise, but even if he could, he wouldn't come for me.

I was a means to an end. A barrier between him and his mate. Brother or not, Ronan wouldn't come for me unless it was to finish the job. This was well and truly the end.

I couldn't help feeling . . . dissatisfied. For such a long life, it was uneventful. What did I even have to show for it? A few dozen lovers strung along, tens of thousands of supernatural servants, a city, an abundance of wealth—more than one man could need . . . but it was meaningless. Empty.

In the end, Ronan would have the one thing that mattered. Because I fucked that up too.

Luci. Lucifer. The Morningstar. The devil.

A ten-thousand-year-old disappointment.

It was no wonder Aeshma rejected me, and while Piper might have eventually taken me as her atman . . . it was too late for that now too.

The universe threw me a bone, and I pissed all over it instead of wooing her like I should have. How I was supposed to woo a girl whose world I was the sole cause for destroying, I'm not sure. But I could have. I should have.

And it was too late.

So I used the last of my energy to focus on something other than that.

It was a strange and pleasant surprise to find that

while the little witch may not have looked like much at first glance, there was something there at the second. Something in the way she spoke. The way she reacted.

Her eyes may have been a shadow from my past, but the way she looked through them was new, and despite the impending death waiting for us—I was intrigued.

She tipped her head back and let out a chuckle. Hoarse, but sultry. "Carissa," she said after a moment. "She never liked me."

"Why?" I asked, turning my face fully to stare at her. She pulled herself up to lean back against the brick wall for support. Her hair was messy from sleep and dirt smudged her cheek. Her left eye was dark and sunken in. That blue-purple splotch discolored around her cheekbone and temple, turning an angry red around the edges.

"I'm different. Weird. My magic sucks, but instead of apologizing for it, I moved on. I became my person, and I think at the heart of it, that's why she doesn't like me. Even with shitty magic, I made a life for myself, and she's just a pretty puppet on a string."

There was no resentment in her tone. No residual anger. Not even sadness. She spoke matter-of-factly and shrugged when she was done, before going back to looking around our prison.

"You don't seem very upset for someone that was kicked in the face," I said after a moment.

"There's no point in getting angry," she replied without looking in my direction. Her forehead scrunched in concentration as she regarded the four brick walls that surrounded us, and the pentagram that held me. "Angry people lash out. They make stupid, rash decisions. My family drugged me for a reason, and it probably has to do with you, which means I need to find a way out of here. Getting angry won't help me do that."

"There isn't one." I sighed, starting to lose interest.

"We'll see."

I narrowed my eyes, regarding her again. "Do you know of one?"

Her lips curled upwards in a sly smile. "You do realize this is my parents' basement, right? I played in these tunnels as a kid and hid in them when I wanted to get away as a teenager. Few people, if any, know them as well as me."

Her confidence was striking, and once more, I found myself gravitating toward her.

"One would think your family would know this before putting you down here, seeing that they didn't bother to secure you," I pointed out.

She ignored me as she climbed to her feet. She used her hand to brace some of her weight as she hobbled around the edge of the circle toward the wall opposite of her.

"If you step into the circle, it will alert them—"

"I know this may come as a surprise to you, but as nice as your voice is, I'm going to need you to be quiet so I can think."

My lips parted. I took a breath and held it.

Only three times in my long life had a woman talked to me that way.

The first was Aeshma.

The second was Piper.

And the third was this little witch.

Maybe it shouldn't have surprised me, given she smelled of my atma. Piper had escaped with her. And then I recalled the way they'd clung to each other . . .

"Are you and Piper in a relationship?"

"What?" she said, surprise flitting across her features.

"Your hearing is quite good for a witch. I know you heard me. Are you two fucking?"

She closed her eyes and exhaled once. "No, Piper and I are not *fucking*, nor are we in a relationship. Piper's my . . . friend."

I'm not sure why, but I breathed easier at that knowledge . . . which was a strange thing for me, and something that I didn't want to look deeper into. Not that there was much point in introspection when I was so close to dying.

"Besides, I'm fairly certain it's only a matter of time until Ronan wears her down."

I didn't like to hear that, but it also didn't hurt as much as it should have.

Perhaps it was because our bond was made and not natural. Perhaps it was because I knew if I died, she would need someone—even if it was my bastard brother.

Or perhaps it was something else.

Something I also would not put a name to.

The witch snorted, and I narrowed my eyes further.

"What are you laughing at?"

"You. Them." She chuckled again. "You're all very predictable. Take you, for instance. You don't shut up until I bring up Ronan and Piper. There's so much unnecessary drama between the three of you. Really, you should all just bond and fuck, and then everyone can move on with their lives. But no. You all have to make things difficult." She rolled her eyes, and my brows furrowed.

"Demons don't share," I told her.

"Yeah, well, Piper wasn't born a demon, and last I checked, they weren't made either—but apparently they can be." She started tapping bricks and humming under her breath as she did so. I watched in curiosity.

"Even if sharing was an option, she wouldn't have done it. Piper isn't like that," I said on a tired sigh.

One final tap and the bricks began to shake. Dust fell in puffy clouds. The clay bricks receded back into the wall as they shuffled to the side in a wave that spread outward until a six-foot tall and four-foot-wide gaping hole was there instead.

"That's true. Piper isn't like that. If it makes you feel better, between you and Ronan, I don't think you ever stood a chance. They have something, and if she can ever move past her issues, I think they'd be good together. Maybe not, but at least the sex would be good," she said, turning and crossing her arms like she didn't just open a door that could be her escape.

"I—you—what are you doing?"

"At a loss for words," she murmured. "Now there's a first. Don't worry, though, I won't tell anyone that the devil needs relationship advice."

"I don't need advice," I said. "I want to know why you're not leaving. You've spent the last five minutes telling me that Piper and I aren't right together. I'm trapped in this circle with no way out, when you clearly aren't. I've only ever been horrible to you and your kind . . . so why aren't you leaving?"

Her honey eyes watched me for a long-suspended moment. But it wasn't the color or the shape that made me stare back and really see the woman before me as more than a witch, or a girl, or even a tool to be used like so many before her.

It was the expression on her face.

And one I would never forget . . . if I somehow didn't die before the end of this.

"Because I can't. You and Piper would be awful together. She would never be able to fully forgive you, but regardless of that—you share a bond. You are her atman."

"She has another one," I pointed out, though really, I shouldn't have. Part of me just wanted to see what she'd say to that. What she'd do.

"It doesn't matter," Nathalie said softly. "Tell me, Lucifer, is it true all supernatural bonds are merely weaker imitations of the atma bond?"

Her expression was sharper, keener than I'd expect for someone who'd been kicked in the head. I felt like prey under this witch's watchful gaze, and I wasn't sure if I disliked it or not.

"I can't attest to if they're truly weaker. I've never experienced one. But they do come from the atma bond. Magic seeks balance. Without it, we all lose to chaos."

She nodded once, like that was the answer she expected.

Then she stepped into the circle.

"Don't—" I tried to protest, but there was no point. She'd already triggered it.

"Precisely," she said, crouching at my side. "Which is why I can't leave without you. If you die . . . so will part of Piper. I won't do that to her."

The air hissed between my teeth as she placed her hands on the chain linked to my right wrist. The metal turned red hot and began to burn. My teeth clenched as I swallowed the pain down.

"If there was a way out of these chains, don't you think I would have done it?" I said. "It's impossible. It's—"

"That's not true. Nothing is impossible. It's simply very difficult, and you're not being helpful right now. You said yourself they'll know I'm in here. Maybe they'll come down. Maybe not. Either way, I'd rather be long gone by the time my parents figure out what happened. So are you going to help me, or am I on my own for saving your ass here?"

Her words were a cold slap across the face. I took a slow, shallow breath and swallowed down the fire threatening to boil my skin and eat away at bone.

"These chains were made specially for me. They used my blood. It might not be impossible, but you forget—I've tasted your blood. I know what you are and how much power you hold. You're not strong enough for this, little witch. It would take the caster themselves to break these chains, but I can promise you she won't."

I knew, but I scented her on them when they first chained me.

I hadn't recognized her voice when I first heard it that day I was taken. It'd been a few hundred years, but her scent—that was something I knew. I remembered.

Black cherries and mulled wine. Rotting flesh and spilled blood.

She smelled like an oxymoron, which was fitting for what she was.

It was the reason I knew this was the end.

Piper had all but stripped me of my powers, leaving me open to the lion waiting in the shadows. And then *she* sprang.

"Who was the caster? Can you tell?" Nathalie asked after a long moment. I wondered if she would ask what she was. If she would give in to that curiosity I could see burning in her eyes. She didn't, and it said a great deal.

"Morgan Le Fay."

For centuries, that name had caused near as much terror among supernaturals as my own. She was almost as infamous. Twice as bloodthirsty. Madder than a hatter, and more possessive than even a demon could be.

She was a witch, but she'd stripped herself of all humanity in order to become more. She cast off her human beginnings, and all but killed that side of herself to be immortal.

Most witches would have turned and run at her very name. But not this one. And that intrigue I felt—that pull toward her—it strengthened and took form.

For the second time, she surprised me.

Because she smiled.

"My family must really think so little of me. It would be insulting under different circumstances."

"And it's not insulting because?" I trailed, partly because words were becoming harder to form the more the iron burned. Fire seared my flesh and scented the air.

"Because I don't look a gift horse in the mouth," she said, pulling up her sleeve and extending her wrist. She placed it on my lips, warm and inviting. "Bite me."

The scent of jasmine and lilac made my mouth water.

"You don't know what you're asking for," I murmured, lips skimming her heated skin. My tongue darted out, the tip trailing over her pulse. I felt it skip, and her skin pebbled.

"Bite me, but don't take too much. I need blood to smear over the chains. It should be enough to release you."

My heart jolted.

"Are you sure?"

"No," she replied in an honest, shaky laugh. "But I think it will work. I'm related to Morgan Le Fay. Weak or not, her blood runs in my veins. There's a chance the magic will take."

No, there wasn't. I might not have studied witch magic, but I did create the first witch, and another dozen or so since then. I knew enough to know that what she wanted to try . . . it was a long shot. An impossible shot.

Even for her.

But with her skin pressed to mine and fire burning through me, I felt want and desire beyond a passing fancy for the first time in a long time. I wanted to kiss every inch of her skin and feel her writhe beneath me. I wanted to see what made her jump and learn what made her moan.

That wasn't an option, though. I knew that.

So I took the next best thing she offered: her blood.

My fangs pressed down, and she held her wrist firm as I pushed them into her skin. Copper blossomed. Sweet ichor touched my tongue.

The initial taste was sweet and crisp, like a breath of fresh air. But it was what lived beneath it that came after; the very magic in her veins that lurked like a secret hidden in the night. I pressed my lips to her wrist and took a hard pull. Her magic, while weak, still pulled at me. It wasn't the fire that

Aeshma and Piper boasted. It wasn't boisterous or loud.

It was a gentle breeze. The sun on my skin. Snow melting to make way for new life, and a lullaby that gently guided you into sleep.

"Lucifer," Nathalie's voice said in a hoarse cry. "Lucifer, you need to stop. I need to get your chains off."

I didn't want to stop.

In fact, it was the last thing I wanted to do.

But if I took more, it could actually kill her.

My jaw opened on its own, and my lips parted, releasing her. Blood ran freely for a few seconds, dripping onto my lips. I ran my tongue over them, feeling more clearheaded than I had in days. I opened my eyes to stare at her, almost entranced by what I'd just experienced.

But she wasn't even looking at me.

Hunched over, she swiped her wrist over each of my chains and muttered words in languages I'd learned and forgotten ten times over. Determination pushed her brows together and sweat dotted her temple. The heat coming from the chains was reaching an all-time high. That bitch Morgan really knew how to get to me, but I didn't let it.

Instead, I focused on Nathalie Le Fay with everything in me.

It was easier than it sounded since I was hard as a rock from drinking her blood.

"Motherfucker," she grunted. "Son of a bitch. Peace of sh—"

"I told Mother we should have tied you up," another voice said. "You never knew when to leave well enough alone."

I didn't look because it didn't matter. I'd never let myself truly hope there was a way out, so I continued to focus on the witch even as her whole body went taut. The muscle in her cheek twitched, and I wondered if she bit it.

"Katherine," she said through gritted teeth. Blood touched her tongue, so she must have. "I'm going to assume you're not just here to gloat."

"Unfortunately not," the other one said. She sounded like her, but the voice was all wrong. The tone. The inflection. I didn't find this other person half as agreeable. "I've been told I get the *honor* of preparing you."

"Preparing me?" she asked, and to some it might have seemed innocent. Stupid, even. But there was intelligence in her eyes and a lilt to her voice. She was fishing. Despite being caught, she still looked for a way out.

It was no wonder I couldn't hold on to her and Piper. The two of them together . . . I really had no chance, as much as I hated to admit it.

"Yes, dear sister. You wanted to claim your birthright so badly. It looks like you'll get your wish," the other voice sneered.

"My wish?" Nathalie lifted an eyebrow defiantly.

"To lead the coven," Katherine said, pausing for dramatics. "You're going to perform the sacrifice and open the portal."

"Open the . . ." Her voice trailed off. Her eyes took on a faraway stare. "Where are they trying to open a portal to?" She spoke softly, then. Quiet. Like she knew but hoped she was wrong.

"Hell, of course. We're going to find the source of magic."

22

DESPITE THE EXHAUSTION weighing me down, sleep didn't come easy. Dressed in the thin excuse for a dress, the cold of January in New Chicago bore down like a hungry beast. I rubbed my stiff hands together, prickles of pain shooting through them. They'd lost feeling more than an hour ago. The skin turned red, then white, but blue was edging its way around the tips. I healed fast. Faster than a mortal. I wondered if hypothermia would have already set in had it not been for the magic coursing through my veins. I rolled again, groaning from the stiffness in my shoulders. My knees came up to my chest, and I wrapped my arms around them, trying to conserve warmth.

If I died like this when I could have burned that bitch to ashes, I would haunt them. Morgan. The Le

Fays. And Ronan. I'd haunt him most of all for stopping me when I could have ended this.

The buzzing in my head intensified. While I couldn't see much in the dark room, black spots appeared in my vision. Heaviness dragged me down, and as much as I wanted sleep, I fought it—because I worried I wouldn't wake up.

After being unconscious for a week, then put under again via a sleeping spell, then brutalized, starved, and now left in single-digit temperatures, I didn't have a choice. There was no strength for me to pull on. No reserves of energy that could power me through. Hatred burned in my soul, but it wasn't enough.

The darkness claimed me, and my only consolation was that it wasn't the darkness I thought it was. Instead of whatever lay beyond this existence, I stepped into a memory. Or at least part of one.

To anyone else, this would just be a street in the middle of nowhere. A road just outside of New Chicago. But I wasn't just anyone, and this place wasn't just a spot on the side of the road.

It was where my life as Piper Fallon ended, and where the Witch Hunter was born.

"This is where your parents were killed," a voice said behind me.

Death may have been waiting in the wings, but it was Ronan who joined me.

I stared at a spot on the pavement, and while there were no bodies now—I remembered what they looked like then. The odd angle of my mother's neck. The twin bites on her throat from a client that had been too rough the night before, the purple bruising illuminated by the sun.

Humans were taught to be scared of the dark, but the worst day of my life took place at ten in the morning.

Part of me wondered if that was why I never feared the night like I was supposed to.

At least there I knew the monsters were waiting. I blended in with them, and that day, I became one of them.

"How are you here?" I said without turning. "She said the chains confined your magic."

"My magic," he replied, voice like gravel. I sensed him behind me, his presence like a shadow that followed wherever I went. "Not yours."

My eyebrows lifted in acknowledgement, but I didn't turn. I didn't say anything more. There was nothing to say. Nothing to—

Calloused fingers wrapped around my jaw, pulling my gaze away from the five-foot section of asphalt that chilled me to the core. He faced me toward him, planting his feet in front of me, his height and wide shoulders blocking everything else from view.

"Look at me, Piper."

I pressed my lips together, debating the merits of ignoring him. After all, if my magic brought us here, I should be able to leave when I wanted, right?

The thing was, I didn't know how to control that part of it. My visits to Lucifer showed that much. So instead of acting like a petulant child because I couldn't mentally walk out, I lifted my chin—and I let him see my anger. My fury. My hate.

He didn't blink in surprise or appear taken aback. If anything, the lack of reaction pissed me off more because it was almost like he expected it. Yet, he showed no guilt or remorse.

His eyes were all steel and winter nights. Not an ounce of apology.

For all that I'd told myself I couldn't trust him . . . that he would ruin me . . . that it was just magic, and nothing more . . . part of me had started to think there might be more to it.

Maybe.

He hadn't hurt me before, not truly. But this? It cut deeper than any knife could.

All at once, that rage—that fire that burned so bright—simply died out.

I turned away, or I tried to. But Ronan held my jaw in his grasp.

"You bastard," I said, wheeling toward him, feeling out of control as my hands went flying.

Punches landed, and he took them all without a wince. "You *coward*. How dare you—"

His second arm came up to wrap around my waist and pull me inward, and despite the struggle, our chests pressed together. My breath came in hard pants as I twisted against him, trying to land another punch.

"I didn't break your trust, Piper."

His words stopped me cold. My body went limp. I tilted my head back to look at him, to accuse him of being a liar. The word was on the tip of my tongue when he spoke again.

"If she killed you—if you die—I will lose complete control. My magic . . . it's more than this world can handle, and it will lash out at the loss of its atma. I couldn't stop myself from doing it, even if I wanted to—which I won't. So before you call me a liar, that's the truth of it."

My heart hammered. My breath came quick. Part of me, the smallest sliver, unwound at his words, but I wouldn't give in to that. Give in to him.

"You're weak," I spat, wrenching myself away. This time he let go.

I stumbled back, ignoring his angry gaze. I sensed a storm brewing there, and maybe if I got him angry enough, he'd do something about it. Or, in all reality, I was angry with myself and taking it out on him.

"Weak?" he repeated. An unspoken threat never sounded so sensual. "I'm many things, atma. Cruel.

Brutal. Unforgiving. We're well met in that, you and me. Which is why I know this is you lashing out. You feel *weak*. You feel *cowardly*. You—"

"I think I'm immortal," I said. The words came out as a whisper, but I had to stop him. I couldn't hear it anymore.

It was one thing to know my own faults; to have the self-awareness to recognize what I was doing, even if I didn't try to stop it or change. It was another to watch him pick me apart so acutely. He'd always had the power to unsettle me, but this ran deeper.

The truth always did.

Because the fact of the matter was—the only one that ever seemed to lie in this relationship was me.

This relationship?

I might have laughed at myself if Ronan hadn't spoken then.

"What makes you think you're immortal?" he asked, our prior conversation left on hold, if not forgotten. I didn't believe he'd leave it. He liked to poke and prod at the weak points in my armor. He liked to cause pain, but it was a different kind of pain. Not born out of cruelty, but something else.

"The second blood exchange. It did something to me," I started slowly. "I noticed when I woke up after the crash. It wasn't the same as the previous times. It was easier. Then I stepped on glass in the pits, except when I went to remove it later—the wound had healed. I had to reopen it to get it out."

"And that wound?" he prompted, his attention fully engaged by the prospect that I might not be mortal anymore. He probably liked the idea. I would be harder to kill and live . . . longer than I cared to think.

"Healed within seconds. Just like yours. You know what this means, right?" I turned, and he was further away than I'd expected. I looked down to see I'd wandered over to the spot where my parents died. "Morgan's curse might not kill me."

Ronan's expression darkened. "Might," he said. "That doesn't mean—"

I doubled over, pain erupting in my stomach.

My knees would have hit the pavement had Ronan not been there.

Strong arms wrapped around me.

"What's going on?"

My insides twisted. Fire coiled around my organs, as if they were being pulled apart. I gasped.

"I don't know."

The vision started to fade. The pavement beneath my feet crumbled. I still felt Ronan's arms around me, and his voice in my mind telling me to breathe and not do anything rash, when a loud crack jarred me fully awake.

My bittersweet vision dissipated, leaving me in the cold dank cell where I'd been before.

I lifted my head, putting a hand to my temple. It pounded like a jackhammer was being taken to it.

"Get up. The Morrigan desires your presence."

I was certain there were worse things to wake up to, but for the life of me, I couldn't think of a single one.

23

My feet dragged across the concrete floors.

"Hurry up," the man behind me grunted. Since Rafi, my werewolf guard, had failed to escape with the rest of us, I'd been assigned a new jailor. One that made Meatface almost seem friendly. A hand slammed into my back, and I stumbled forward, catching myself on the edge of a doorframe. The walk from my cell had been excruciating. The burning in my stomach ever-present, but thankfully not any worse. I wouldn't have been able to walk at all if it were, and I could all too easily imagine what would happen then.

I brought a hand down to press on my abdomen, taking a slow steady breath.

My eyelids fluttered as I lifted them to the scene before me.

My airway constricted, and if dread could have filled me anymore than it already did, it would have. But at a certain point, there was only so much stimuli the body could take. Even as my situation went from bad to worse.

"Ah, entertainment," a sultry sweet voice said, making me cringe. "Just in time for dessert."

"I told you to hur—" the man behind me said. I lunged forward, sheer will keeping me on my feet as I entered what could only be described as a party. The room wasn't particularly large, but only a few couches and a king-sized bed took up the space. A dozen or so witches and warlocks were scattered around like accessories. Their bodies positioned on overstuffed pillows and draped languidly across the furniture. Only a few stood, and judging by their mostly naked bodies that were adorned with enough jewelry to pay for my apartment ten times over, it was likely they were pleasure slaves.

And yet, I was the entertainment.

This was going to suck.

"Apologies for the delay, Morrigan. The human is slow."

Slow? I gritted my teeth against a retort about how slow he'd be if he were starved and left in the cold without his thick jackets and fur-lined boots. Not to mention injured and enduring whatever was going on with my stomach.

I clenched the hand pressed to my belly, and it twisted in the fabric. I had to be careful not to tear it.

"You're dismissed," she replied with a wave of her hand. A door slammed shut behind me, and then it disappeared. I peered over my shoulder at the blank wall where it should have been.

She'd either cast an illusion or transformed it without words. Just a flick of her wrist.

The kind of power she must wield . . .

I straightened my spine, sensing eyes on me.

"Come, Witch Hunter, join us. If you behave, I'll feed you."

My feet were leaden as I slowly turned my cheek. She sat on the singular armchair, one bare leg draped over the arm, the other hanging loosely over the male chained at her feet.

Ronan.

My heart thudded.

The fire in my stomach lurched, threatening to suffocate me. Despite the hunger gnawing at my insides, I was fairly certain I couldn't eat even if I wanted to.

Still, I made my feet move and tried my damnedest to blank my face.

Sneers and whispers followed my every step as I shuffled forward into the center of the room. Morgan Le Fay lowered a hand to Ronan's head, running her fingers through his black hair like he was her most prized pet. The silver of his eyes glowed white hot with rage, but he didn't move. He didn't shudder. He stayed still as a statue, because to do anything else would provoke her ire, and then she'd fuck with me.

Unfortunately for both of us, it looked like she was going to anyway.

"Do you know why I've called you here?" she said softly, not looking at anyone in particular, but instead staring out the long window that overlooked what I could only assume was the Underworld. It was dark out, and the glass was streaked from snow that melted against it, creating a depressing, dreary image.

"Because you're bored already," I replied, unable to keep some of the bite from my tone. If only the searing pain would ebb . . .

The Morrigan smirked, then cackled. "If my servants were half as observant as you, they'd likely live twice as long," she said. "But now that I have you, there isn't much need. At least for a few decades. Or until you break . . ." She trailed off, her eyes flicking downward as Ronan tensed. I wanted to tell him to quit playing into her hand because his reactions were the real reason I was here. By myself, I was just a human to her. Expendable. Replaceable. But with Ronan, I was a bargaining chip. An ace up her sleeve for anytime he acted out.

"We had a deal," Ronan said, his voice a quiet hush of night in an otherwise vibrant party.

"That we do," Morgan Le Fay murmured, her pale fingers fisting in his hair. "You be good, and Piper here doesn't get hurt. Not physically, at least." Her lips curled up at the corner in a cruel smile. "Still, it's such a momentous occasion. I want to celebrate. After thousands of years under Lucifer's thumb, we are finally free. Tonight marks the emancipation of not only witches, but every supernatural in the world."

I frowned, and her smile sharpened.

I wanted to ask, and yet I didn't. Morgan was baiting me with tiny pieces of information, trying to draw me out—but I was a hunter, and I knew when I saw a trap.

My lips pressed together, both to keep from speaking and to hide the wince that ran through me when that searing sensation traveled up my abdomen all the way to my sternum. I slowed my breaths, trying to keep myself on my feet, but the world was swaying.

Irritated I didn't bite, Morgan Le Fay snapped her fingers, and a tray of desserts appeared in front of me. Cake and cream puffs and crème brûlée, each piled together on tiny plates and crammed on a gold platter that suspended in the air.

"Don't drop it," Morgan said, a wicked glint in her eye as the tray started to fall. My hands whipped out, faster than I thought I'd be able to, considering my state. I caught the platter and righted it. My breathing was sharp and uneven.

"I take it I'm supposed to serve you," I said, my tone steady but grated. She scrunched her nose.

"No, you're supposed to serve *them* in any way they wish." She jutted her chin toward the males at the back. The pleasure slaves.

I would have snorted in derision if I weren't so focused on not dropping the damn gold-plated serving tray. It would figure that I wouldn't be there to serve the witches of upper society, but instead their slaves. I was only a human. Worthless in their minds, apart from labor.

The image of my mother on the warm pavement, the vampire bites on her neck so stark against her light skin jarred me. She was so pale . . . cold to the touch.

She was told to serve them too.

Told that her human body was only worth what her blood could afford and her hands could clean.

My breaths ramped up, and I stuffed the image down as I shuffled forward presenting the tray.

One of them reached for a cream puff, then paused. "Feed it to me."

I lifted both my eyebrows. "Feed it to you?" I repeated.

"Is that a problem?" Morgan chimed in.

Breathe, I coached myself. *In. Out. In. Out.*

"No problem," I answered, hoarsely.

I angled my arm to hold the tray with one hand and picked up the cream puff. My hand shook slightly as I extended my arm. He opened his glossy lips, and took half a bite, then chewed slowly before swallowing.

I hoped he choked on it.

However, fate was not on my side because he opened his mouth again, this time swallowing the rest of it and sucking the tips of my fingers softly.

I snatched my hand away, and a growl rumbled through the room.

"Are you sure?" Morgan asked, no one answered. I couldn't tell if she was talking to the servants, to Ronan, or to me.

Chancing my odds, I lifted my head and looked her straight in the eye. "I'm sure, right, Harvester?"

Snow fell. My chest felt like it was being ripped open and blood was pounding in my ears, but you could have heard a pin drop.

Except Ronan didn't answer. I got the feeling if he spoke, all that would come out were death threats and worse—but the non-answer didn't help either of us.

If anything, it was only going to make the situation worse.

I wished I could communicate and tell him to

shove that alpha male bullshit down long enough to agree, but I couldn't, and he wouldn't.

"Right, Harvester?" I repeated in a harder tone. Sweat dotted my temple, and despite the cold, I felt hot. Burning. But not with rage.

"He can speak for himself, human," Morgan replied, back to referring to me by my species. "Continue as you were."

I turned back to the men before me. The next one took a seat on the couch. His muscles gleamed in the low light as he moved to sprawl his legs out and then patted his thigh.

My lips parted, but despite the slight trickle of conversation that had restarted, I knew that no one was actually lost in their discussion. All eyes were on me. I was the entertainment.

I clenched my jaw and swallowed my pride, perching on the edge of his knee. A bare hand came up to grasp my leg. He pulled at it, tugging my legs apart so that I straddled him.

"Stop," Ronan bit out.

"I don't believe I asked your opinion," Morgan replied, a satisfied smile curving her lips. "I asked for entertainment," she added toward the slave.

The man I was sitting on leaned back and wrapped an arm around my waist. Sweat slicked my skin and my fingers trembled. As much as I disliked this, whatever was happening inside me was far worse. My stomach twisted and turned like my organs were being pulled out.

"I want cake," he demanded. His jewel-green eyes moved from the platter I held to my parted lips.

I switched my hold again so I could pick up a piece with my hand, but then, he said, "Chew it first, and feed it to me with your mouth."

A sound like thunder shook the room, but it wasn't the storm.

My eyes flashed from the piece of cake to Ronan as I tried to convey a look of warning that he completely ignored.

"Get your hands off—"

I took a bite of cake and chewed twice, the sweetness nauseating me. That made it easier for me to press my lips to his, letting my gag reflex force the food into his already open mouth. He flung his arm outward, pushing me off of him. Both the tray and I toppled to the floor as he choked. I pulled myself up onto my elbows, noting how no one moved to help him or offer him something to drink. He was still a servant to them, even if he was technically getting to play master.

I lifted my head and met Ronan's hard gaze.

His eyebrows creased as if he was finally seeing that something wasn't right.

"Tell me, Harvester, do you like seeing your atma this way?" Morgan asked, speaking as though the warlock wasn't still coughing hoarsely. Her leg curved over Ronan's shoulder and down the length of his bicep, angling so that she could press her foot into his groin. "Lucifer dressed her like this. I would have thought you'd share his taste, but it seems the human *is* a poor excuse for a mate, otherwise you'd be hard."

It was only then that I noticed the room was spinning.

Shaking.

But no one seemed alarmed.

Could they not feel it?

When Ronan came for me, Sasha had realized it was him when the Underworld began to break apart. We knew. We all knew, but this time, it was like no one noticed.

I pushed myself up on my knees and pressed a hand to my head, trying to steady myself.

"Abuse is not attractive," he said, his voice rough. "And I am not my brother. Her pain only calls my rage."

"Hmm," Morgan hummed thoughtfully. "How boring. Lucifer didn't know how to keep it in his pants, and you're practically neutered." She scrunched her nose in distaste. "Perhaps I'll find another demon to take as a pet. Oh, I know. I could have a whole harem. One for every kind of magic.

Now that would be interesting."

"Another demon?" I rasped. I was sweating bullets now. The skimpy dress clung to my skin uncomfortably, and the sweltering heat bearing down on me wasn't from this world.

I needed to latch onto something, anything, because my heart was beating faster. Racing toward that inevitable stop.

"Yes," Morgan purred, seemingly happy that someone asked her. She really was batshit, and more than a little narcissistic. "You see, my line is doing a little siphoning spell tonight. Right now, in fact. As we speak, Lucifer is being drained of his blood so that my heir can open a portal to Hell. We'll take the source of magic for ourselves, and with it, control every demon in existence—"

"Morrigan," one of the witches said. Her voice sounded like a slur. "I think something's wrong with the human."

Really? What gave her that impression?

If I weren't on the verge of blacking out, I might have said it. As it was, my consciousness was slipping, as was my control.

"Maybe she's hungry. Feed her the cake she so carelessly dropped on my Persian rug."

"Me?" I vaguely heard the same witch's voice ask.

"You are the one so concerned about her," Morgan Le Fay replied acidly. Meanwhile, my head was swimming. The room spun, around and around—

"Eat this," someone said in my face. Bile rose in my throat.

"No," I breathed, pushing the hands away.

"No? No?"

For a moment, I floated. The pain drifted away, carrying all my worries with it. I sagged forward, my face hitting the ground. My muscles uncoiled and the nausea faded.

For a brief second, there was relief.

Then a hand grabbed me by the hair and hoisted me up.

"How dare you refuse my hospitality," Morgan hissed in my face. Her light brown eyes narrowed. She tilted her head. A quizzical look appeared. "Your eyes . . ."

Her face smoothed, and I knew without a doubt what she'd seen.

The hand holding me suspended let go.

My knees slammed back into the floor, and I caught myself as my palms slammed into the ground. Pain ricocheted up my arms. Exhaustion weighed me down.

I registered the snap of fingers, followed by the words, "Bring me chains. The second set made for the Harvester."

I wanted to laugh. I wanted to cry.

All of this could have been avoided.

But instead, I did everything right. I swallowed my pride, I begged, I fought, I *won*—and she still figured out that I wasn't a human.

And now I was going to be chained.

Cold metal wrapped around my wrists and ankles.

"You were good," Morgan Le Fay said. "Very good. I didn't think he'd done it. You were a mere human. Unworthy of a demon's blood. But you must have some in you for your eyes to change. Tell me, Witch Hunter, what is your gift? What are you?"

She crouched in front of me, cupping my face between her hands.

"Tell me," she commanded, and I felt magic in that voice. A siren's call reminiscent of Lucifer himself, but if I could deny the devil, I could deny his bitch.

I spat. A wet glob hit her smack in the face.

To say I'd not learned my lesson after doing the very same thing to Lucifer was an understatement.

Agony tore through me. A searing, undeniable pain.

I blinked past it to see Morgan pressing a knife into her arm, drawing thick lines down her bicep to her elbow.

"Try to use magic all you want. Those chains were created from the blood of Lucifer, the Harvester, Crom Cruach, and my late husband, Dagda. Any descendants or creations of the four will be rendered powerless."

I gasped, the acid eating through me.

And then I started to laugh.

And laugh.

And laugh.

"To think . . . you thought me a-arrogant. You sh-should remember. Don't talk shit . . . until the deal . . . is done."

Lightning struck in the distance. Thunder rolled. The winds kicked up, and a howling scream pierced the ears of all who resided in New Chicago.

But my heart, my stupid, human, heart—it didn't simply stop.

It felt like it was being torn out of my chest.

My skin was being flayed from my body.

My bones cracked under the immense pressure.

I was dying, or at least it felt like it.

For all my self-control, or lack thereof, this change wasn't on me, and I tried my damnedest to shove it down. But nothing would.

Not the chains.

Not the Morrigan.

Not Ronan.

"Think of Bree, Piper. If you do this—"

I lifted my head, and no one was laughing. The words halted on his lips.

"I can't stop," I whispered. My voice didn't even sound like mine. There was nothing human about it.

Only rage.

Only hate.

Red tinted everything.

And then there was fire.

24

FOR SO LONG, the city of New Chicago was shrouded in darkness. Magic brought that here. It created the divide and plunged us into a new dark age. The fall of technology was the fall of humanity. We were regarded as property. Bodies to be used. Never-ending sources of blood and sex and labor.

Supernaturals took my world from me. They took my family. My future.

They created an abyss inside of me that nothing could fill.

Or so I thought.

Then there was light.

It was as if a switch had been flipped. A handle turned. Power flooded my system. Magic filled my veins. It hemorrhaged from my pores—and there wasn't a power in this world or the next that could have stopped it from exploding out of me.

Everything turned white.

Fire raced down my arms and torso, eating away at the scrap of a dress. It leapt from me to the floor to the walls. Glass shattered. No one even had time to scream.

The chains around my wrists and ankles melted instantly, pooling to the ground like liquid mercury.

My abdomen contracted as I forced myself to sit up and then to stand. I didn't even need to fight. I simply needed to exist.

The body could only take so much before it shut down, and mine? It had passed that point. The pain had become so all-consuming, so unending, that I didn't feel it at all . . . because I became it.

My brands glowed red hot like the end of a poker pulled out of a fire. A sizzling warmth spread through the small of my back, telling me that another one had just formed. That my name and my soul and everything I was had changed once more.

I looked not at Ronan, but at Morgan Le Fay. She knelt before me. The skin on her face blistered. Pieces burned and others melted. Black wispy strands of magic drifted off of her.

And for the first time, she didn't smile or laugh.

On the contrary, she seemed remarkably calm for a dying woman.

"How?" she whispered, not in fear or awe, but raw jealousy. Her light brown eyes raked over my brands with acute interest. "You were human. Even if he changed you . . ."

"He didn't change me," I replied. "I changed myself."

Crimson brands curled around my pale flesh as I grabbed either side of her face.

My blood was turning to acid. I hardly felt it, but I knew from the pockets forming and healing on the surface of my skin that her curse was at work.

"If you survive this, I'll be back for you," Morgan Le Fay said, her tongue darted out to lick her blistered lips.

"No, you won't." My voice was an echo from above and below and all around. "Whether I die or not, you're not coming back from this. You're not hurting anyone ever again. Certainly not me."

She grinned maniacally even as the fire ate away at her.

My hands clenched into fists. Her skull cracked.

Like an egg under pressure, the fissure spread before it popped. The light left her eyes as the flames engulfed all that was left of the Morrigan.

Her remains slid from my fingers, but they never hit the floor. Her bones dissipated in a shower of ash and black smoke. I uncurled my fingers, letting the blackened particles fall.

My skin split. Blood flowed. Gaping wounds appeared as her curse came into full effect. But I didn't fear it.

Life was hard. So fucking hard.

Twenty-six years flashed through my mind. The beginning. The end.

I had a lot of regrets. A lot of red on my hands. A lot of horrible things that I did to witches and warlocks and supes in the name of my family. Some of them probably deserved it. Morgan Le Fay certainly did. I wouldn't regret killing her even if it meant my own death. There would be two less monsters in the world.

But if there were an existence after this, I would feel guilt there for the people I didn't save. The ones I couldn't help.

"I'm sorry, Bree," I whispered into the flames as I fell to my knees. "I'm sorry I couldn't save you. I'm sorry I'm the reason you need to be saved. I'm just . . . sorry."

"No," a voice responded. A hand reached for me out of the flames. Nails tipped in black, he hooked them in the concrete and dragged himself forward.

A lone figure of shadow in an otherwise world of light. Beautiful. Horrible. Pristine white filled my vision as the fire pouring out of me eclipsed and died like a sun going bang one last time.

I may have healed fast, but something told me I probably wouldn't come out of this one.

But Ronan? He still fought. Tooth and nail, he clawed his way forward.

"You don't get to die," he said. Hands grabbed at my shoulders, but I didn't feel them anymore than the acid eating away at me. "You hear me? You want to save Bree? Save Nat? Then don't die. Pull it together." His voice was gruff, thickened with emotion I didn't want to feel.

"I told you, I can't stop it. The fire. The power . . ." I tried to swallow, but my mouth was dry, and I was losing all feeling. My muscles trembled. My teeth chattered. Either the crash or death would claim me, and only time would tell which. "I'm as much a slave to the magic as you are. I guess we're both . . . weak."

"Liar," he spat. Voice fading in and out. "Coward. If you really loved them, you'd fight."

"The same could be said about you," I breathed, not knowing if he could hear me or if I was already gone.

Darkness was closing in. The silver of his eyes was the last thing I saw, and I smiled just a little. Not that I'd ever tell him if I somehow survived, but there were few sights nicer to look at while dying. And even fewer that brought me some measure of comfort.

ONE WEEK

TWO WEEKS

THREE WEEKS

FOUR WEEKS

FIVE WEEKS

25

RONAN

THE SUN ROSE and fell thirty-five times.

The moon waxed. It waned. It was empty and now approaching full once more. I watched it with unseeing eyes as I sat at her bedside.

Waiting.

Wondering.

Would she wake up? I had to think she would. Because if she didn't . . . my free hand clenched into a fist, knuckles white and veins bulging. The only thing that kept me stable was the flutter of her pulse. I kept my left hand on her wrist day and night, feeling that tiny blip. It was the only thing that calmed the darkness. The chaos.

My magic and I were one, and we were both irrevocably bonded to her. In the same way my mind told me she wasn't dead, my magic simmered on the edge of a boil because it knew she wasn't here. Not truly. Not since that damned night.

She'd burned so bright. So angry. But she'd exhausted her own source of magic in doing so, and barely had enough to keep herself alive. She wouldn't have survived it if not for me. Her blood turned to acid over and over and over again.

I gave her my blood each time.

I pried open her limp jaw and poured what I could down her throat. It was enough to stabilize her through the worst of the curse until eventually the witch's magic fizzled out, but it wasn't enough to wake her.

It seemed that power was with Piper, and Piper alone.

Two knocks at the door made me blink slowly. The witch didn't wait for me to respond. The door opened and closed quietly, soft footsteps trailed over the wood floors.

"Any change?" she asked, her voice both hesitant and hopeful.

I opened my mouth to say no when Piper's heartbeat picked up. It was half a second faster, which before might have meant nothing—but now . . .

I leaned forward, studying her flawless porcelain skin. Looking for any change at all, a twitch of the lips, a flutter of her lashes. Anything.

But after a moment of staring, the hope dwindled. It shriveled and shrank as if set on fire.

I let out a tight breath that I'd been holding. "No," I murmured. The same answer I'd given twice a day, every day, for five long weeks. That was how often she came to the penthouse because I wouldn't let Piper out of my sight.

The witch was faithful to her own. Not those that shared her blood, but those she claimed by choice. And just as Piper had asked me to save her with what she thought could be her last breath—Nathalie did not give up so easily either. I'd give her that. But right now, all I wanted was to be left alone with my atma.

"Soon," she muttered. I wasn't sure if it was meant for me or herself. Perhaps both. "It has to be."

"You don't know . . ." I trailed off.

There it was again. That blip. That abnormality. It was only a half second, but that was twice her pulse had sped up at the sound of Nathalie Le Fay's voice.

"What is it?" she asked, concern coloring her tone. She appeared on Piper's other side and reached for her other hand. "Something happened, didn't it?" She leaned over, peering into Piper's face. The bridge between her brows puckered as she frowned. "Piper?" she said softly, not waiting for my response. "I need you to wake up, asshole. You left me in this shithole with the mess you made."

I narrowed my eyes and would have told her to

leave if not for the sudden rapid-fire beating of Piper's heart. It was a series of gunshots in my ears. A clap of thunder over a cloudy sky. It was the most responsive she had been in five weeks.

I faded into the back of my mind, feeling for the tether that connected us.

I'd tried to pull her from her sleep more times than I could count. I'd also tried to enter it just as many, but shields surrounded her mind. Walls as high as mountains and trenches deep as oceans. Whatever that output of magic had cost, her brain had tried to protect her from it by shutting me out.

I understood why, though it didn't make the process any easier.

It was the singular reason I didn't push or pull or try to break my way past them.

But now, with her pulse quickening and the uptick in her breathing, I tentatively reached down that bond, and lifted my hands to her shields.

"Piper," I said in a whisper from mind to mind.

It stretched across the void. Two syllables held together by nothing but space.

One breath passed. Then two. When no answer came, I turned back internally and sighed in frustration.

My hands clenched at my sides. My nails curving and sharpening to claws.

Then I felt a tug.

It was soft, and so slight at first that I almost missed it.

My head whipped around, and I surveyed the chasm between her mind and my own once more.

Another tug pulled. It was fast and as fleeting as a kiss. It hit me hard and filled my lungs with fire and ash. I inhaled sharply and took one step toward the void.

And then the wall fell. Brick by brick, it cracked and crumbled.

And the trench as deep as the sea filled. Rock and dust and mortar piled up. Slowly but surely, her mind unfurled.

The wall reached the ground, and the ground reached the wall, and there in the emptiness she stood.

Her long blonde hair was braided back. A cut scraped her cheekbone. She dressed in a white tank top and jeans that clung to her long legs. Her black bra peaked over the edge. It was a stark contrast from the Piper I'd become accustomed to seeing.

Gone were the black pants, combat boots, and long-sleeved shirts.

Her brands twisted and twined around her arms, black tinged with red—as if the magic refused to calm after the last episode.

I stared at them, stared at her, and then—

"Did you do it?" she asked, breaking the silence.

I frowned. "Do it?"

"Did you save them?"

Her eyes. Her damning, haunting eyes. They were blue-tinted violet windows that stared straight into me, but this time I let her see. I wanted her to.

Because this time I did exactly what she wanted.

"I did."

She didn't blink or act surprised. The apathetic expression never left her face as she took that in and then nodded.

Piper turned on her bare heel and walked into the dark.

"Wait!" I called, crushing through the barrier between us. "Where are you—"

My words faltered as she peered over her shoulder. The shadows kissed her skin with longing, and a small half smile dragged up her lips in amusement.

"It's time," she said. "Time to wake up."

26

AWARENESS DIDN'T RETURN SLOWLY as it had in the past. For weeks I'd been surfacing, but my body was too weak to respond. My mind too closed off to reach out. I was a prisoner to my magic. It had risen like a tidal wave to protect me.

And so I waited in the shadows of my mind, unfeeling to the world around me, though I sensed time passing. It was a strange thing to be locked inside the void. I both hated it and yet didn't. I hated that I couldn't tell whether Nathalie had made it. I hated that it was only myself for company, and my own thoughts and memories that could fill the silence. That I hated most of all because it forced me to come to grips with some things.

The first was that maybe it wasn't magic itself I

hated. I seemed to rely on it an awful lot. Perhaps it was less magic and simply just people. Bad people.

Which led to the second. Not all supernaturals were evil.

Nathalie was my case and point. While there were plenty that weren't good, she, the twins, Ronan, and somehow even Lucifer all went against that. They may not have been good in the traditional sense, but neither was I—and I was once human. So perhaps it was not as black and white as I'd led myself to believe.

That brought me to the third and final realization.

My entire life had been built on systemic prejudice and speciesism. It colored everything I did, from the decisions that led me to find and take power for myself—to my family dying as a result—to the subsequent decade I'd spent hunting the people whose ranks I had joined. Every single thing I did, and even the guilt I harbored, was because of it.

Including the many, many lies I told myself.

Lying was easier. It was softer. Kinder. You found a way to manipulate the reality, and you made yourself believe it. Say the lie ten times, then twenty—and one day, you would no longer question it.

But it would come back. The past always did. In the end, the truth would always find you.

In the deepest recesses of my mind, it found me, and it made me take a cold, hard look in the mirror and ask myself what I saw.

I didn't like the answer.

It was only then that I saw another truth. I was stuck in my mind for so long because of myself, and no one else. I feared what I'd done because I lost control. I feared what Ronan didn't do. I feared that the guilt I would wake up to would be too great.

It was only with that realization that the barriers began to crumble, and I heard her voice, and I felt Ronan's touch as his mind brushed against mine.

The crash may have been what dragged me under, but it was the words '*I did*' that pulled me out.

I still wasn't sure if I would tell him that, or anyone for that matter, when I opened my eyes for the first time in what I was certain had been a very long time.

All I knew was that I couldn't keep going this way.

I wouldn't.

And it was time to wake up.

I WINCED INTO THE LIGHT. After so long of staring into the dark, even the softest flicker was still bright. Painful.

My dry lips parted. I inhaled deeply, ignoring the strain in my throat. If I thought it was dry before, that was nothing compared to now. While my head didn't pound from dehydration, my ashen skin and chapped mouth made me feel more like a corpse brought back to life. I'd have wondered if they turned me into something like a vampire, if not for the steady thundering of my heart.

The sound of it pounding as it pushed blood through my veins calmed me. I took a few deep breaths before trying to sit up. A wave of dizziness hit me instantly, and hands grasped my shoulders. "Take it easy," a deep voice rumbled. Goosebumps pebbled my skin. Even half dead, my body still responded to him and his presence.

"Where am I . . ." The light gray walls and dark curtains were wholly unfamiliar, and yet not.

"Ronan's penthouse. You've been out a long time. He wouldn't let you out of his sight," a feminine voice scoffed. My chest tightened, then released. I blinked a couple of times to clear the haziness and wait for my vision to focus. "You gave us a scare this time. You really are an asshole."

Despite feeling like a train wreck, a harsh raspy chuckle slid between my lips. I'm pretty sure I sounded like I was choking, given the growl that elicited from Ronan. His narrowed eyes slid sideways to glare at Nat. She shrugged her slender shoulders, completely unfazed. The soft golden glint in her eyes spoke of mischief, like she knew exactly what she was doing.

"Judging by the fact that you're here, I take that to

mean the coven's attempt to open a portal failed?" I asked. Her easy smile dimmed, and her eyes flicked downward. Avoiding.

I frowned, concern and confusion filling me. Ronan must have sensed the difference because he replied quickly, "Yes and no. They managed to open a portal, but they didn't find the source."

"I see," I rasped. "And Lucifer? Where is he? I would have thought after he was freed—"

"I didn't free him," Ronan replied. I lifted my eyebrows in silent question, preserving my already aching voice.

"He died," Nathalie said. Her body slid back, away from my side, as if needing to put some space between us suddenly. "The siphoning killed him. I tried to save him. I tried to—" She broke off very abruptly and took a harsh breath. "He died," she repeated. "He wasn't strong enough to bolster the corridor. They managed to open it but couldn't keep it open. It collapsed when his magic gave out. Several of my family members and the Pleiades Coven were on the other side. The rest fled shortly after when Ronan came for me."

Silence filled me. A loss I didn't understand. There was a hole in my chest, not as deep or wide as what I felt at the loss of my sister and parents, but still there, nonetheless. I didn't understand it.

"His death is the reason you lost control," Ronan

said softly. My head jerked up. "Nathalie told me you'd entered the first blood bond with him. It would have been enough to trigger a response similar to a true atman dying. It's why you were in so much pain, and why you couldn't stop it."

I wasn't sure what to say. I barely knew him, and yet part of me seemed to grieve. I felt the truth in his words, and it made sense in a way. Mates often lost control and went mad when their other half died. If the atman bond was a deeper mate bond, it surprised me that I was okay.

"Will I go crazy?" I asked, not wanting to voice the concern, but needing to be sure.

"I don't believe so," Ronan answered, his bare thumb skimming over my shoulder where he still held me up. A thin long-sleeved shirt kept us from making contact, but my pulse raced. My breath hitched.

This response I had to him. It was electric. Magnetic. It was . . . magic. But then, so was Lucifer and my bond to him, yet I didn't feel this way. There wasn't even a speck of trust or true desire.

I could lie to myself. I was good at it, but when I woke, I said things would be different—and I meant it.

"Because of you, right?" I said, lifting my face to look him in the eye. "Your bond with me, that's what will keep me sane?"

The silver seemed to intensify in his gaze.

"Partially," he acknowledged. "I believe that because he wasn't your true atman, your magic won't degenerate rapidly either way. It was a made bond, not a natural one. There's also the fact that you weren't born a demon that may impact it. It's possible that even my own death wouldn't do it."

"Does that bother you?" I asked, unabashedly. Nathalie let out a cough and muttered something about getting me water before stepping out of the room.

"No," he answered almost instantly. "Because it means that you're safe from the worst once the bond is complete. I won't be a weakness for you."

I couldn't help but stare. He meant it. Every word.

Ronan may want me, even need me, but he could acknowledge that once it was done, I wouldn't need him. Something about that settled in me, burrowing deep under the skin.

"Demons are hard to kill. Near impossible, it seems. I wasn't even sure if they could die," I said.

"We are resilient," he agreed. "Me more so than most," he added with a hard twist of his lips. It was a makeshift smirk, but it didn't hold the same arrogance as before. What had happened in the Underworld had rattled him. That much was clear.

"Why is that?"

"Because I'm the Harvester," he said simply.

"You've yet to tell me what that means," I rasped.

"You've yet to earn it," he replied. This time the taunting smirk was genuine.

"You said yourself it wasn't my fault for losing control this time. I didn't exactly enter stasis by choice." I shuffled back, pulling away from him. He let his hands drop as I settled against the onyx headboard. One of them rested lightly on my knee, his strong fingers wrapped around it, heat radiating through the comforter.

"Stasis wasn't, but you chose to go after the witches alone in the first place—and that is your fault," he rumbled.

"We had no way of knowing that they were trying to capture her as bait for me." Nat's voice floated in from the cracked door. She entered the room a few seconds later, carrying a steamy cup.

I wrinkled my nose.

"What is that?"

"Jasmine tea with a teaspoon of honey," she said. "And before you complain, understand that this single cup would cost two thousand dollars, so you'll drink it with a smile on your face because I'm dipping into my own profits here."

I accepted the cup even if my lips were pursed. I'd never had tea before, for obvious reasons. It was a luxury expense. Something I couldn't afford as a bounty hunter.

The mug warmed my hands. "So, why exactly

were they after you?" I asked her, taking a sip. The scent was strong, and the taste a little strange, but not unpleasant. I swallowed it down, and my parched throat thanked me immensely. I hummed under my breath.

Nathalie seated herself on the edge of the bed and crossed her legs, picking at a piece of lint on her pants that wasn't there. "My magic," she said. "Or rather, my ability to manipulate it." I frowned but didn't say anything as I took another sip.

"She's a chaos witch," Ronan said. I nearly spat my tea out, but the sharp look on Nat's face told me to swallow it down, surprised or not. At two grand a cup, the poor person in me really didn't want to waste it on principle.

"Chaos witches aren't real," I said. "They're a fairytale. A fiction—"

"Well, you're looking at one," Nat said. "Apparently my parents knew my whole life. They just let me think I was a crappy witch when in reality, my magic was completely different. It's comparing apples to oranges or—"

"A gray witch to chaos?" I added. She nodded. "Hmm. Well, we knew you were weird. I suppose it makes some sense. You suck at spells but can do magic without words."

"Thanks," she said sarcastically.

"You're welcome," I replied with saccharine

sweetness. My next sip of the tea went down the wrong pipe and I spluttered a cough. My shoulders shook and eyes watered.

"That's what you get," Nathalie said with a twist of her lips, hiding a smile.

"For?" I rasped, taking quick breaths to clear my throat.

"Being an asshole. As always."

I snorted, took another sip to soothe the scratchy feeling, and then took a long slow breath. "Why would they need a chaos witch to open a portal? I didn't even think they're real, so I don't imagine they're common. There couldn't have been one when I summoned Aeshma . . ."

"Because they weren't simply trying to open a portal," Ronan said. "A portal, as you know it, is a one-way door that a demon can choose to enter and cross to this side. They wanted to create a *corridor* for them to cross through into hell. A tear, such as a portal, takes a modicum of magic, but a corridor that allows passage back and forth? That would have taken considerably more, something that only a true demon would be powerful enough for. Because Lucifer was severely depleted of his magic, he wasn't able to maintain it. His magic burned out, and when a demon's magic is gone, so are they."

"While that explains more about Lucifer, that doesn't explain why they needed Nat specifically.

They went through a great deal of trouble to get her when it sounds like they only needed Lucifer. I don't understand . . ."

"Chaos is the fifth magic. It consists of all four magics: desire, spirit, death, and the one you're most familiar with, rage. Because of that, chaos witches can control the magic around them," Nathalie said on a heavy sigh. "It's the reason I was able to kill Dara Lightseeker in the pits. I returned her magic lightning back to her. They needed me to control Lucifer's magic and make the corridor. A black witch can do many things, but they can't control the magic of a demon, especially not one that was the source for their power."

"His blood made them witches," I said. "He could control them because of it. Clearly, they found a way around it, though."

"They did," she said. "Or rather, the Morrigan did. She created a spell that could block Lucifer from reading her mind or influencing her. Throughout the last couple hundred years, she's been slowly testing and integrating it into the black witch lines that follow her. It's the reason Barry claimed to have helped them. They told him if he betrayed me, they could free him from Ronan's control over him—so he would have gotten the power he bargained for but wouldn't have to pay the price. The block allowed all of them to conceal their true intentions so that Lucifer didn't know all these years—and Ronan couldn't learn the truth from Barry before they had a chance to open the corridor. Either way, they needed me because my magic doesn't come from Lucifer like theirs. Which meant whatever sway he could have over them, he couldn't over me."

"If the chaos doesn't come from him, where does it come from?"

"Magic itself," Ronan said. "The magic Lucifer passed on through blood was desire. The magic you took from Aeshma was rage. The woman you call the Morrigan mentioned Crom Cruach and Dagda. If they are the demons I believe them to be, that explains the presence of death and spirit magic in this world. However, chaos does not pass through the blood. When a supernatural is born or created, they have the same magic as their parents—unless chaos intervenes and chooses them, just as it does in Hell."

Hell. Where demons came from. Where magic came from.

"So there are chaos demons?" I asked.

"Yes."

"But she didn't get this magic from them?"

"No," he answered solemnly. "Somehow, some way . . . the magic chose her. Despite coming from a line of mostly death and desire magic, she didn't end up with one or the other as nearly everyone does. Even demons born from two parents of different magics only ever end up as one. Except when chaos comes into play. It makes her magic utterly different because she can control all of them. She's not even a true witch in the same sense. More of a conduit for something greater. They needed her to open the corridor because she's likely the only one in the world that could."

I watched Nathalie while he spoke. While she didn't seem surprised by this knowledge, she also didn't seem pleased. Something told me there was more going on with her than I currently knew about. Ronan's face didn't reveal much of anything, but Nathalie's wasn't flat. Behind the many masks she wore, I saw an inkling of something she wasn't trying to show.

Guilt.

But what she felt guilty about, I couldn't say. Surely, it wasn't Lucifer's death? I wasn't sure what there was to feel guilty about, although the thought of it gave me mixed feelings. With all that I knew, part of me did mourn him. I mourned the loss of New Chicago having someone to look out for it. Someone that wasn't afraid to be the monster; to keep the other monsters in line. I mourned for the small piece of me that was in him, and him in me.

But I didn't mourn him on a deeper level. I didn't know him or even like him. I simply couldn't.

So why was it she seemed guilty?

"Is there something you two aren't telling me?" I asked them eventually.

Their shared look told me a great deal, as did their silence.

The worst thoughts came to mind.

I lurched forward. "Is it Bree—" My eyes flew to the door out of instinct. The hand on my knee tightened, holding it in place as I started to move my legs to get out of bed.

"It's not Bree," Ronan said. "She's perfectly safe, just as you left her."

I breathed out, letting go of my initial panic. "Then what is it?" I demanded, running my free hand through my hair. I regretted it almost instantly. I may have been alive, but they clearly hadn't washed my hair in some time. It felt gross.

"A lot happened that night. Things I did. Things you did. New Chicago isn't the same." Nathalie spoke like she was trying to tell me something while still not saying it.

"Well, Lucifer's dead, so I imagine it's not. He's ruled it unofficially for as long as—"

"That's not what I'm saying," Nathalie said a little sharper than I think she intended. I lifted my eyebrows, silently telling her to go on. "Yes, Lucifer died. But his death had implications."

"Such as?" I prompted, trying to pull the truth from her.

"The Underworld burned down," Ronan said without remorse or much feeling at all. "And every supernatural whose power came from Lucifer died, or was otherwise severely impaired by the loss of magic."

I opened my mouth, but suddenly didn't know what to say. Did I ask about what burned down the Underworld? I already knew the answer. That place was made of concrete and steel. No normal fire would have burned it all. No . . . I did.

These were the repercussions. I'd assumed Nathalie and Bree's death were the only ones, but that wasn't true. They were just the only ones I couldn't face.

"How many people?" I asked.

"Over five thousand died in the fire," Ronan said softly.

Five thousand.

That number was crushing. Suffocating.

I couldn't breathe. I couldn't think.

How many were human?

How many were slaves?

How many didn't deserve it—

"Four hundred thousand is the current estimate that have died as a result of Lucifer's death in New Chicago alone. Outside sources are reporting millions throughout the country, and millions more that are crippled by health issues. Those who took blood from him directly or were supernaturally long-lived died instantly. Mixed blooded humans seemed to have stood a greater chance, depending on age and how much magic they carried. There's still a lot unknown, and I'll be honest that I didn't pay much attention to it in the early weeks. I was preoccupied by you still being in stasis." Ronan's words washed over me, but it wasn't his attention that I sought. For all his years, his power, he lacked in empathy and understanding toward emotions that were very real to me. Perhaps he didn't feel them anymore because ten thousand years had hardened him. Perhaps he never did. But I looked at Nathalie and I just knew she understood. As great a debt as that five thousand felt, it was *nothing* compared to the look in her eyes.

"I couldn't save him," Nat whispered. "I couldn't save the devil, and millions of people are dead because of it."

"It's not your fault," I told her as I reached for her hand.

"I know," she said. "Just like the fire wasn't yours. It was my family's fault. They took him. They made me do the siphoning and open the corridor. They made me kill him, not intentionally, but they did. It's their fault, and I know that, but . . ."

"You still feel the guilt," I said.

She nodded once, then swallowed hard. Her eyes didn't water, and her mouth didn't quiver, but her fingers wrapped around mine and we both held tight.

Five thousand was too large a number to really comprehend them all.

Millions were infinitely beyond that.

It felt like a void of despair. Worse than the worst deed. More wicked than anything I had ever done.

She spoke the truth. Neither of us were at fault, but we both contributed.

We both made decisions that led us to this juncture.

And we both would have to live with the consequences.

27

Hot water scalded my flesh. I scrubbed my arms
and legs raw, then tackled my mass of hair. If it wasn't
so easy to braid back, I might have hacked it all off.
My arms were sore by the time I finished shampooing
and conditioning it. My fingers shook, struggling to
grip when I turned the silver handle. The water
stopped running. Droplets fell from my skin onto the
decorative stone floors.

I stood in the large walk-in shower, breathing
harder as the exhaustion caught up. While I was truly
immortal now, it seemed that five weeks of lying in a
bed still affected me. I was pitifully weak. My muscles
exhausted after so little effort.

I spent years honing my body into a weapon to
fight the damned, but five stupid weeks was all it took
to lose it.

Bitterness sat heavy on my tongue, traced with a melancholy that refused to lift.

I stumbled forward, pushing at the glass door. It swung open easily. Droplets of water scattered, running streaks through the fogged glass. I reached out with an unsteady hand to wipe at the mirror. It wasn't clear through the condensation still clinging to it, but my own warbled reflection looked back.

My eyes were blue as the day I was born, but the subtlest shade of violet tinged them. I frowned at myself, standing there dripping water all over the place.

My hand swung out and rubbed lower, where my chest and abdomen were. The black brands were stark as ever against my skin. Pieces of my past were literally imprinted there. My beginning. My first kill. My first loss of control. My first friend.

I looked at that one. It was Nathalie's brand. She still didn't know about it.

Then I turned and looked over my shoulder at my lower back.

That one was new. It appeared when I made the decision to kill the Morrigan and leave my future in Ronan's hands.

It was the moment I decided I trusted him, more than he seemed to trust himself.

While I had said I was okay dying, part of me believed I'd make it through. Ronan wouldn't let me die, and he didn't. He even went for Nat, just as I'd asked.

He didn't burn my world.

I did that all on my own.

Perhaps it was all the more fitting that a blazing star of black fire was now etched into my lower back. Not necessarily a brand for him, but for the change in me. In who I was. While I was still a creature made of muscle and bone, something deeper had changed that night on a fundamental level.

I brushed my fingers over the marks.

A gentle knock at the door made me jump.

The door cracked before I could tell her to go away.

"You've been in here a long time," Nat said, stepping inside. I moved to put an arm over my tits, and she snorted, grabbing a towel off the shelf over the toilet and throwing it at me.

"You forget, I'm the one that dressed you when we escaped from the Underworld that night. It's not like I haven't seen your boobs before."

I didn't stop glaring at her even as I wrapped the towel around myself, tucking it in under the arm. She picked up another, but instead of throwing it at me, she pointed at the toilet. I lifted an eyebrow.

"Sit. You're barely staying on your feet. I'll brush your hair."

Warmth ran through my chest, followed by an

uncomfortable sensation. I frowned to myself as I shuffled toward the toilet and took a seat.

"Why are you being so nice to me?" I grumbled, feeling the need to take a shot at her because this felt too intimate. Too genuine. It felt like . . . something I hadn't had in a long time. Something I felt guilty in having with her.

"Ah, the asshole has resurfaced. I figured it wouldn't be too long now." She patted at my hair with the dry towel, drawing out the excess water. "You don't like it when people get close, and it bothers you that I've slipped past all those pesky barriers you surround yourself with."

An ugly truth if there ever was one.

"Caring about people is a weakness, and that's assuming they deserve it. Look at what happened with you and Barry," I pointed out.

Her hands stilled. For a moment I thought I had gone too far, then she continued patting my hair down a second later.

"They can be," she agreed. "Barry and I were very close growing up. I should have realized sooner that they'd eventually find a way to use that against us. He always wanted acceptance with his family. He would have seen a spot in the Pleiades Coven as a way to be recognized, and he would have traded anything for it, even me."

Well, now I really felt like an asshole.

"He said he did it because of Ronan—for the block—to be free of him."

"Excuses," she said, but her voice wasn't bitter. "I asked Ronan what he bargained for to begin with. He bargained for power. That bargain is the only reason the Morrigan was able to confine Ronan in chains, though. She was able to use that tiny bit of magic he gave Barry to create chains that could contain him. Lucifer might not have died if he hadn't done that. You wouldn't have lost control. The corridor wouldn't have been opened . . . he made a choice that contributed to millions of deaths, and he'll have to live with it."

Her voice sounded so sure. So steady. In more ways than one, she was wise beyond her twenty-two years.

"He survived?" I asked softly.

She picked up a damp lock of my hair and rubbed it in the towel. "He did. Barry was half fae and half witch. He got the fae half. Spirit magic, not Lucifer's desire magic. Combine that with the tiny bit of magic Ronan put in him . . .Barry survived. I saw him run when he knew the corridor was collapsing."

"Are you going to go after him?"

"No," she answered firmly. "He betrayed me . . . but what we had was good before that. His friendship was what kept me sane through most of my child- hood. One really shitty thing doesn't undo who he was to me then, even if we'll never be the same again."

"That's very mature of you," I said, wondering if I would be the same. It was something I was probably better off never knowing. "Ronan will probably hunt him down, though. His actions also led to me being in the pit. He doesn't seem to take kindly to people endangering me."

"He won't," she said. I frowned at the certainty in her voice.

"How do you know?"

She set the towel down and picked up the hairbrush off the counter. "Because I made a bargain with Ronan." My hands flexed. I opened then closed my mouth, considering my response. She didn't wait for it. "He found us that night coming back from the Underworld. We were halfway down the hall when he stepped out of the elevator behind us. Instead of taking you from me, we made a deal." My hand whipped out to grip the back of the toilet to keep me from doing something stupid. Namely strangling her.

"Why would you do that? Why are you telling me this?" Words fell from my mouth then.

"Because Barry betrayed me for power, and I don't want you to ever think I did the same to you." She brushed out the ends of my hair, slowly working up with complete calm and utter confidence. I didn't share it. "Ronan could have taken you and killed me in a second. I knew that. So when he offered a bargain instead, I took it. Except I didn't bargain for power. I asked for a favor because I had a feeling I'd need it one day if I was going to stick with you. I used that favor to spare Barry because I want him to live with the consequences."

"You lied to me," I snapped. "You told me demons couldn't find us there. That nothing could penetrate the wards."

"Nothing can," she replied. "*Now*. Ronan reinforced them. That's why my family couldn't enter my building, let alone my apartment, and just take me. He reinforced them and left you with me because he knew you wouldn't accept him. In return, I had to periodically inform him where you were and that you were safe. It was a good deal, all things considered." She tugged at a particularly wicked snarl in my hair, making me wince.

"That bastard," I muttered.

"Yes, well, not everyone can be as awesome as me."

I turned to narrow my eyes at her over my shoulder, and she tugged harder, making my head turn straight.

"You're on my shit list right now."

"I'm aware."

"I may not forgive you."

"You will," she said. "You will because I told you,

and you know I'm right. As much as it sucks to learn he's been watching over you this whole time, he could have killed me and made you a prisoner. Guy might be kind of intense, but he's not that bad as far as alpha males go. I'd say you ended up with one of the better ones. He puts up with your bullshit."

"What the fuck, Nat?" I snapped, really twisting around in my seat.

"What? It's true. Not every dude would have gone to such great lengths to do what you wanted. There's some fucked-up people out there. He doesn't even come from this world. I mean, relatively speaking, he at least seems to be trying. He saved me, didn't he?"

"Well," I spluttered, not knowing how to respond. "I told him to save you. I don't know if that's the same."

She rolled her eyes. "You were dying, you know? He seriously jumped out of thin air, grabbed me, saw that Lucifer was dead, and then brought us all back here to give you a blood transfusion because your skin was peeling off and your blood was straight-up acid. I have a scar from you." She lifted her forearm to show me a four-inch section of molted and discolored skin that did indeed look like acid damage.

"That's what you get for lying to me," I said stiffly, not feeling even an ounce of sympathy.

She threw her head back and laughed so hard there were tears coming out of her eyes.

"You're a real piece of work," she chuckled, wiping her eyes with the back of her hand. Then she fisted my hair and turned my head forward, pushing my chin down to my neck so she could brush out the tangles at the base of my skull. "I'll give you that I lied, but I never betrayed you in the real sense of the word. I didn't tell him when you went for those morning coffee runs even though you weren't supposed to, or when you'd get off calling his name—"

"I did not," I snapped at her.

She chuckled. "So you say. I don't believe you, but the point is, I didn't betray you for power or for the hell of it. He wanted to keep you safe, and I rather liked the idea of neither of us dying, so it didn't seem like such a bad deal. I got a favor from a demon too. Yes, I suppose he has some power over me now, but I'm thinking once you're a full demon, I can suck your blood and cancel it out—"

"I'm sorry, but you're going to have to back up to that whole *suck your blood* bit. I'm not a vampire. That's disgusting."

"Says the woman who grows fangs and ripped out one of my coven member's throat in front of me. Not to mention the blood I saw on your face after you visited Ronan for the second *blood exchange*—"

"That's different, and it doesn't mean I'm going to just let you suck my blood."

"You're arguing semantics. I'll get some blood from you, and then you should technically have an equal hold, so I don't have to report to him anymore. It's a win-win."

I scrunched my nose. "We don't know if my blood even works like a normal demon's. What if you just end up with a double dose of Ronan's?"

"Then I'm utterly fucked, but at least I didn't have to make a deal with him for it. Besides, he can hear our entire conversation and he hasn't stormed in here yet, so I can't imagine he's that against this."

As if on cue, I heard a grumble come from the kitchen.

"I'm surprised he hasn't killed you yet," I said.

"He won't. You care about me, and my voice is what woke you up. He knows that. He'll growl and grumble all he wants, but at the end of the day, he won't hurt me because I'm important to you."

That uncomfortable feeling was back, but not as strong as before. Despite the change of time, the weight we carried, and the millions of deaths, we'd settled in like nothing had happened. I wasn't sure if Nathalie just had a gift for it, or if that was our dynamic, but I was thankful either way.

"Everything would have been easier if I'd just shot you," I pointed out as she finished brushing my hair.

"Probably, but you're stuck with me now." I heard the grin in her voice and chuckled. The brand on my chest seemed to burn as a reminder that I was indeed stuck with her. Not that she knew it. "All we need is for you to get this third exchange out of the way so you're a full-fledged demoness, and I can suck your—"

"Nope," I said solemnly. "Still not calling it that."

She moved away and started rummaging through the drawers. "But the third exchange?" Nathalie said lightly. Pointedly.

"I'm planning to . . ." My words trailed off when I turned my cheek and saw her finger dragging across the mirror.

Her earlier words played over in my mind.

He can hear our entire conversation.

Son of a bitch. She was clever. More than I ever remembered to give her credit for.

Her finger slowly moved across the mirror. The letters running almost instantly as she did, but I still managed to make them out.

I know how to save Bree.

"You're planning to . . ." She paused, leaving it open-ended, implying for me to answer.

"Do it," I said quietly. "The third exchange. I want to do it tonight."

The noise coming from the kitchen went quiet.

I mouthed, "*How?*"

She spelled out: *Siphoning. Need 3 exchange. Open Portal.*

She stepped away from the mirror and gave me a meaningful look.

"Are you sure?" she asked, sounding like the concerned friend. "You just woke up. It may put you under again."

I stared at her words, a visceral need filling me.

"When I was trapped in the Underworld, I had to pretend to be human. I was scared to use my power because then she'd confine it. I was also scared to use it because then I'd crash. I couldn't win. I was power-less . . . I won't let myself be powerless again, even if it means I'm under for multiple months. I have to do this."

I said it, and I meant it. I'd chosen this path before she told me what it could do. That it could save Bree.

That I could save my sister.

"Good," she said lightly, picking up the towel off the counter and wiping the mirror down. "We should go out there. Ronan made dinner. You're going to need it, it sounds like, for all that blood you'll be sucking tonight—"

"Ugh. I'm going. You're gross."

I got to my feet, feeling a little stronger. A hell of a lot more confident.

Nathalie's eyes twinkled with mischief as she opened the door. She was having way too much fun with this, I decided. That, or she was that much better of a liar than I was.

Anticipation thickened in my gut as I dressed in an oversized sweater and sweatpants. It didn't escape me that Ronan had filled half the master closet in clothes my size. Nathalie navigated easily, pulling the pieces out and tossing them to me.

I left the damp towel on the floor beside the bed and stepped out into the hall once I was clothed. Nathalie followed behind me, whistling eighties music as she went. I truly didn't know how she kept up with herself. It was exhausting enough being around her.

The scent of garlic and tomato registered before we entered the living room.

Ronan hovered over a stove with his back to me, stirring something in a pot that smelled mouthwatering. My steps slowed as he pulled something out of the oven without grabbing a mitt.

"I hope you like spaghetti. It's one of the few things I know how to cook," he said in that voice of midnight.

"I'm not picky," I replied. Nathalie stepped around me when I slowed to a stop, and she grabbed bowls out of a cabinet.

"I am," Nathalie said, filling one with noodles and sauce. She tossed a couple of pieces of garlic bread on top and then handed it to me.

"What are you doing?" I asked, as she stepped around me and grabbed a jacket off the couch.

"Make sure she eats. She's not as grumpy when

she's fed. Don't give me that look," she added, directing the comment at me as she zipped up her jacket. "I have a date with my tea and a trashy romance novel. My favorite Chinese place is still open, so I'll grab that on the way home. On the off chance you don't crash," she paused to pick up something else off the couch that I quickly recognized as one of my pistols and a holster, "I brought one of your guns. You'll need to walk or get Ronan to bring you over. It's cold outside, and I'm not crossing the city tonight unless you're dying."

With that, she tipped her chin and walked out the door, leaving me with one intense demon and a lot of awkward silence.

I moved over to the couch and plopped down. Hunger rumbled from my mid-section, and while my stomach was in knots from nerves, the food smelled amazing. I picked away at it, only pausing to look up when the couch sank. My eyes slanted sideways to where Ronan sat.

He wore sweats, and a white t-shirt clung to his muscled frame. I swallowed harder than necessary on my bite of noodles and sausage.

"You're not eating?" I said, noticing his lack food as he put his arm along the back of the couch.

"Not hungry."

All right, then.

"Where'd you learn to cook?" I said, trying to ignore the lump in my throat that was forming.

"Stolen memories from different Antares Coven members," he replied in the same tone. I chewed slower this time. Digesting that information.

"Can all demons steal memories?"

"No," he answered, leaning forward. The steel in his eyes looked lethal and cruel, cutting as a blade, cold as winter skies. "It's actually incredibly rare. The only one I've known who was able to was the Harvester before me."

I took another bite of spaghetti, chewed, and swallowed. "Before you? What happened to him?"

"I killed him."

His clipped response made me want to poke and prod. For once, he was offering information up freely instead of trying to bargain with me. I wondered if that was because he knew he was getting his third exchange either way, or if this was more getting to know me by way of judging my reactions. Something made me think it was probably a bit of both.

"Why?" I asked, settling back against the corner, just out of range of his outstretched arm.

"Because I had to," Ronan said, like it was really that simple. "The only way to become the Harvester is to kill the Harvester."

I twirled my fork in the noodles, frowning at them. "That seems like a shitty job," I said bluntly.

Ronan chuckled darkly. "It's the single most powerful position in all of Hell. Some might say the benefits outweigh the drawbacks."

"Power isn't everything," I murmured.

"Isn't it?" he questioned, that lovely and terrible voice giving words to the nagging feeling in my mind.

"No," I answered firmly, despite the niggling sensation in my chest that felt very much like a lie. "It's not."

He curled his arm up to run his knuckles over his chin, then under his bottom lip as he assessed me. "If not power, then what? Love?" he asked, clearly in jest. "Hate?" A flush crept over my chest, and despite the sweater that covered me from wrist to neckline, I could swear he saw it.

"Survival," I said. "Both love and hate are strong contenders, but they're brittle. Love can be lost. Hate can be shaken. But survival is an instinct. It runs deeper than fear—"

"And yet, you would have willingly sacrificed yourself so I could save the witch and your sister if need be." His response was measured, but I sensed darkness lurking beneath the neutral tone. "Survival can't be everything, or you'd be better at it," he added.

I looked away, setting the bowl aside.

"This from the demon that allowed witches to chain him," I said after a moment, lifting my chin.

If we were going to go there, I wasn't pulling punches.

"Ah, but I never claimed survival was all—"

"No, you said power was everything. So tell me, Harvester, why did you don chains? You could have killed her yourself and possibly still saved me, but you didn't. So is it really power? Is it love?" I repeated it back in the same mocking tone he'd used when he asked me. His eyes flashed in warning, reminding me of my own white fire. I didn't listen. But I did watch. "Or maybe it's control. If the Harvester is the most powerful position in Hell, it stands to reason you chose it because no one can control you. And then there I went, blowing apart that plan by being your atma. The one person you can't control—"

"You don't know that," he said gruffly.

"Oh, but I suspect. Nat thinks you're a good guy deep down. I'm not buying it. You may not be bad, but you're not the white knight that saves the princess from the dragon. You are the dragon—and if you thought I'd let you keep me locked up here, you'd probably do it. Because then I'm safe, right? Then you can control—"

He moved so fast I barely saw. Or rather, he moved through the void.

He went from one end of the couch, and then he was only inches from my face as he hovered above me, hunched over and crowding my space.

"You're grasping at straws," he said softly. "Reaching for something to make you feel in control of this situation. You think that by breaking me apart, that might keep you together. That we'll cross through the third exchange, and you'll be unscathed because you can convince yourself that I want to control you." His hand brushed over my forearm and up my bicep, curling around the edge of my shoulder before coming to wrap around my throat. It wasn't an aggressive hold nor was it meant to intimidate. It was intimate. Purposeful. Possessive.

"Don't you?" I replied, not mocking, but serious. He wasn't wrong, and I wasn't going to deny it.

Something simmered in the depths of his eyes.

"No." His thumb came up under my chin, tilting it back. "If I valued control more than anything, I never would have crossed through the portal. While we have instincts, a demon can ignore them. Aeshma did. She rejected Lucifer because he was weak, and she thought bonding with him would make her weak. You're right that I can't control you, but you're wrong in thinking that I want to." His thumb slid across the underside of my jaw as his hand changed its hold. The rough pads of his fingers pressed to my bare flesh was distracting. Disorienting. "I controlled much of my world for a very long time. I was the sole reason it ran as it did. And for a while, I won't lie, I enjoyed it. The power.

The control. There's a rush that came with being the Harvester, but much like all other brittle emotions, it faded quickly. That control became just another chore. Running Hell was simply something to do. I wasn't living." He loomed closer. The scent of fire and brimstone and scattered ashes swept over me as our breaths mingled. "Then you called. You created the door, and I didn't even have to think. Hell could be in ruins by now. Odds are it eventually will be unless another Harvester is chosen, but I don't care. You'll come to find there are not many things that hold my interest, Piper, and even fewer that I truly feel something for. In that, there's only one. You."

A steady beat thundered in my chest. It was a ritual drum, signaling something to come.

"For a demon that mocks love, that sounds a lot like it," I said, mouth dry and head pounding.

"I've felt love," he said. "When I stole the Antares Coven memories, some of them had loved and still did. That thing they felt, it's nothing like what I feel. This need—it's raw. Visceral. I want you at my side and in my bed. I want to be the one you fight for. The one you laugh for. Smile for. You've given the witch a piece of yourself and it taunts me . . . because I want every piece. I want to own you—make no mistake." His voice was deceptively soft, and a chill ran over my skin. "But I don't desire to control you. I want you to give me those things willingly because I know that's the only way I'll get to keep them."

My lips parted. Warmth bloomed in my chest, but it wasn't gentle. The feeling was closer to fire.

"Maybe love was the wrong word. Obsession sounds a lot more like it," I said hoarsely, trying to talk past the lump in my throat.

"Call it what you want, Piper. Love. Obsession. Infatuation. There's nothing I want more in this world or the next than you. And I think you know that. I think you counted on that when you killed Morgan Le Fay and asked me to save the witch—with what you thought was your dying breath. You knew I would find a way because you wouldn't forgive me if I didn't. So say what you want, lie to me if you must, but I know the truth."

I licked my chapped lips, and his eyes followed the movement.

"What's that?" I said.

"You're the one that craves control, but with me, you know you have it. You know you're safe—because as long as I want you, you get to make all the rules in this little game we've been playing."

Most men said they loved a girl and made it sound almost like a burden. Like she owed them something for that love. They didn't give it freely. They expected her love in return, without even understanding what it was.

But Ronan, he gave me these truths that weren't sweet, or soft, or gentle. He was right. That it wasn't love. But it was all he had, and he gave it freely, without expecting anything in return.

As dark and depraved as it was, I preferred it.

A small part of me might have even loved it.

But that thought didn't just scare me. It terrified me. I once said that Ronan wouldn't just be a bad decision; he'd be a devastating one.

And there I stood, on the edge of the cliff, swaying in the wind.

My heart beat heavily. Adrenaline rushed through my veins.

I might drown in guilt later. My resentment could very well eat me alive.

But I couldn't stop myself.

I jumped.

28

I SHOT UP, closing the gap between us. My hands reached, threading through his onyx locks. Ronan released a growl as my tongue parted the seam of his mouth.

Broad hands grasped my waist, the pointed tips of his clawed nails biting into my flesh. I yanked downward, and he pulled me up. I felt the cool chill of the void as it wrapped around us. His magic brushed against my skin, lighting it aflame. I groaned into his mouth, and he pulled me close enough that not even a sheet of paper could fit between our bodies. My legs wrapped around his waist, ankles hooking at the small of his back. There was nothing small about the demon. From his broad shoulders to his massive hands, and six and a half feet in height, he wasn't simply large. He was just larger than anything or anyone else in this life. His very presence echoed strength and authority.

The Harvester.

I still didn't know what that meant, not truly. But I knew he wasn't even an ordinary demon. If there were such a thing. Even among the strongest and most powerful beings my world knew, he was other. More.

He was holding me by the small of the waist and devouring my mouth like it was his source of air. Our tongues clashed and then twined. I breathed him in, and he breathed me out.

The pounding grew louder.

My blood pulsed.

I shifted up and then down, rocking into him.

Then the swift and bitter bite of cold wind slapped my skin. I gasped, pulling back.

The dark of night surrounded me, but it wasn't truly dark. A night sky filled with thousands of stars looked down on us, flaming balls of gas, burning as I did.

Blackened ruins surrounded us on every side. I slowly turned my chin, surveying what I was fairly certain had formerly been the pits.

The wide glassy floor beneath us was a dead giveaway.

I turned to Ronan. He was watching me, waiting for the question I undoubtedly would ask.

"Why here?" My words came out in a white fog as my warm breath turned to ice.

"There's nothing here," he said. By nothing, he meant no one.

Because my fire had already killed them all . . .

The thought crossed my mind, bitterness dampening the lust in me.

"I see," I murmured, turning my face away. I didn't want to look at him, but I didn't want to look at the devastation either. I settled for staring at the stars. That seemed an appropriate way to mull over one's actions.

"You can't go back. You can only go forward," he said, teeth grazing my jaw. I took a shuddering breath. "Isn't that why we're here; so this never happens again?"

I sensed there was more beneath his words. Like he was searching for some confirmation that something in me had changed.

"Tell me," I murmured, angling my neck to give him better access. His lips paused at the sensitive spot just below my ear. "What happens after the third exchange?"

"Our bond is unbreakable," he whispered, then sucked on that patch of flesh, sending a shiver through me. "You're mine. At least as far as magic is concerned."

"Will I change more?" I asked, a sliver of fear

creeping into my tone even as his wicked lips kept the worst of it at bay.

"Probably," he said. Honesty. I appreciated it. "But you'll still be you. Just stronger. More in control. Your magic won't rule you the same. At least that's my hope."

"And you?" I asked. "Will you be stronger?"

He didn't answer at first. His lips disappeared from my neck, but then his face loomed in front of mine. "I don't know, and I don't care. I have enough power of my own, but if I have to sacrifice some of it so that you'll be safe—then so be it."

He meant it. Every bone in my body knew he was speaking the truth. He really, truly, didn't care. He was going to complete the bond with me come Hell, high water, evil witches, or my own damn prejudice.

"There is one other reason I chose this area," he continued. The way he said it made me more alert, despite the very hard shaft pressed against me.

"Why?"

"Your magic lingers here. It should give you an advantage, if you need it . . ."

Understanding washed over me. "You think you won't be able to control yourself?"

Something close to guilt crossed his face but was gone so fast it could have been any number of emotions. "I gave you my blood again and again when the acid ate at you, and each time it was harder to not take yours and force the exchange. After two exchanges, an atman's instincts are so acutely focused that I can think of little else when you're even near."

"Ronan . . ." I paused. "I don't think I'll be able to control myself any more than you, lest we forget last time. Just remember, this doesn't change anything. It's only sex."

His eyes darkened. The silver flashed. Lightning struck in the not so far distance, and the wind whipped around us.

His hold on me tightened, not just in lust, but in anger too.

He didn't like what I'd just said. Not one bit.

Instead of arguing it, his lips slammed back to mine. He devoured me with a brutality that made them feel bruised.

But when I pulled away to gasp for breath, he wasted no time.

Sharp pain lanced through my neck as he punctured the artery. The scent of copper hit me . . . followed by all-consuming desire and rage.

My heart skipped a beat and then stopped.

There was no preamble. No moments of indecision.

The fucker bit me, and then he drank his fill.

My back hit the cold glass of the pit. But I was burning. Red tinted my vision as I stared up at the sky, back bowed and body weeping.

He released me faster than expected. I was almost disappointed when he pulled back on his knees. Ronan stared down at me, eyes hard.

I knew then that this wasn't going to be like any other time.

He was angry, and he was going to fuck it out of me.

I welcomed it.

His hands released my waist to grab the edges of my sweater. I expected him to push it up my chest and pull it off. Instead, he tore it down the middle, and my nipples hardened.

He leaned over, taking one tight bud in his mouth. My hips bucked off the ground, the cold long forgotten. He pressed one hand down on my lower abdomen, holding me there.

"Just sex, right?" he said, whirling his tongue around me.

I moaned. He slapped his bare hand over my sex. A shock ran through me, and I groaned as my core tightened, disappointed to find nothing to ease the ache.

"Right?" he repeated, voice hard.

"Right," I bit out.

It was going to piss him off, but I didn't care. He'd still do this. I knew he would.

Pain flashed through my breast. I looked down my

chest to his teeth buried in the side, red welling around his mouth.

The flames fanned hotter because he watched me as he did it.

I pushed against his lower hand, my hips straining for him, but he was as immovable as stone, holding me in place.

Ronan took a long pull from me, and I growled.

He slapped my pussy again, drawing a much less frightening sound that made him smirk.

His lips made a popping sound as they released me. I glared. Not that he seemed to give a solitary fuck. He moved onto my other breast, continuing with this slow torment that had my nails clawing at his back. They dug deep, shredding him.

He groaned, the sound reverberating through the nipple in his mouth.

I lifted one of my hands. His blood dotted my nails.

Thunder clapped over us. Fire ignited as I brought my fingers to my lips.

A warning shone in his eyes. He reached for the hand with his blood, but I wrapped my lips around one of my fingers before he could get there.

My body trembled.

Flames ate away at the rest of my clothes.

Wind slapped at my skin.

The ground itself seemed to shudder in response to me.

And then came rain. It poured down on us as I sucked his blood from my fingertip.

It couldn't have been more than a drop or two, but it did the trick.

I hooked my legs around his hips and rolled us using a move I'd learned in Jiu Jitsu. His back hit the glass, and I wondered if it would shatter and break.

It didn't.

I pushed one hand onto his chest, holding him down, my claw-tipped fingers pressing into him.

I think we were both a little surprised when he didn't budge.

My knees pressed into his sides. I arched forward, my long hair falling around us in a curtain. The world could have been breaking apart in that very moment, but it wouldn't have reached us.

I leaned forward, my lips only a hairsbreadth away.

"It's only sex because it has to be," I whispered, my lips brushing his. "I could tell you it's more. I could lie. My body may want it—hell, I can even admit part of me likes the idea because you're right, Ronan. I trust you despite everything in me saying I shouldn't. You saved Nat. You saved me. And here you are, saving me again even though you know when this is done, I won't need you. That's why I won't lie. I may want this to be more, but there are things I have to do. To figure out. I'm damaged goods—and you may be the dragon, but I'm no princess." A dark chuckle slid from my lips. I reached around to thread my free hand in his hair once more and pull tight. "I can't promise you more, Atman. I just can't. Not right now. But I can give you this."

The word fell from my lips before it registered, and I knew I'd just fucked up.

The coldness in his expression melted.

Everything in him changed.

Because of that single, damning word.

I'd never even let myself think it, but clearly at some point, I started to believe it.

He grabbed me roughly by the hip. His hard cock pulsed between us, already prodding at my entrance.

"Say it again," he growled.

My lips parted, but words didn't come out.

"I said, *say it again.*"

When the word got stuck in my throat, he dragged me down and thrust up.

A mix between a scream and a moan was all I managed as he filled me in one swift movement. My body tightened. My legs spasmed, threatening to give out.

"Stop being a coward, and fucking say it," he snapped, not letting me recover. His hands moved me up and down, dragging me over every thick ridge. I wasn't going to last long if he kept it up. My hands on his chest clawed at the place where his heart should be. He didn't seem to even notice, or if he did, he was into it. His hips thrust up, pumping into me.

I canted forward, my face falling to the crook in his neck where it met his shoulder.

My teeth itched to bite. I parted my lips.

"Not a chance in hell," he uttered.

Our bodies flipped. Glass pressed against my back again, but I couldn't even feel the cold. I was too warm. To taut. Feverish, even. I arched up, but he pulled out.

"You want my blood?" he said, his face appearing in the haze. "My cock? You want to use me? Fine. But you're going to fucking say it, Piper. I'm not asking for much."

I crumbled.

And that word stuck in my throat came out as a whisper that may as well have been a roar.

"*Atman*."

His head dipped, and his eyes closed in victory. Ronan pushed back inside me, giving me exactly what I wanted. His shoulder was close enough for me to lean up and bite . . . and I did.

Blood filled my mouth.

I detonated.

My entire body tensed, locking tight before releasing.

Rain soaked our bodies. His hips slapped into mine and the resulting sound was thunder. Every thrust a bolt of lightning.

I wish I could say I was being dramatic, but the sky quite literally followed our push and pull. My core contracted with the most intense orgasm of my life, and I blacked out.

I wasn't sure how long truly passed. Seconds or minutes. But when I came to, he was turning my body over.

He grabbed my ass, hauling me up on my knees. My arms were weak as I pushed myself up. Our reflections stared back at me, surrounded in black fire. It melted with the sky. His eyes glowed white hot as he lined me up from behind. Mine glowed red as he thrust in me.

One hand gripped my hip, holding me in place. The other wrapped around my long blonde locks, holding me up when my arms threatened to give out. The bite of pain hurt, but it made that second orgasm all the better because I got to see his face as I fell apart.

He was right. Whatever he felt, it was visceral and dark and possessive.

Lust shot through me. Before my orgasm was even over, he bit my shoulder. He hardened further, filling me more. My lips parted in delicious agony.

I lifted a shaking hand to my clit, rubbing it in stilted, jarring movements as I tried to find relief.

And then the strangest thing happened.

His mind brushed against mine and I felt what he felt. The way my channel clenched and fluttered around him. The warmth of my hip beneath his rough palm. My slick hair, tight in his fist. My magic pulsing through his veins, mixing with his own.

I felt that need he spoke of.

And I knew that no matter what I'd told myself, he was never, ever letting me go.

Because he felt me too.

He felt my barriers crumble and my walls turn to dust.

I might have meant what I said. *This* was just sex. But *us?* We were more.

Maybe not now. Not yet. But beneath the lust and guilt and complicated history between us, there was something there. Something that felt permanent, like the brands on my skin.

He released my shoulder to let out a roar as he pulsed within me. His release triggered my own, and my consciousness wavered as fire wrapped around us.

This was when I usually burned out. When the magic ran dry. Body ravaged by its power.

Not this time.

Instead of disappearing without a trace and

pulling me under, it slowed to a trickle that left me weak, but conscious and sated.

I sagged to the ground, and Ronan followed with me.

The fire winked out.

The rain stopped.

The wind calmed.

The ground went still.

I laid there, stuck in that moment with Ronan, where the starry sky hung over us because for the first time in a decade, I wasn't a slave to my power any longer.

I was free.

MY KNUCKLES RAPPED against the door for the third time, and a sigh of frustration left me when there was still no answer. Ronan had dropped me at her door, naked as the day I was born, after the worst of the tremors in my muscles petered out, and the exhaustion lifted. It was half-past three in the morning, but I had no desire to stay the night with him. That just felt too real.

After a short argument, he relented, but I had a feeling it had more to do with the presence in the back of my mind where he now permanently resided. It seemed that our final exchange had carved him out a space there, one he occupied like a king upon on a throne. He lurked like a shadow, watching me. I knew he wouldn't leave, even if I asked. I could push all I wanted, but it was the price of my freedom. The result of our completed bond.

He'd warned me before that each exchange would have an effect on me. It seemed ours had formed a bridge of sorts from one mind to the other.

I wasn't sure exactly how it worked since I refused to cross it, and instead focused on shutting him out as best I could.

Easier said than done when I felt his amused chuckle as though he were standing behind me, lips pressed to my skin. I ignored the sensation and lifted my hand to knock for a fourth time. At this rate, I'd have to pound the damn door down all because she hadn't left me any keys.

Once upon a time, you could use a credit card if the lock was shitty. Thanks to the bomb I'd strapped to the door, all that would do was land me in a world of pain I wasn't interested in experiencing.

But I also had no desire to ask Ronan for help. He'd done enough, and I needed space; both for what was to come and what had already happened.

Before my knuckles could make contact with the fake wood panel, the door to my left opened. I turned my cheek, glancing over my shoulder.

Señora Rosara peered through the couple-inch gap in the door.

She regarded me shrewdly, expectedly unamused at seeing my naked ass before dawn.

"If you're here to yell at me about the noise—" I started.

"You killed the Morrigan."

"I hope you weren't friends," I said, knocking on the door once more.

Her thin lips curled upward, the wrinkles around her eyes growing more pronounced. Call me crazy, but it seemed like the old lady had grown fond of me. There was a saying about distance, though, and how it made the heart grow fonder.

"She killed my sister, Rosalina. Sacrificed her."

I nodded along as I silently hoped Nathalie would wake the fuck up.

"Yeah, she was a real piece of work," I said, my voice a little more neutral. I didn't exactly enjoy talking about Morgan Le Fay, or my time with her, considering how it ended.

"I killed her once. She didn't stay dead. I hope she does this time, for your sake, *Diabla.*"

I froze, sucking in a sharp breath. Ronan's presence brushed against me instantly, a silent question in it. I quickly pushed him off with a mental shove, thankful he couldn't truly read my thoughts unless I wanted him to.

Footsteps sounded on the other side a moment later. She stepped back with a nod of respect and closed her door right as Nat's opened.

"Sorry," she croaked, sounding not all that sorry. A

shiver worked its way up my spine, and I shook it off, deciding to ask the Señora about her warning another day. "I stayed up late reading. Wasn't expecting you for another month or two, if I'm being honest—"

"Nat, not to be an asshole or anything, but it's cold as shit and I'm naked."

She blinked, her light brown eyes dropping down to my bare chest. My nipples were hard enough I was fairly certain I could cut glass. I lifted both my eyebrows, motioning toward the door when she lifted her chin again to look back at me.

Her mouth slanted into a smirk, a sly expression entering her features. "Well, judging by all that red on your tits, you really did let Ronan suck your blo—"

I couldn't hear her say it again. I whacked the door with one hand, and it shot back, the handle burrowing in the wall. Both Nat and I paused, then looked sideways at it.

I slipped past her while she was scratching the back of her head. "Is this thing going to blow up if I just pull it out of the wall?" she called after me. I continued down the hall toward the shared bathroom.

"Not if you're careful," I called back. Then I thought better of it, and added, "Probably."

Her curses followed me into the shower, but after a quick rinse and dressing in my own clothes, I returned to the living room. I hadn't heard a bomb, so

I was fairly certain she was fine, the gaping hole in the drywall notwithstanding.

"You know, I go to your bedside twice a day for five weeks, and *this*," she motioned to the door, "is how you repay me?"

"I'm still sore on the fact that you spied for Ronan. Don't push it."

"Oh, let it go. That's old news now," she said, putting a kettle on. "Besides, now that you're a full-fledged demon, we're going to rectify it."

"The bond is complete. I'm not sure if that's the same thing as being a 'full-fledged' demon—"

"Close enough," she said, dumping some dried leaves that looked like potpourri in a cylindrical ball with holes. "Now that the bond's complete, does that give him access to your mind?"

"Parts of it," I said grudgingly.

"Fascinating," she murmured, dropping the ball in a mug. "Can he read your thoughts?"

"Not unless I want him to. It's more of just a general feeling. I get the sense he's watching my emotions closely."

Nathalie snorted and then let out a witch-worthy cackle. "Of course he's watching. You just bonded, and then you up and left him. And by the way you looked when I opened the door, don't even try to lie and tell me nothing happened. You fucked."

I didn't deny it, instead opting to pick at a hangnail on my thumb.

"Are you done here?"

"I'm not the one that showed up at three a.m., dude. You're lucky I'm just wired from being worried that my apartment was going to blow up after that crap you just pulled with the door—which by the way, if that's a demon thing, you're going to have to work on it. I'll pay for the damage this time because you just got a power up, but we're going to have to work something out if this becomes a habit—"

"Nat," I interrupted. "As much as we both know how you love to drive me fucking crazy—I didn't show up on your doorstep this early in the morning to talk about Ronan or the exchange." I gave her a pointed look while she poured the hot water from the kettle into the mug. The scent of jasmine and vanilla perfumed the air.

Nat inhaled its aroma and then sighed. She set the mug back down and walked over to her coat rack. Unzipping a small satchel, she pulled out a familiar hairbrush that was covered in long brown hair.

"I guess it's a good thing I gambled you wouldn't enter stasis again and stole this out of Bree's room this afternoon." She set the hairbrush on the kitchen counter. "I don't suppose you'll let this wait till morning?" She gave me a hopeful look, then cast one toward the hall where her bedroom was.

"No," I said firmly. "I've been searching for answers for a decade, and my sister isn't immortal. For all we know, the morning will bring some new enemy to our door, and I just can't chance it. Time is never on my side. I have to do this."

She blew out a tired breath, unsurprised but still put out that she couldn't sleep more. "All right, but I need to finish my tea. You'll need me awake to do the summoning." Nat reached over and clasped a plastic handle, pulling a serrated knife out of the block on the counter. "In the meantime, decide where I'm taking blood from and what our deal will be. Then grab a tarp out of the greenhouse."

I frowned. "What do you need a tarp for?"

The look she gave me was pitying. "The way we're going to get her back is the same siphoning I used on Lucifer with some minor tweaks. I spent the time while you were in stasis working on it. Tailoring it to find her. But even with my changes, I couldn't get around the blood price. I won't lie to you, it's a lot. Are you sure you can pay it?"

"Is this really a question? You know I will," I said, furrowing my brows in confusion. "Where is this going? Because you already know the answer."

Nathalie sighed, then took a sip from her tea. "There are things to consider here."

"Such as?"

"All the shit that can go wrong, Piper. I'm fairly

confident this will work, but let's talk about the what ifs here," she said.

I pinched the bridge of my nose. "No."

She smacked her hand on the counter. "Yes."

I raised my eyebrows, assessing her in that moment. I exhaled, annoyed and feeling like she was trying to talk me out of it. I waved my hand at her, telling her to go on.

"Aeshma didn't go as planned when they summoned her. That's why you're here. The summoning with Ronan didn't go as planned, and we all see how that is working out. My arrogant family siphoning Lucifer didn't go as planned . . ." she trailed off, momentarily lost in thought. Clearing her throat, she went on. "Basically we have nothing but failure to compare this to. Not once has it worked out the way anyone has planned. I know you will do anything for her. I know it. I won't try to talk you out of this, but I have to say these words out loud. Can you truly pay whatever price this will cost?"

I didn't hesitate because to me, it didn't matter if I could or could not.

I would find a way through sheer force of will.

This would not fail because of me.

"I can," I said in a hushed voice, the edges of the serrated knife glinted in the lights of her kitchen.

"Then get the tarp. I'm not ruining my floors when it can be avoided."

30

I SAT cross-legged on the floor across from Nat. Between us were two blades: the kitchen knife and a ceremonial athame. Hundreds of candles formed a circle around us, casting a soft glow over the apartment. Inside, we lined the circle with salt.

"Have you decided?" she asked, her light brown eyes turning golden in the dim light.

I picked up the serrated blade. "I have."

"And?"

I took a deep breath, trying to center myself. Three months ago, I wouldn't have believed it if someone told me I'd be binding myself to a witch and letting her use my power to open a portal to Hell. I looked back and knew what led me here, but I didn't relate to it anymore. It felt like another life. Another person entirely.

My words were strong and steady when I lifted the knife and my hand, looking Nat in the eye. "I ask for unyielding loyalty and honesty in all matters that pertain to me. In return, I give you my blood so that you may shed your ties to all others. Nathalie Opal Le Fay, do you accept this bargain?"

Magic reverberated in my words. It was in every exhale of my breath, wrapping around us both in the makings of a bond. An oath.

"I do."

Her words were a flick of a thumb over a lighter. A spark of flame over gasoline. The magic that had been tentatively weaving itself snapped taut, very much alive.

I turned my index finger to press it to the edges of the knife. The pointed metal dug into my flesh, a slight prick of pain. I pressed harder until two drops of blood welled between my finger and the blade. Then I carefully pulled it out, taking the magical ichor with it.

I extended the blade to Nat. She took the handle from me and without fear, licked the drops off the blade.

I gasped as an invisible tether snapped between us. It wasn't the bridge that Ronan and I had, but instead a tight rope. A lifeline. There was something intimate about it that I didn't expect.

"Every bargain is different," she said quietly. "The

bonds formed are different. The nature of the bargain and relationship between the two people matter . . . I could get around Ronan's with twisting my words and weaseling my thoughts out of the way of his magic whenever he probed past the surface. I don't think I could do that here, though. You chose to base yours around intention, rather than bind me in absolutes."

She regarded me with a shrewd expression for a moment, then shrugged.

"I don't want to own you, or anyone for that matter, and I don't think I could search through your mind if I tried. I just don't want you reporting to Ronan about me."

She nodded and tossed the blade outside of the circle. With that part out of the way, it was time for the real finale. My heart sped up a little and my magic grew restless. I sensed Ronan watching my emotions flutter and fluctuate, I tried to push the nervous anxiousness down, but it did little good when Nat picked up the athame.

"Once I start, I can't stop. I can't pause. We have to follow it through to the end—otherwise we run the risk of losing control and unleashing your magic on New Chicago."

My mouth went dry. I nodded stiffly.

"Piper," she sighed. "Are you sure— "

"I'm sure," I snapped a little harder than I meant. I knew she was just concerned. Worry permeated her features between the drawn together eyebrows and pinched lips.

"I'm going to do my best to go slow enough to give your body time to heal as we go. The further along we get, the more the magic will start urging me on. I can't stop, but if you fear you're going to black out, snap your fingers three times."

The reason for the snapping made sense when she lifted a clean rag I was meant to bite down on. A cold flush broke out over my skin.

"We have to start," I told her. "Ronan can sense me even if he can't read you. If we take too long—"

"Say no more." She lifted the athame and pointed at me. "Strip down so that all your brands are visible."

"Do I need to do anything during the siphoning?" I asked, shucking my sweater off. The cool air made me stiffen.

"No. I'd probably try to focus on Bree since she's the reason you're doing this. Gives you something to hold on for."

I wasn't a coward, nor was I scared of a little pain, but I also wasn't a masochist. Nathalie had spared me the grisly details of what she would do to me so that she could harness my magic and single-handedly open a portal.

It shouldn't kill me. Shouldn't. Nathalie wouldn't do it if she weren't confident she could keep me alive.

But even all the confidence in the world wouldn't

matter if the spell went sideways. I just had to hope she was right.

"Let's do this."

She straddled my waist in baggy sweatpants and a hoodie. Her long hair was tied up into a messy bun, and sleep still lined her eyes, even if they were bright and calculating. She lifted the knife and pressed the tip to my sternum.

A cold wind blew through the living room, but the windows were closed.

Every candle went out.

And my heart stuttered.

Ronan was here.

"I'd hoped you would at least wait till morning," he murmured.

Shock ran through me.

"Wait. What?"

I eyed Nathalie suspiciously, like she was the cause for his presence. She lifted her hands, athame and all, in a sign of surrender. "Not me, dude. I kept this from him while you were in stasis."

Which meant—

"I'm ten thousand years old, Piper. Did you truly think you could keep this from me? I knew you two were up to something, and I'd already worked out that a portal was the only way to bring your sister back. Here you are, as expected, and you don't even have her body," he said.

My cheeks heated, and I was thankful for the dark in that moment.

"Congratulations, Harvester. You outsmarted two twenty-somethings. Would you like a cookie or a bone?" I said acidly.

Nathalie stifled a laugh, attempting to mask it with a cough before she spoke. "I don't need Bree here, Ronan. She just needs her body to return to. Was it ideal that she'd wake up in your apartment? Not really, but beggars can't be choosers. It's not like you would have just handed her over."

"You didn't bother asking," he said quietly.

Tired of the back and forth, I asked, "So good for you, you're here to stop us. What now?"

"Actually, Atma, I'd like to help."

I shot up, and Nat fell back, catching herself on her wrists.

"Forgive me for having a hard time believing that—"

"What's so hard to believe?" he questioned, stepping forward. The hundreds of candles that surrounded us illuminated once more when he entered the circle. In his arms was my sister, Bree. He took two steps to the right and twisted to lay her body on the couch. His muscles bunched and contracted as he lowered her, and then he turned around. "I tried to keep you safe, and you fought me harder, almost dying multiple times in the process." Silver eyes turned glacial as he looked over my half-naked body with unmasked possessiveness and something else. "I might be stubborn, but I'm not dense, and I won't make the same mistake twice where you're concerned. You would die for your sister if you thought it would bring her back. I see that. Just as I would if it were you." He turned his cheek to look at Nat, who sat on my legs and was looking back and forth between the two of us. "Which is why you're going to use both of us."

"Both of us?" I uttered.

"I would do it alone if you'd let me, but—"

"Not a chance."

He smirked. "I suspected as much." Ronan dropped onto one knee. He was already shirtless himself. "Which is why you'll go first."

I narrowed my eyes. Inside, I was screaming this was too good to be true. But a smaller voice whispered, *what if it is?*

He'd given me the third exchange so I wouldn't be a slave to my own power.

Now he was going to help get my sister back.

The things he did for me weren't hearts and flowers. They were as deep and raw as this thing between us. They were *real*.

And while I didn't love him, they made me feel something.

"All right," I said. "You want to help? Fine, but I'm not giving you anything in exchange for it."

His smirk widened. Ronan dropped to his knees and cupped my cheek, then dropped his hand lower to grasp my throat. "I already have everything I want," he said, the meaning in his gestures clear.

I narrowed my eyes, and Nat cleared her throat.

"If we're going to do this . . ." She made a laying down motion.

I pulled back, and Ronan held me there for a moment—just to prove he could—before releasing me. My back settled against the scratchy tarp. Warm fingers wrapped around mine.

I tilted my chin to look over at him in silent question. He returned my stare, unwavering. He shoved the clean rag between my parted lips.

Then metal pierced my skin.

Nathalie began to chant.

My breath lodged in my throat.

Rage *burned*.

"Breathe," he commanded quietly. His hand gripped mine, hot and hard with a staunchness that kept me grounded.

Nat kept cutting. The blade swept over my skin like a paint brush, tracing the lines of my brands. If she meant to do them all—

I hissed in pain as she dragged the tip over the side of my breast.

Her eyes said what her words couldn't. She spoke faster. Stronger. Louder.

Magic filled the room, and the more blood of mine that spilled, the more that magic wrapped around us.

The pain was starting to mix together when her legs slid over my lap. She nudged my side for me to turn over. Ronan helped me, and she used the blade to trace my sides carefully as he did so.

She worked her way over my ribs, then up my spine, before going back down. When she only had the arm he was holding left, we maneuvered again. I couldn't count the number of times I screamed and moaned. Each sound drew a frown from Ronan. His jaw clenched, but he didn't try to stop her.

I should have been focusing on my sister—but it was Ronan that occupied my mind and held me there.

When the blade moved from the edge of my wrist directly to his, I knelt at his side and held his hand the same as he'd held mine. Our blood mixed and mingled, but with the third exchange out of the way, I didn't feel the overwhelming desire to drink it like before. Certainly not with the open wounds on my chest, back, and arms still bleeding. My sternum was only just starting to close.

The breath hissed between his lips as Nat traced the athame over his brands.

I ripped the rag from my mouth and shoved it toward his. He shook his head once, and I glowered, tossing it aside.

If he wanted to risk biting his tongue off, let him.

Soon, another magic was filling the space beside mine. Where the rage in my veins felt like fire and burned like hate, this other magic was unruly. Dark, yet not evil. It felt like temptation and the edge of choice. It was adrenaline and desire. It carried hints of rage, of spirit, of death—but it wasn't them. It was wholly different.

While in the throes of our exchanges, I never had the head to pay close attention to what his magic smelled or tasted or felt like. But I did now, exhausted and weak as I was.

It brushed against my skin, both taunting me and calming me simultaneously.

"Chaos," I whispered beneath Nathalie's haunting chants. "You're a chaos demon."

Ronan's eyes flashed in recognition, not that Nat herself seemed to notice. A glazed look had taken over her face. One of rapture. The magic she was wielding had pulled her entirely under.

A sliver of uncertainty crept into me as she climbed over Ronan's body without even seeming to notice what she was doing. Her hand grabbed his naked side, pushing it in silent request for him to turn.

She kept cutting as he hauled himself into a sitting position.

On her knees, she shuffled behind him. Her hand whipping the blade around so fast, I found myself transfixed by the movements. Her voice washed over me, and it was only Ronan's claws pinching into my hand that kept me from being carried away to wherever in her mind she'd gone.

Thunder boomed overhead.

Lightning struck in quick succession just outside the window, the light casting the three of us in a horrific picture painted by our blood.

I sensed that the spell was near its end. My wounds were almost healed, and our magic began swirling around us.

Like the beat of my heart, it went faster. Faster. Faster.

Lightning continued to strike.

Thunder clapped, one boom after the other, without any break. If I looked out the windows, I would have expected to see rain.

But all I could focus on as everything in me pulled tight was the near-serene expression on Ronan's face as Nathalie twisted the knife with one last stroke.

Time collapsed in on itself instantly.

Our magic clashed, folding and merging as one before exploding outward.

I'd been to two summonings in my life, and I

could say with certainty that they were nothing like this.

Those covens had harnessed only a drop of power compared to the veritable black hole that formed before me.

Wind blew outward from its center, carrying the scents of a faraway land. I couldn't see anything, but I could feel it. The call.

Ronan gripped my hand tighter.

I couldn't tear my eyes away from it, even to watch as Nathalie sliced her own hand and then yanked a clump of hair from my sister's hairbrush.

Her voice echoed with immeasurable power as she whispered a single word.

A name.

"Bree."

True silence expanded outward of that raging hole that led straight to Hell. I couldn't hear my heart, or the storm, or Nathalie's voice—if she was even speaking.

It was silence. Utter silence.

We waited.

I waited.

But the corridor churned, and no Bree appeared.

I inched forward. Desperation starting to eat at me.

What if we'd failed?

What if this didn't work?

What if—

My hand reached for the inky strands of magic. My fingertips just barely brushed them when Ronan grabbed me by the waist and pulled me to him.

I strained.

This was my chance. My one chance. I couldn't leave her there. I couldn't stop. We had to—

Everything in me froze when the warbled whisper of a girl echoed from across the corridor.

"Piper?"

It was her. It was—

"BREE!" I screamed at the top of my lungs.

I lurched forward, and the silence ended. Time caught up. One moment I was reaching, tumbling, falling toward that voice, and the next, the corridor collapsed.

The magic fizzled, breaking apart.

It was only when it settled, and I was left standing there turning in circles, that I realized our magic hadn't run out. The corridor hadn't simply closed.

"Where did it go?" I demanded, my voice hoarse.

"You were going to cross—" Nat started.

"Where. Did. It. Go?" I repeated.

"Piper, I couldn't let you run into Hell. We'll try again if we have to. We'll find another way—"

"There isn't one," I said, voice breaking. "Don't you know that? I've looked. For a decade, I've hunted every witch and warlock I could get my hands on to find a way. This was it." I took a sharp breath, trying to calm the rising rage that threatened to do something I would regret.

"Piper," Ronan urged.

"No!" I snapped. White sparks danced over my clenched fists. Nathalie took a step back, and for the first time since the night we met, she looked scared of me.

I looked down at the bolts of power that zapped harmlessly off my skin.

It wasn't fire this time, but lightning.

I took a deep breath, calming myself and my agitated magic. There was no telling what I could do now, and as angry as I was—I didn't truly want to hurt her.

"You've got to be fucking kidding me," a voice behind me said.

Everything in me jumped to alertness. My magic cut out. I turned around.

On the couch, pressing a hand to her head, was Bree.

With one major distinction.

Her waist-length brown hair was now as white as fresh snow.

"Bree," I breathed her name in relief. I fell to my knees at her side, wrapping my arms around her.

It took a moment for me to see past my joy and

realize that she hadn't moved. She wasn't hugging me back.

I pulled away a fraction. The lack of happiness on her face was a knife to my stomach.

"Where am I? Where is Lorcan?"

Her eyes were hard as they darted around, taking in each corner of the room. It was like she knew but didn't want to admit it.

"You're on Earth," I said in a whisper. "I brought you home."

At that moment, her eyes stopped searching for a way out. They closed, and she took one deep breath before releasing it back out. When she opened her eyes again, that knife to the stomach twisted.

"I know it's been a long time, and I look different than I used to, but it's me. Your sister. Piper." I motioned to myself, my voice thick with unspoken fear. Not fear of my sister, but fear of what I sensed coming.

"I know who you are," Bree said. "What I want to know is *what did you do*?"

The same blue eyes as mine stared back . . . except there was an emotion I didn't recall ever seeing on her face before.

Hate.

To be continued . . .

Piper's story continues in:

Blood be Damned
Magic Wars: Demons of New Chicago Book Three

Preorder Book Three Here

AUTHOR'S NOTE AND ACKNOWLEDGEMENTS

I know if you're here after that ending, it's likely to find out more . . . probably regarding why the next book isn't here until May.

This series started as a passion project for me. As a writer, I don't give myself many of those—but this one was—and in my determination to keep it that way, I swore I wouldn't overextend myself in writing it. I've done that with several past series where I never wanted to look at them again, and that's such a hard feeling to experience as an author. I want to love all my work, but I'm also not superwoman. Writing, editing, and marketing are a full-time job—and the faster I go, the less authentic my work tends to be.

All of that said, with 2020 and the challenges it has brought to me, my work pace has taken a hit. So I'm scaling down a tiny bit so I can breathe. Haunted by Shadows took me four months to complete. This is probably the longest a book has taken me since Scion of Midnight. While I loved the journey Piper went on, and I'm happy I gave myself the space to find it, I also recognized that mentally I need more time to work on Piper's third book, because man—there's a lot to be told.

I do want to take the time to thank my editor, Analisa Denny, for not only holding my hand through this book, but making sure all the necessary changes were done in time, even when I couldn't do it myself. You're a total rock star, and I'm in awe of your ability to make it happen.

I'd also like to send a thank you out to my lovely PA, Maegan Kelish. She's the reason I have the time to write and focus on my books. The work she does behind the scenes often isn't "seen", but it's so crucial to my process, and I'm utterly thankful to have her on my team.

People behind the scenes tend to get overlooked, but they are just as valuable. They help me as a friend, and as a writer. Courtney Lummus, Amanda Pillar, Graceley Knox, Kayla Perkins, Heather Renee, Amber Lynn Natusch, and Coralee June are just a few of the people that deserve thanks for checking in on me and being there when I needed them.

That said I don't think anyone has done quite as much as my husband and best friend, Matt. He has been my rock through this crazy shit storm we've all faced, and I don't know what I would do without him.

Last, but not least, I'd like to give you—the reader —my greatest thanks. You guys made this series an instant international bestseller. You preordered and talked about it with your friends and family—and really made it possible for me to spend more time in this world. That's right, the Magic Wars universe will have more series to come, and that is truly all in thanks to you guys for showing me the love you have for these characters. I am so incredibly thankful to have you as a reader. Every single one of you is a ripple that became a tidal wave to help this series grow, and I am humbled by that.

Until we're back in New Chicago together,
Kel

Complete Series Boxset

ABOUT THE AUTHOR

Kel Carpenter is a master of werdz. When she's not reading or writing, she's traveling the world, lovingly pestering her editor, and spending time with her husband and fur-babies. She is always on the search for good tacos and the best pizza. She resides in Bethesda, MD and desperately tries to avoid the traffic.

Facebook Group
Newsletter